HE COULD NEVER BE HERS

"Mr. Radcliff, I believe it's my turn. After all the lady is with me."

Kathleen's heart slammed in her chest at Rian's voice, at his words, and then again when Beau left graciously and Rian slipped his arms around her.

"I'm afraid that we won't have much time before dinner," Rian said.

She nodded, conscious of the strength of his arms and the heady mixture of scents that were his.

"Did you enjoy your dance?"

Her gaze sought and found Beau Radcliff where he stood off to one side, conversing with a young woman with dark brown hair. "He thinks a lot of himself, doesn't he?"

Rian's grin transformed his features, making Kathleen's pulse race. "Aye, that he does," he said, sounding very Irish.

She melted. How she loved this man—her cousin's fiancé!

"It's dark outside. I imagine the house would look more beautiful if we were to walk out and view it later."

Was that an invitation?

"Could we?" she asked, daring to be bold.

"Aye." His expression made her breath catch. "We could."

Kathleen wanted nothing more than to walk out in the warm, dark night with him. . . .

Other Zebra Books by Candace McCarthy

Fireheart
Wild Innocence
Sweet Possession
White Bear's Woman
Irish Linen
Heaven's Fire
Sea Mistress
Rapture's Betrayal
Warrior's Caress
Smuggler's Woman

With stories in these Zebra collections:

Irish Enchantment
Baby in a Basket
Affairs of the Heart

IRISH LACE

Candace McCarthy

ZEBRA BOOKS
KENSINGTON PUBLISHING CORP.
http://www.zebrabooks.com

ZEBRA BOOKS are published by

Kensington Publishing Corp.
850 Third Avenue
New York, NY 10022

All Kensington titles, imprints and distributed lines are available at special quantity discounts for bulk purchases for sales
promotion, premiums, fund-raising, educational or institutional
use.

Special book excerpts or customized printings can also be created to fit specific needs. For details, write or phone the office
of the Kensington Special Sales Manager: Kensington Publishing Corp., 850 Third Avenue, New York, NY 10022. Attn. Special Sales Department. Phone: 1-800-221-2647.

Zebra and the Z logo Reg. U.S. Pat. & TM Off.

First Printing: June 2001
10 9 8 7 6 5 4 3 2 1

Printed in the United States of America

For Keith and Jennifer . . . and the love that you share and the dreams that you have that will make your life together truly wonderful.

With love,
Mom

Prologue

"Meara Kath-leen! Meara Kath-leen!" Rian Quaid taunted her as she passed where he sat on a rock, throwing stones into a stream.

The red-haired girl froze and turned to him with a scowl. "Don't call me that!" she cried. She was younger than he by four years, but still Rian liked to irk her.

"Why not? 'Tis yer name," he insisted. "Meara Kathleen Dunne."

"Stop it!" Her elfin face puckered into a pout. "I don't like it. I'm Meara. Only Meara."

"Well, I've a fondness fer Meara Kathleen, and I'll call ya by that name if I want!"

"I hate ya, Rian Quaid." Blue eyes flashing her fury, Meara crossed her arms and glared at him. "You're an awful beast. I hate ya!"

Fifteen-year-old Rian smiled with a sureness that unsettled her. "Nay, ya don't hate me, Meara Kathleen."

"I do!" she insisted.

He raised an eyebrow. " 'Tis a pity, then, isn't it? Fer it doesn't bode well fer us, does it, Meara Kathleen, since we're to be wed someday."

"Wed ya!" she exclaimed. "Never! I'll never have ya to be me husband."

" 'Tis not what Da says." He turned from her to pick up another stone, tossing it into the water and watching its splash create ripples. He swung back to her with a smile. "Our granddas want us to marry."

Disturbed, she hugged herself with her arms. Nay, she thought, shaking her head. But Rian Quaid was entirely too smug. Meara narrowed her gaze. What did he know that she didn't? Grandda wouldn't do such a thing. *Would he?*

They were in the field on her father's land, not far from the family manor house. Rian's family had come to pay a visit. Rian, his father, and Michael Quaid's English wife. It was true that their grandfathers were friends, had been for years. But surely they didn't hope for more.

A connection between their families, perhaps? a little voice inside jeered at her.

"Nay," she murmured, aware that Rian continued to study her with those disturbing green eyes of his. She raised her chin, refusing to be intimidated by him . . . refusing to believe him.

"You're wrong, Rian Quaid," she said. "Grandda would never do such a thing without askin' first." She didn't like Rian Quaid. She didn't! She didn't like his grin or the intent way he watched her all the time. He was entirely too good-looking to be humble.

Rian's green eyes caught hers, held her mesmerized so that she couldn't look away. He bothered her, but she wouldn't let him see. His gaze made her feel jittery inside, a sensation that frightened her. He bothered her, but she wouldn't let him know.

"Nay, we'll not be wed," she whispered.

"We'll see, Meara Kathleen," he said, his voice soft and confident, his green eyes gleaming. "Believe me or not, it matters little, fer you'll see soon enough." Then he grinned as he added, "Meara Kathleen."

His answer shook her to the core.

One

1846

Kathleen Maguire sat on the bed built into the ship's bulkhead and held on to her churning stomach. She'd been at sea for weeks with no sickness. Why was she feeling poorly now?

It must have been something I ate, she thought. Perhaps the fish stew she'd been served for supper.

Despite her illness, Kathleen realized that she had nothing to complain about and everything to be thankful for. Just seven months ago, she'd been alone in County Roscommon.

"Just tryin' to stay alive," she said with a shiver. If not for her uncle Sean, she'd be wandering the hills of Ireland without friend or family, her parents having died within a year of each other.

Her stomach grumbled noisily with nausea, and Kathleen lay back, closing her eyes. But the motion of the ship, while she was in that position, made her feel worse, and she sat up again, groaning.

Kathleen tried to focus on something other than her stomach. She forced her thoughts back to the day she'd received her uncle's missive. Uncle Sean was her mother's brother and a wealthy landlord in County Clare.

His letter had been a shock to her, for she'd not been aware that he'd known of her existence. She certainly recalled little of Uncle Sean, only a story or two about him as a boy.

Kathleen smiled, remembering the events that led to her being aboard the *Mistess Kate* headed for America. Her uncle's letter had been kind, offering his sincere condolences on the death of her mother.

"Your aunt Shannon and your cousins, Shamus and Meara, are anxious to meet you, Kathleen," he'd written. "We'd love for you to make your home with us. You'd be very welcome. We've plenty of room for you to live with us—your family."

After the initial shock, she quickly rejoiced at the invitation, which she'd accepted with a prayer of thanks. Her gratitude increased when she learned that Uncle Sean had arranged for her transportation from Roscommon to the Dunnes' residence in Clare.

Upon arriving at her uncle's estate, she'd been amazed by the vastness of his lands and the evidence of his wealth in the fancy manor house with its lovely furnishings. She wondered why her mother had given up a lucrative life to marry her father. Recalling her tenant father's disparaging comments about landlords made her wary. But Uncle Sean's kindness and caring had quickly banished her misgivings, and she was glad she'd come.

She immediately became companion to her cousin Meara, who was two years younger than she. Despite the obvious differences in their upbringings, they took an instant liking to each other. Kathleen might not have had the privileges afforded by money, but she'd had her parents, two wonderful people who'd lavished love and attention on her. And in that, she'd felt as wealthy and blessed as her cousin.

For months, Kathleen had enjoyed a privileged life with her uncle's family until disaster struck again with the repeal of the Corn Act. The change in law, along with the terrible conditions suffered by the country people because of the potato blight, even had the landlords struggling to survive.

Uncle Sean had begun to evict his tenants in favor of raising cattle instead of grain. The tenants retaliated, venting anger and frustration in an uprising that threatened the well-being of the entire household.

Sean, afraid they were in real danger, decided it would be best to send Kathleen and his daughter to America and Meara's betrothed, Rian Quaid. The cousins were taken to Liverpool, England, where they'd boarded the *Mistress Kate*, and sailed off to a different world: Maryland, in the United States of America. She didn't mind the long voyage or the changes in her life. She was happy that she'd been promised a future in the Quaid household after her cousin's wedding. She would continue to be Meara's companion and have a fine home.

Where is Meara? Kathleen wondered as thoughts of Meara brought on concern for her cousin's whereabouts.

Meara had been gone for over an hour. It was raining up on top deck. Where on earth had her cousin gone?

Her stomach settling, she rose from her bunk, then clutched a post to steady herself as she swayed on her feet.

"Please don't let her be with Robert," she murmured.

Kathleen frowned. As of late, Meara had been spending time—too much time—with Robert Widham, an American they'd met when they'd boarded the ship in England. Meara's behavior in keeping company with the man was most unseemly. Her cousin was a betrothed woman; it wasn't right for her to be seen with another man.

Kathleen fought back the premonition she'd been having lately that something dreadful was going to happen. It was her mother who had possessed such intuition, knowing when something bad was about to occur, not she.

She shivered and hugged herself, trying to banish her own fears. Fiona Maguire had predicted the demise of her husband and her own death.

"Nay!" she murmured, still trying to deny it. " 'Twas something that just happened." No one—except perhaps fairies and witches—could predict the future, and her mother had been neither. *Certainly not Mother and most definitely not me!*

The cabin door flew open, and Meara burst in with a startling, breezy laugh. "Kathleen!" she gasped, out of breath, grinning.

Kathleen narrowed her gaze. "Where have ya been, Meara? I've been half out of me mind with worry fer ya."

Meara looked neither repentant nor contrite. "I was on the upper deck. 'Tis a beautiful day. The rain has stopped, and the sun feels glorious!"

"Meara, 'tis not proper fer ya to be up and about without an escort."

"I had me escort," her cousin said cheerfully.

Kathleen's sick feeling now had nothing to do with her earlier nausea. "Who?"

"Robert."

"Meara! Ya know 'tis not proper fer ya to be spendin' so much time with him. Not ye—an engaged woman!"

Meara smiled, but not her eyes. "Well, then 'tis best ya know that I've no intention of marryin' Rian Quaid.

He wants only me dowry. He'll be happy enough to have it without a wife."

"What?"

"Aye, ye heard me right, cousin. I'll not wed Quaid. I don't love him, and I'll not be forced to enter a loveless marriage."

"But Meara!" Kathleen exclaimed. " 'Tis all arranged! You and he are to be man and wife. He's expectin' ya!"

"Nay, cousin. I'll be marryin' Robert Widham or no one!" Leaving her cousin gaping with horror, Meara left the cabin as abruptly as she'd come in.

Kathleen stared at the closed door, her heart pounding. "Uncle will never forgive me if I don't see that you are delivered to yer betrothed, cousin," she said, swallowing hard. "What am I goin' to do? *What am I goin' to do?"*

They had two days left till they reached America, which meant she had two days to change Meara's mind, to make her cousin see reason.

"And why would Robert Widham be willin' to marry ya without a dowry?"

She would point out that bit of logic to her cousin and pray that Meara had the good sense to listen to her father and accept Rian Quaid.

Two

Green Lawns, Kent County, Maryland

Rian Quaid stared down with a dark scowl as he read from the piece of parchment he held.

"What's wrong, Rian? Bad news?"

Rian glanced toward his neighbor John Foley. "Nay, not bad news exactly," he said. " 'Tis a letter from my betrothed's father. Meara, it seems, is on her way to me. 'Twas to be expected eventually, but not now, not when I've enough worries on my mind."

"Your betrothed!" Elizabeth Foley, blond, pretty, and considerably younger than her husband, entered the room. "I didn't know you were engaged."

"Aye." Rian lowered the letter to his side. "Her name is Meara." His lips curved slightly. "Meara Kathleen Dunne."

"She's Irish," John said.

"True, that she is," Rian replied. "As I am." The brogue in his speech had lessened over the years since he'd first come to America.

"I meant no offense—"

"None taken, John," he assured his friend.

"When will she arrive?" Lizzy asked.

He shrugged. "Could be anytime. I can't get away to Baltimore now. I'll have to send Jack Peterson. She could come as soon as this week or next." He didn't need this now! A recalcitrant fiancée was the last thing he needed when problems with the plantation took up most of his time. *Why now?*

"If there anything I can do to help while she is here," John's wife offered graciously.

"Yes, Beth can assist by making Meara feel at home." John glanced with fondness at his wife.

"I may call on you for help," Rian said with a smile of gratitude as he set Sean Dunne's letter on a nearby table. "Thank you."

Smiling slightly in return, she nodded, then turned toward her husband. "John, I think Rian has enough on his mind without worrying about entertaining the likes of us."

John nodded and raised his large frame from the sofa cushions. "Thank you, Rian, for your hospitality." He held out his palm, and the two men shook hands. "We'll talk business later, when my dear wife isn't about to listen to such boring talk."

"John," Lizzy protested, "you know I don't mind when you discuss business with your friends."

John beamed at her. "Yes, I know, dear heart, but I suspect the children feel differently."

Lizzy glanced down with fondness at the little girl who played quietly on the floor, not far from the sofa where her father sat. Eight-year-old Jason had gone outside earlier to visit the stables and Rian's horses. She'd just come in from checking on the sometimes-mischievous child, after being assured by Rian's groom, Thomas, that he would see that Jason behaved himself.

"I suppose you're right. Emma's getting tired." She reached down and picked up the little girl. "Come on, sweetie. Time to go home for a rest and treat. Last night,

Mama baked cookies for you and your brother." She nuzzled her face against her daughter's neck.

"Wanna stay," Emma insisted. She grabbed hold of a strand of her mother's blonde hair as Lizzy raised her head.

"No, sweets, it's time to leave. But we'll come to see Mr. Quaid again." She flashed him a smile. "If he invites us."

"You're welcome at Green Lawns at any time," Rian replied with a grin.

As John bent to retrieve his daughter's toys, Rian studied the Foley family with interest, marveling anew at their relationship. Although John was old enough to be Elizabeth's father, the couple appeared happy and content with their marriage.

He smiled as the little girl wrapped her arms tightly around her mother's neck, then kissed her cheek. It was obvious that the Foley children adored their parents.

He thought back to the travesty of his father's second marriage and felt his smile slip. Did the Foleys ever argue? After his mother had died, his father had married a woman who was nothing more than a shrew. No matter how hard he tried, his father could not make Priscilla happy. Her beauty had bewitched him, but she had ultimately made their life miserable.

Rian supposed it was the reason he had conveniently forgotten his betrothal to Meara until receiving Sean Dunne's letter. Now the agreement was back to haunt him, to threaten the good life he'd worked hard to create.

He didn't want to get married. It was a rare relationship that ever survived marriage.

"The only way to escape marriage is to convince Meara Kathleen that she and I aren't at all suited for each other," he murmured.

Perhaps it won't be a problem, he thought. On the last occasion they'd seen each other, Meara hadn't been at all enamored of the idea of marrying him.

Then why was she coming to America now? She could have just written if she had wanted to put an end to the engagement.

"John, will you call for Jason?" Lizzy said, interrupting Rian's thoughts.

"Ri-an!" her daughter crooned, holding out her arms.

Rian grinned and took the child from her mother. "You really don't have to leave, Lizzy. Henny's about to fix lunch. Won't you stay?"

"Thank you, Rian, but no," John said as he placed his hand at the small of his wife's back. He regarded his daughter in his friend's arms fondly. "She likes you, Rian."

Rian nodded. "She's a sweet thing."

"You'll make a good father," Lizzy said.

Surprised, Rian could only look at her.

"Well, you've a fiancée, Rian Quaid, so I imagine the notion will be entirely possible at some future time," she said with candor.

"Perhaps next week you'll come to visit us," John suggested.

"Tuesday?" Rian asked, mentally reviewing his schedule.

John smiled. "Fine. Tuesday, it is."

Rian followed the Foleys toward the door.

"I wonder where our boy has gone to?" John said as they stepped outside.

"I suspect he's still in the stables." Lizzy smiled. "He obviously loves your horses, Rian, and I can't say I blame them. They look fine."

"You're welcome to come riding anytime, Lizzy," Rian offered, surprised by her compliment.

"Thank you, but John recently bought me a mount of my own."

"From the Joneses of Grayson Manor," John said.

Rian approved. "Good people who raise fine horse-flesh."

"Jason!" John called as he spied the boy near the side of the house, on the path that led to the stables. But Jason either hadn't heard his father or had pretended not to as he ran away.

"I'll get the boy for you, Mr. Foley," one of Rian's workers said as he appeared from the opposite side of the house.

"Thank you, William," John said, recognizing the young man as a field worker who was also one of the groom's helpers.

With a brief wave of his hand, William continued toward the stables.

"Are you sure you have to go?" Rian asked, drawing the Foleys' attention.

Lizzy smiled at him sweetly. "Yes, I'm sure. I've work at the house, and we're keeping you from yours."

"Dad!" Jason, his face smudged, his sandy brown hair tousled, and his eyes sparkling, came hurrying toward them.

"Time to go home, Jase," John Foley said.

The boy climbed into the carriage without protest. "You should have seen Mr. Quaid's black stallion," he told his family with excitement.

"Midnight," Rian murmured as he placed little Emma into her mother's waiting arms.

"Do you think I'll be able to ride Midnight someday, Mr. Quaid?"

"That depends on how responsible you can be for your mother," he said with an amused look for each of the boy's parents. "And whether or not your folks say it's all right."

"Can I?" the boy asked.

"As Mr. Quaid said, Jason," Lizzy warned, "it will depend on whether or not you can be a responsible young man."

"I am responsible."

"You'll have to show us," she said. "For one, you'll have to do your chores without being reminded."

The boy's face crumpled with disappointment. "But . . ."

"No buts, Jason. Your mother's right," Rian said. "It's the best way to show me that I can trust you with Midnight."

"All right," he said.

"We'll see you on Tuesday, then, Rian," John said.

Rian nodded. "Take care, now."

" 'Bye, Mr. Quaid," Jason said.

" 'Bye, Quaid!" Little Emma echoed her brother. " 'Bye-'bye!"

As the Foleys left, Rian turned toward the house, his thoughts once again on his fiancée. "What am I doing to do with her?" he murmured as he reentered the house. He picked up Sean Dunne's letter from a parlor table and finished reading the last paragraph.

Meara will not be traveling alone. She'll have a companion with her, Sean had written. *I trust you will find a place for her in your household.*

"Aye, Sean, a place she'll have," he said, "for as long as your daughter is at Green Lawns." He scowled as he set the letter down again. "As if I've a choice in the matter," he said, the Irish in his voice thick with his concern.

Rian knew that this time of confrontation between

Meara Kathleen Dunne and himself would come sooner or later, for the marriage had been arranged when they were children. He had almost believed that Sean Dunne had forgotten about the betrothal and allowed his daughter to marry another.

"Apparently not," he mumbled as he dropped down into the nearest chair. Sean Dunne must have been waiting for the time when he believed his daughter was ready to wed.

Closing his eyes, Rian got an image of a pretty girl with bright red hair, a freckled face, and blue eyes. Meara Kathleen Dunne. How he'd loved to taunt her when he'd been younger. Would she take to his teasing now better than she had eleven years ago?

He had suspected that Meara Kathleen had never forgiven him for being right about the betrothal arrangement between their grandfathers.

Had things changed? Had Meara Kathleen Dunne come to terms with their engagement?

Rian frowned. He hoped not. For he couldn't afford the time to change the dear lady's mind.

Three

Port of Baltimore

"Surely ye are jokin'?" Kathleen tore her gaze from the bustling crowd on shore to gape at her cousin. "Ya really don't expect me to give him yer dowry, do ya?" She eyed the box in her cousin's hands warily.

"Aye, cousin," Meara said, her gaze narrowing. " 'Tis the least ya can do."

"But yer father!" Kathleen exclaimed. "He expects ya to wed Mr. Quaid."

"He's not here and in a position to argue, is he?" Meara softened her expression. "Me father loves me, Cousin. He'll get used to the idea of another husband fer me. I'm not concerned with his approval."

A ship's officer barked commands at members of the crew, making it difficult for conversation.

Kathleen raised her voice to be heard. "Why would Robert marry ya without a dowry?"

"He loves me. Only me," Meara replied loudly. "And he has plenty of money of his own." The commands stopped suddenly, making her cousin's voice seem overloud. "He doesn't need what me dowry can bring him."

"But—"

"Go!" Meara said, shoving the box at her until she was forced to accept it. "We'll be waitin' fer ya within

yards from that flower cart over there." She leaned
against the ship's rail as she pointed toward the vendor
hawking colorful blooms from a wooden cart onshore.
"Meet us there when ye're done. And don't look so worried, Kathleen. Make no mistake; Rian Quaid will think
ye're me. We both have the red hair of our grandmother.
Rian hasn't seen me since we were children. Ya look
enough like me to pass as me sister."

"Meara—"

"Enough!" The young woman tossed her red hair—a
shade brighter than Kathleen's—and dismissed her
cousin's misgivings with a flick of her right hand.

Her heart pumping hard, Kathleen ducked below some
rigging and started reluctantly toward the gangplank.

Meara grabbed her arm to stop her. "I think that
Robert and I should leave first. Just glance toward yer
right, to the cart, when you are done and you'll see us.
We'll not move from that spot. We'll be there waitin' for
ya."

Kathleen hated the position Meara had put her in, but
she had little choice but to follow her cousin's instructions. What else could she do? She was a penniless re-
lation, one who had to rely on Meara's generosity to
survive. If she angered Meara, she'd lose the only relative
she had in this strange new land.

What would she do if she didn't have a place with her
cousin? she wondered. She bit her lip to keep from arguing with Meara further. 'Twas bad enough in Ireland.
In America, she'd be lost and destitute without anyone
to whom she could turn.

As much as it galled her, she needed Meara. And she
would pretend to be her cousin until she'd carried
Meara's dowry and the bad news to Rian Quaid that he
and Meara wouldn't be marrying.

Uncle Sean is not going to be happy, she thought. Kathleen had the awful feeling he was going to be furious with his daughter, perhaps more so with his niece for not delivering Meara safely into her betrothed's hands.

"Why must I be the one to tell him?" Kathleen asked. She wanted nothing more than to be safe somewhere and with all of this behind her. The voyage had been a long one, and there was nothing she would like better than to soak in a tub and forget all about her cousin, Robert Widham, and Rian Quaid.

"Robert's jealous, and he does not want me talkin' with him." Meara wore a smile on her face that made her look like a satisfied cat. Kathleen thought she heard her cousin purr like one.

"I don't like this, Meara. It doesn't feel right . . . pretendin' to be you . . ." She tightened her grip on the box until her knuckles hurt.

Meara's good humor vanished. "Oh, do stop frettin', Kathleen. What are ya worryin' about? You've got a home, haven't ya?"

Kathleen eyed her warily. "Aye, thanks to you, I have—"

"Well, do what I ask, then," Meara snapped irritably, "and yer circumstances won't change. Refuse to do it and . . ."

Paling, Kathleen could only nod and stare down at the box in her hands. She was conscious of the sounds of the ship and the passengers as they disembarked, but the noise seemed far off in the distance.

If she took some of the dowry money, she thought. But she quickly dismissed the idea, as it was wrong, more wrong than what Meara was asking of her.

"Kathleen? Kathleen!" Meara exclaimed. As she regained her cousin's attention, she sighed with exasperation. "Do ya think himself would be happy knowin' that I wouldn't speak with him?"

Kathleen looked up. "Why should it matter?" she challenged. "Ya said he wanted only your money." The burning in Kathleen's stomach intensified.

"Aye, and so 'tis true. Rian Quaid never did care fer me, 'tis certain. The last time I saw him, he was rude and ungracious. He's only eager to wed me now because he needs funds to keep his precious land."

"But what if you are wrong and he is devastated by yer betrayal?"

Meara snorted, but the sudden gleam in her eyes suggested that the image appealed to her. "I'm not wrong." She began to study Kathleen thoughtfully. "Why concern fer a man ya don't know? If you're so worried about Mr. Rian Quaid, then you marry him."

"What!"

"Aye," her cousin said, her voice softening, her look smug. "The prospect doesn't sit well with ya, does it. 'Tis different when it's about you now."

"But 'twas not me who Grandda arranged the marriage fer," Kathleen said.

"Aye, and ye've the right of it, Cousin. Just as it wasn't me wishes that were taken into consideration when the arrangement was made. 'Twas only the wishes of two old ornery grandfathers—Galvin Quaid and me own. Why should either of us care if we do not follow some old men's dictates?"

Meara could have a point, Kathleen conceded. But she knew that she herself would have done anything for her family if she'd only had someone left to do something for.

Isn't Meara yer cousin, girl? she thought. *Aye, but this is different. This is deceitful.*

Meara should have told her father that she had no intention of marrying Quaid. To escape marriage in such a way was wrong and hurtful.

She would do what her cousin asked because she had no other choice. She would do it, but she viewed the time with dread. When she was done, she would find a church and ask God's forgiveness for deceiving the man.

For she didn't care what Meara said; Kathleen just couldn't believe that Rian Quaid would have consented to marry if he truly didn't want Meara for his wife.

Tomorra afternoon, 'twill be over, she thought. Then she could get on with her life without thinking of the terrible thing she'd done to poor Rian Quaid.

Four

"She's in! The *Mistress Kate*!"

Rian was in a shop in Baltimore when he heard the cry. It was a coincidence that he'd come to the city. It had been over a week since he'd sent Jack Peterson, Henny's son, to wait for the arrival of the ship. There had been another sailing vessel in port during the past week, Jack had informed him, but it hadn't been the one carrying Rian's betrothed. Rian couldn't be certain if this one carried Meara Kathleen and her companion, but for some reason he had the feeling that it did.

He paid for the items he'd selected, then left the store and headed toward the docks. He saw Jack standing among the crowd waiting for passengers to disembark, and he approached the young man.

"I'll see if she's come, Jack," he said as he reached the young man's side. "Here, take these." He handed him his purchases. "Put them onto the *Windslip* and tell Martin that I'll be there as soon as I'm able. If Miss Dunne has arrived, we'll be leaving for home shortly."

Eager to please, eighteen-year-old Jack bobbed his head vigorously. "Yes, Mr. Quaid."

"Thanks for staying in Baltimore, Jack. 'Twas a man's job I sent you on, and you've handled it nicely."

He beamed. "Thank you, Mr. Quaid."

Rian smiled. "I've been told that your mother was to

bake a berry pie today. Perhaps we'll be home in time for us all to have a piece."

Jack grinned. "I hope she baked more than one, sir."

"I'm sure she did, Jack. I'm sure she did."

As the young man ran off to do his bidding, Rian searched the deck for his betrothed. It should be easy enough to spot her, he thought. Her red hair would stand out brightly in a crowd.

Had she changed much over the ten years since he'd last seen her? He'd encountered her only once since the day he'd teased her about marrying. She'd not been happy to see him. It had galled her to learn that he'd been right about the betrothal arrangement between their grandfathers. She'd been furious upon learning that he hadn't been lying about the engagement. The grandfathers might have made the arrangement, but their parents had agreed. The Dunne and Quaid families would be reunited through the marriage of their two offspring—Rian and Meara.

Had Meara come to terms with the arrangement? Or would she be just as recalcitrant, trying his patience, as she had as a child? Would she have come all this way if she hadn't wanted to come?

How could he know what was in the mind of Meara Kathleen?

His gaze swept the deck and gangplank in his search for her. And then he spied her, with her glorious mane of dark red hair. She stepped onto the platform hesitantly, clutching something between both hands and looking lost. She looked up, and he saw her face. And Rian felt his heart slam into his throat.

Meara Kathleen Dunne had indeed grown up, and she was beautiful.

* * *

Kathleen saw her cousin and Robert slip past her and hurry onto shore. Meara was unrecognizable in a poke bonnet that covered her hair and her face and a gown that was one of Kathleen's, a garment simpler than the dresses Meara usually wore. She watched as the couple hurried toward the flower cart, where they'd promised to wait for her. When she turned back to the milling crowd, she saw him in the distance. Lean, powerful, and striking, the man was. She didn't know why she felt sure it was Rian Quaid, but she did. Still, she was surprised when he approached her.

"Meara Kathleen?" he said, his deep voice making her tingle.

Startled that he'd called her by her given name, she gaped at him until she recalled that both she and her cousin had been named after their grandmother, Kathleen, from whom they'd received their red hair. Her cousin was born Meara Kathleen Dunne, and she, Kathleen Mary Maguire.

She nodded in answer. "Are ye Rian Quaid?" she asked.

The man was stunning. The sun shone on his brown hair, making it glisten with gold highlights. Eyes so green and crystal clear that Kathleen felt that she was looking at the reflection in a lake of a summer's forest. He was lean and lithe, and he filled out his clothes nicely. He wore a white shirt with matching navy waistcoat and trousers. Kathleen's gaze fastened on his throat as he swallowed. Embarrassed by her interest, she quickly looked away.

"Ya mean to say that I've changed that much, Meara Kathleen?" he said, sounding amused, his Irish lilt more pronounced.

She felt her face flame. "I recognized ya, but I wanted to be sure."

His slow smile made her feel warm and fuzzy inside. "Have ya a trunk with yer belongings?"

"Aye. Still on board," she said with a glance toward the flower cart. Her heart thumped hard. Meara wasn't there. And neither was Robert Widham.

"Come and I'll arrange for it to be brought to the *Windslip*," he said, his Irish accent no longer present.

"The *Windslip*?"

"My sloop."

Kathleen groaned inaudibly at the thought of heading out to sea so soon again. "Is it far to yer home?" She looked up to find him studying her with an intensity that thoroughly unnerved her.

"Would you prefer to stay the night at an inn before we head for home?"

Home. She felt a longing for something that would never be. "You would stay," she asked softly, "fer me?"

He frowned, clearly disturbed by something she'd said.

"I don't mean to be a bother—"

"Since when did it ever upset you to bother me?" His voice was soft. He touched her cheek, and the caress warmed her, making her feel strange inside. "You must be feeling poorly to be so amicable, Meara Kathleen."

"Have I been so terrible in the past to make you think ill of me?" she asked. What didn't her cousin tell her about their relationship?

He raised an eyebrow. "You need to ask?"

"There is little I remember about our relationship, Mr. Quaid."

. He appeared shocked. "Did you have an accident?"

"You could say that," she said. Another glance toward the flower cart confirmed that her cousin hadn't returned to wait for her. Kathleen knew for certain then that she'd been abandoned.

I'm alone with no money and me cousin's fiancée. What was she to do? She couldn't use some of her cousin's dowry, for neither the money nor the family jewels she carried belonged to her. They had been Meara's and were now rightfully Rian's.

It's the least Meara could have given Rian fer discardin' him so easily!

"One of the crewmen will see that your belongings are brought to my ship. Is there anything in your trunk that you need before I find you a room at the inn?"

Kathleen shook her head. He started to turn to issue instructions. "Rian," she called, stopping him, using his familiar name for the first time. "There is no need to stay here this evenin'. We can leave fer yer plantation. Green Lawns, is it?" she asked.

He nodded. "Are you certain you feel well enough to travel?

"Aye," she said, but she was weary indeed.

The thoughts she entertained since discovering her cousin had run off frightened her as much as they excited her. She would go to Green Lawns, for she had no place else to go. Once there, she would give Rian Quaid her cousin's dowry money and then explain who she was before deciding her next course of action. Perhaps he knew of someone who would take her on as a seamstress.

Did they need anyone to make lace here in America? She had learned the craft from her mother, who had used her skill before Kathleen was born to help support herself and her new husband.

Her mother's occupation was just another piece in the unfinished puzzle that was Fiona Maguire. Kathleen still didn't understand how her mother had come to be with her father, a good and kind man but someone, she thought, whom Fiona never would have met under the normal circumstances of living in a landholder's house.

She waited for Rian to oversee the transportation of the trunk, then followed him to the pier where the *Windslip* was docked.

The *Windslip* was a beautiful little sailing vessel, her hull and riggings in good repair. Kathleen glanced up at its masts and wondered how far they would have to travel. A cool breeze kicked up its heels, brushing her face and tugging at her hair.

She turned and saw to her dismay storm clouds gathering over the Chesapeake. The last thing she wanted was to travel in unsteady waters. Her illness on board the *Mistress Kate* sufficed for one day. Rian, who had boarded the sloop and gone below, came above to assist Kathleen. She saw him notice the change in the breeze and the air temperature that had cooled somewhat. His gaze went to the horizon, where the sky had darkened, and he frowned.

Then he studied her for a long moment before stepping from the ship. "I'll find us an inn. We'll set sail in the morning."

Kathleen couldn't prevent a sigh of relief. "Thank you."

Rian's gaze narrowed. "If you weren't feeling well, why didn't you say so?"

"I'm fine, Mr. Quaid. Honestly. I'm just tired, is all."

"Rian," he prompted. " 'Tis strange for us to use formal titles. We are betrothed, aren't we?"

Kathleen blushed. "A-aye, R-Rian."

His green eyes sparkled with amusement. "You've changed, Mcara Kathleen. I'm not sure I'll get used to such humble servitude from you."

She sputtered. "Humble servitude!" She glared. "Well, ye'll not be gettin' it from me."

"Good," he said. His soft smile made her heart beat faster. "I like a woman with spirit, Meara Kathleen Dunne."

Kathleen looked away, feeling guilty for her continued deception. Guilty of pretending to be her cousin.

"... offered a humble servitude." She gazed

... il not be sold in front of me."

Five

The first inn where Rian attempted to book two rooms had only one bedchamber available. He and Kathleen left and went to another. After trying several establishments to no avail, Kathleen resigned herself to taking the journey across the Chesapeake in the worsening weather.

Rian, however, had different ideas. He took her back to the first inn, the Jug and Cask, where he booked the only vacant room.

"Rian. . . ." she said when it appeared that he had ideas of sharing the room with her.

"I'll stay on the *Windslip* and come for you tomorrow."

"No!" she said, suddenly alarmed at the thought of being left alone.

He arched an eyebrow. "You wish me to stay?"

She swallowed against a suddenly dry throat. "No . . . yes! Oh, I don't know."

His expression filled instantly with concern. "What is it, Meara?" he asked.

"I don't want to be left alone." Embarrassed, she went to the window and studied the gathering darkness. She had already been abandoned by Meara. What if he didn't return for her?

"I can stay," he said. When she spun to gaze up at

him, he smiled. "I'll sleep on the floor. I've done it before."

"But what will Mistress Wettin' think?" The innkeeper, Mistress Wetting, had studied the two of them intently as if trying to decide whether or not they were a respectable pair.

"I told the dear lady that we were married."

Kathleen blinked. "You did?" She didn't know why that acknowledgment made her feel uneasy. "Why?"

"It wouldn't have seemed proper unless we were married for me to follow you into your room to see you settled."

"Not even if we are betrothed?"

"Alas, no. This is not Ireland. Here in Maryland a lady's reputation would be ruined if a gentleman and a lady were to remain alone together in this room."

"And if you had left? What would she have thought then?"

He shrugged. "She might have thought I found a card game somewhere."

Kathleen studied him thoughtfully, then looked away, still uneasy. "We brought no luggage," Kathleen said, just then realizing how that might appear. "Wouldn't Mrs. Wettin' think it odd?"

Rian shook his head. "I told her we were due to sail home, then thought better of it when we saw the storm clouds. She understands that our belongings are on the ship."

"I see."

"Would you like me to stay or go? It matters not to me; the choice is yours."

Kathleen gazed into his glistening green eyes and saw only a concern for her well-being. Her skin tingled, and her pulse began to race. "I'd like ya to stay," she said. "Please."

He gave an abrupt nod, then suggested they go downstairs to dinner.

They enjoyed a simple but tasty dinner cooked by Mrs. Wetting herself and served by her daughter, Lydia, a shy young girl who said little as she served the food. The public room boasted ten tables, seven of which were filled. Ornate woven baskets and fresh aromatic herbs hung from the ceiling beams, making the inn seem more like a home. Candles burned on each tabletop, softening the expressions of the diners. The low murmur of the patrons' conversation and the occasional clink of tableware filled the air as each guest enjoyed the meals and beverages put before them.

Lydia Wetting's shyness seemed to break a bit when she set a plate before Rian, and he offered his thanks with a smile. The girl beamed as he praised his first sample of the meal. Watching with amusement, Kathleen felt that they received special attention after that, as Lydia visited their table often.

The fare consisted of beef stew with dumplings, dishes Kathleen had never had before and thought quite delicious. When she mentioned it to Lydia on one of her trips to refill Rian's mug of ale, she noted that while the girl's response was polite, she didn't beam at her the way she had at Rian.

"Lydia has taken a fancy to ya," she said to Rian quietly when the girl wasn't within earshot.

Not that she could entirely blame the girl, Kathleen thought. Rian Quaid was a fine specimen of a man. In fact, she couldn't understand why her cousin had an objection to him.

Rian's lips curved slightly. "Jealous?"

Face flushing, she lifted her chin. "Certainly not!"

After a period of awkwardness, which Rian quickly banished with conversation, they discussed Ireland, a place that had once been home to Rian but which he hadn't seen in many years.

"I remember a beautiful place," he told her.

"Aye, 'twas beautiful, and still is in some ways." She grew wistful. "If not fer the pain and hunger, I would never have left Ireland." She felt the intensity of his stare and looked at him. "I didn't mean—" She hadn't meant to offend him. Here she was supposedly his fiancée, and she told him that she wouldn't have left Ireland even for him.

"I know," he said softly. He picked up a pewter tankard and sipped from it.

"Thank ya." Her voice was equally quiet.

He looked puzzled as he set down the mug. "For what, Meara Kathleen?"

"Fer being so understandin'. I was missin' me homeland. 'Twas not me intention to say that I wouldn't never have come . . . to you."

"Now you do surprise me, lass, for the last thing I would have thought was that you cared how I felt."

It was Kathleen's turn to be puzzled. "But we're engaged. Why shouldn't I care fer yer feelin's?"

His long, speculative look unsettled her. She was no longer sure how to act, how to respond.

Rian began to relate memories of his time in Ireland, and again, an awkward moment had passed. He described what he remembered about the hills of their homeland

and the people he knew there. While he talked, Kathleen couldn't help but be fascinated by him.

He was a man to be admired. His hair was clean and shiny, and she had the strongest urge to touch it—to feel if it was as soft as it looked. His eyes, that vivid shade of green, were beautiful, and his lashes, long for a man, were enough to make a woman envious. But despite his thick, long lashes, his features were extremely masculine. There was no doubt that he was all man—one that would appeal greatly to women. Rian Quaid was the only one who had ever affected her in such a way before.

This cannot be good, she thought. *He is me cousin's betrothed. And I've got news fer him.* But if she confessed it now, where would she be? He certainly had no obligation to help her. And his anger at her cousin might transfer onto her, taking away her only hope, her last chance for time to figure out what to do.

No, she would have to continue the charade at least until they reached Green Lawns. Once there, she could confront him in the privacy of his study, hand over Meara's money, then beg him—if necessary—to help find her a position.

"You've become quiet, Meara Kathleen."

She realized then that she'd been staring pensively at her plate while playing with her meat with a fork. "I'm sorry." She looked up and felt a shock as they locked gazes over the burning candlestick on the table.

"Are you too tired to finish eating?"

The thought of retiring to their shared room for the night made her heart pound hard. "I'm fine. I was just thinkin'."

"Of?"

She felt her cheeks flush and held a napkin to her lips as she bent her head to hide her face. She couldn't very well tell him "you" or of her deception. "Actually, I could use a tumbler of water." As the heat in her face dissipated, she lowered the cloth napkin and met his gaze again.

Rian stared at her before nodding. He signaled to Lydia, who appeared instantly at his side, before he had a chance to lower his hand.

"Sir?" she asked, her expression of one eager to please.

"My wife would like a glass of water," he said.

Lydia's smile faltered for only a second. "Certainly, sir." She bobbed a curtsy and left.

"She reacts like a skittish horse, 'cause she finds ya handsome," Kathleen murmured without thought.

"And you?" Rian said with a hovering smile. "Do you find me handsome as well?"

She gave him a haughty look. "I don't think 'tis wise of a lady to give away her thoughts, sir."

His green eyes twinkled. "I've never known you to be shy when condemning me verbally before."

Condemning him? Had her cousin been cruel to him in the past? If so, what must he think of her? *Of me!* she thought. Kathleen frowned.

"As soon as you're ready, we can retire, dear wife. I long for bed as much as you do, I think."

His sudden use of the term "wife" and "bed" had her feeling less bad for his cousin's treatment of him. He really could be impossible at times!

Lydia came with the water, catching wind of Rian's last statement. She saw the girl's eyes widen as she looked from Rian to Kathleen, no doubt imagining the married couple in bed together. "Here's your water, ma'am," she said, setting down the glass within Kathleen's reach.

"Thank you," she murmured, then picked up the glass and sipped from it.

She couldn't control the heat that stained her cheeks or the glaring look she flashed at Rian. He had purposely said it in front of the girl, she thought, leading Lydia to believe that he was anxious to bed her! She was mortified to think that now the girl would return to the kitchen to gossip about them.

"Ye deliberately allowed her to believe that we would be sharin' a bed!" she exclaimed after Lydia had left.

"And wouldn't it seem wise to do so? If the Wettings are to believe we are indeed man and wife, wouldn't it be wise to speak so naturally with each other?"

"About the bedchamber?" she hissed in undertones.

"And why not? Married couples do often share a bedchamber. Or are you planning to demand your own room after we're married?"

She opened her mouth to respond to his taunting, only to close it again. The man was insufferable!

"You've changed, Meara Kathleen," he said, studying her with a half-smile when she didn't answer. "I've never known you to be at a loss of words before, certainly not during any of our past altercations."

Past altercations? Kathleen thought. Just what kind of relationship *did* this man have with her cousin?

Six

Kathleen moved about the bedchamber awkwardly. Her heart thumped hard, and her thoughts raced as her gaze fastened on the size of the mattress. She quickly looked elsewhere. But she was too nervous to appreciate the lovely green floral curtains on the windows and the matching bedclothes on the huge four-poster bed. She was having difficulty breathing. She casually wandered toward the washstand and then ran her fingers over the top of the mahogany dresser next to it.

"I'm not going to attack you, Meara Kathleen," Rian said from directly behind her, making her gasp.

"I didn't think ye would."

"Oh?" His lips twitched as he controlled a smile. "You know me so well."

"I don't know ya at all," she replied. The man was too attractive, she thought, backing away to put some distance between them.

He had removed his waistcoat, and she noticed that his white shirt fit him well. He was tall and lithe, with a body that appeared powerful and strong. "We've known each other since we were children."

She couldn't deny it, for she couldn't without telling him the truth. For a moment, she was tempted to do so, but then what would happen to her? Rian thought she was his betrothed, so there was a measure of propriety in that knowledge while sharing a room. If he'd known that she was not his fiancée, with no attachment to him all, how would he look upon her? As a trollop?

He will find out eventually, she thought.

But then, perhaps he will have discovered her true character. Then, once she explained all, he would forgive and help her . . . being angry with Meara instead.

Don't wager on it, Kathleen, the voice of reason responded.

"It's been a long time since ye've seen me," she said, her voice quiet. *Never,* she thought. *Ya'd never laid eyes on me before in yer life.*

Meara had been right. They looked enough like each other that Kathleen could fool him. It might not have been convincing if it hadn't been eleven years since Meara and Rian's last meeting. Kathleen fervently wished that it had only been a year or two instead, for then Meara wouldn't have been able to force her into this preposterous situation. A situation that Kathleen wasn't sure she could get out of.

"Are you tired?" He startled her with his question.

Her gaze shot to the large four-poster bed—the only bed. "Nay."

To her surprise, he didn't mock her. "Do you play cards?"

"Aye, a bit."

"Would you care for a game?"

She glanced about the room, looking for a place to play. "What shall we use fer cards and where can we play?"

"It is not a problem. I'm sure Mrs. Wetting has cards available for her guests."

"But—"

He held up his hand. "She will think nothing untoward

in a husband and wife amusing themselves with a card game, Meara Kathleen. If you will wait here a moment, I'll find us a deck."

Without waiting for her response, he left the room, and Kathleen was left to gape at the closed door. His use of her name, Kathleen, after Meara, seemed to mock her, as if he knew who she was and sought to taunt her for her deception. But, in her heart, she knew he hadn't a clue, which didn't make her feel any less guilt for the role she'd played in her cousin's betrayal.

He was back within minutes with a deck of cards and Mrs. Wetting, who had graciously brought the couple a snack to enjoy while they had their game. It eased Kathleen's mind when Mrs. Wetting smiled at her fondly before she left.

Rian was a good player, teaching her a variety of games she'd never learned. As they played, Rian and she shared thoughts of Ireland and County Clare. They were lost in the games and in conversation when the tall case clock in the downstairs foyer chimed twelve times on the hour. It was midnight. They had been playing for over five hours!

She swallowed against a dry throat, realizing that the time had come for bed. Kathleen and Rian glanced at the bed, then at each other. The easiness of those card-game playing hours vanished with the new intimacy that suddenly surrounded them.

There was no privacy to dress or undress, and Kathleen wondered what to do next. She hadn't brought any night clothing with her, so she'd have to sleep in her traveling gown. Still, it seemed strange to simply walk over and lie on the large bed.

Despite the recent time she had spent in Rian Quaid's company, what did she really know of the man? Meara hadn't thought well enough of him to stay with the betrothal agreement. Why should she trust such a man?

Rian, who had busied himself gathering and stacking the cards, set the deck to one side of the table. Kathleen trembled when he rose and looked at her.

"I can wait outside the chamber for you to ready yourself," he suggested thoughtfully.

Kathleen knew she should have been grateful for his offer, but his words conjured up images of a bride on her wedding night or a lover waiting for her man to join her.

"Thank you," she murmured. She was mortified and felt her cheeks flush. "I didn't bring a change of clothes."

He smiled, then, to her surprise, reached behind an upholstered chair and held out a satchel toward her. "I found this with your trunk. I thought perhaps it might contain items necessary for your comfort."

Pleased, she gazed at it. " 'Tis mine, thank you," she said, reaching to accept it. The satchel belonged to her alone, unlike the trunk, which was Meara's, and only held some of Kathleen's things.

Where was Meara? she wondered. And how could she have abandoned her that way?

He picked up the tray that Mrs. Wetting had thoughtfully provided earlier. "I'll just take these dishes to the kitchen."

"Oh, but you don't have to—"

"I'll be back in a little while," he said with a smile, then left the room.

Sighing, Kathleen began to rummage inside her satchel. She found her nightdress, which covered her completely. After fumbling to hurriedly tie the garment's ribbons, she scurried under the bedcovers to await Rian's return.

He was gone for a long time, it seemed, before she heard the squeak of the bedchamber door. By then, she felt exhausted, and the sound of his return was comforting to her, as was the noise of the lock clicking into place. She had made him a sleeping pallet on the floor out of some spare blankets she'd found in the dresser. Hearing him leave the doorway, Kathleen rolled onto her side, facing away from him to afford him some privacy to undress.

"Good night, Meara Kathleen," came his thick, husky voice from below her in the dark.

"Good night, sir," she murmured, unconcerned that he'd known she was awake. And she drifted off to sleep.

Seven

There was no opportunity for Kathleen to feel embarrassed the next morning. Rian was gone when she awoke. His pillow and folded blankets had been stacked neatly on the upholstered chair. Kathleen washed, using the ewer of water and basin provided, then quickly dressed and finished her toilette. Rian knocked on the door just as she'd finished packing her satchel.

He came into the room, smelling of fresh air, soap, and a wonderful scent that was all his own. "The weather has cleared nicely. Will you be ready to leave in an hour?" he said. He was polite, as if they were strangers, not a couple who had just shared a room, if not a bed.

"I'm ready now," she told him.

He smiled. "Have you eaten?"

"Nay."

"Good," he said. "Let's sample Mrs. Wetting's breakfast fare before we head toward the *Windslip*."

"I'd like that. Thank you."

At his lead, she preceded him out of the room and downstairs to the dining room, where Mrs. Wetting had already set out muffins and rolls for them. They enjoyed their breads and sweetened porridge. Rian had some eggs and bacon as well, but Kathleen was happy enough with her hot cereal. Afterward, Rian had expressed their thanks to Mrs. Wetting and collected Kathleen's bag from their room.

"Come again, Mr. and Mrs. Quaid!" Mrs. Wetting invited.

"Thank you, Mrs. Wetting. I believe we shall," Rian said.

The warm look he flashed at Kathleen made her insides quiver. The sound of Mrs. Wetting's parting lingered in her mind as they headed toward the *Windslip*.

Mr. and Mrs. Quaid . . . Mr. and Mrs. . . .

This time Kathleen had no qualms about stepping on board Rian's vessel. She'd had a good night's sleep, and there was no trace of any illness or queasiness. The day was so lovely, in fact, that she looked forward to the voyage.

After assisting her on board, Rian introduced her to the ship's captain. She thought Lawrence Bitmen a pleasant man. It was only afterward that Kathleen recalled that Rian had introduced her as his future wife.

And the deception continues, she thought. Wondering how she and Rian were going to come out of this unscathed, Kathleen was more than a little nervous.

The journey took only a few hours, for the wind was perfect for sailing, and Green Lawns was in Kent County, located almost directly across the Chesapeake. It was a warm, springlike day. Kathleen enjoyed the scent of salt and the caress of the breeze on her skin. She had donned a dress made of blue satin, forgoing her crinolines for the comfort and freedom of a simpler style.

As usual, she had decided not to wear a bonnet, although it seemed like all the rage. She detested headwear and wore hats only when it was cold or absolutely necessary. Her hair was up in a topknot, but the breeze over the water had loosened auburn strands about her face.

And the red tendrils teased and tickled against her neck and face.

Rian seemed to be enjoying the journey as well. Kathleen watched him standing not far from Captain Bitmen, his stance erect, his gaze on the horizon, a look of satisfaction on his face. He looked as if he belonged in the captain's position, with the wind in his hair and his booted feet parted to brace himself.

Kathleen was able to study him without the embarrassment of his attention and found much about his appearance that pleased her.

His brown hair, which just brushed the back of his collar, blew in curling tendrils about his face. He had discarded his jacket and waistcoat, and his white shirt bellowed in the breeze, flattening against his chest, the sleeves molding against his hard, sinewy arms. He murmured something to Bitmen, then took the wheel. As she'd imagined, he seemed perfectly at ease at the helm, as if he'd sailed the *Windslip* many times in all waters.

His gaze shifted, met hers. Kathleen felt her heart pump harder when he grinned at her. She returned his smile, and her spirits brightened.

Rian Quaid was a kind man, and he had proven to be a gentleman. Kathleen became hopeful. Perhaps he would understand why she'd pretended to be her cousin. Perhaps when she finally told him, he'd be sympathetic to her plight.

For now, though, she would enjoy the moment with the sun on her face, the wind in her hair, and a handsome man she could pretend was her betrothed for a little while longer. She gazed out over the water, enjoying the sparkle of the sun, the sound of a pair of seagulls circling overhead.

"Meara Kathleen, there!" Rian called, drawing her attention. "Kent County." He gestured toward the mouth of a river. "The Sassafras," he informed her. "Home! We're almost home."

Kathleen sighed as she studied the beautiful land that lay ahead.

Home, she thought. If only Green Lawns in Maryland were actually her home.

Kathleen rubbed the back of her arms to ward off a chill. Then she forced a smile for Rian as she shared in his delight in his homeland.

Green Lawns was breathtaking. The property, she thought, deserved a more impressive title than Green Lawns. But as she continued to stare while the small ship docked within sight of the manor, she noticed that the vast expanse of green lawns surrounded the house as far as her eyes could see.

The name suited Rian's property, after all, she decided.

The manor house had been built of brick and whitewashed a bright white. Dark green shutters flanked each window, and the massive double entrance door was of a matching dark green. The building was two stories high, and Kathleen suspected it had attic rooms under the roof peak. The five second-story windows paralleled the four windows and center door on the first level. Huge unpainted brick chimneys sat at both ends of the building.

The structure was lovely and kept in good repair, but it was still the surrounding lawns and gardens that had captured Kathleen's fancy. An array of summer flowers bloomed riotously, brightening the side and front gardens. She was eager to explore the house and had a feeling that nothing she saw would disappoint her.

Smiling, she turned to Rian. "Aye, Rian Quaid," she told him. " 'Tis a beautiful place . . . a magical place."

"I'm glad you like it, Meara Kathleen." The warmth in his green gaze told of his pleasure with her.

"Can ya not call me Kathleen?" she asked.

He looked puzzled. "I thought it was Meara that you preferred?"

She blushed slightly and turned away to stare at the manor house. "Ah, well, I've changed me mind over the years. I was named after me grandmother. A lovely woman, so I've been told."

"You're not angry with her anymore, is that it?" he said, sounding surprised.

"Why should I be angry with her?" *Especially when I've never met her,* she thought. When he didn't immediately reply, Kathleen looked at him, saw that he had extended a hand to help her disembark from the *Windslip*, and avoided his gaze as she accepted his assistance.

"I'm amazed that you've asked me such a question about your grandmother, Meara Kathleen," he said, "since it was the woman's husband who helped to arrange our marriage. I was always under the impression that you blamed her by association. You were so furious with him."

Kathleen didn't know how to respond. Apparently, she'd been ignorant of Meara's true feelings toward her grandparents, especially her cousin's feeling for their grandmother. Meara had spoken of them with affection— Kathleen was sure of it.

She captured Rian's gaze. "I think yer memory is

faulty, sir. I love me grandmother. And if I was angry with me grandfather before, I'm not now."

"I see. That explains it, then." But he looked puzzled, as if he didn't understand her at all. The length of his penetrating look finally made her look away.

Kathleen began to fidget. "Will ya show me your house?" she asked, hoping he couldn't read her thoughts.

"Of course." He released the intensity of his look and smiled. "Are you hungry?"

She allowed her lips to curve. "Aye." After living in a land where food had become scarce, she fully appreciated the gift of a good meal, and she wasn't going to pretend otherwise in order to appear ladylike to Rian Quaid or anyone.

"Henny will have dinner ready soon. Henny," he explained, "is my housekeeper. Her husband, James, is my head foreman, and their son, Jack, helps in the fields and stables."

Kathleen suddenly felt nervous at the prospect of meeting with all of the Green Lawns residents. She hated to continue the deception, but what choice did she have? Would the lies never end? And what would happen to her once everyone found out?

Henrietta Peterson was a woman in her late forties, Kathleen surmised, with a stern countenance and a sturdy frame. As Rian introduced them, the housekeeper eyed her critically before smiling and offering her hand. The smile changed Henny's face, brightening her expression and warming Kathleen as she, in turn, offered her hand in friendship. The woman's grip was warm and firm. Kathleen liked her, and it seemed that Henny felt the same way.

"Welcome, Meara Kathleen," she said pleasantly. "It's good to have you here."

"Thank you." Kathleen smiled. "I'm glad to meet you."

"Sure as it is that Rian needs a wife. You'll do fine for him."

Kathleen reddened, and a quick glance at Rian Quaid told her that he was amused.

She met and shook hands with James, then several other employees, and Kathleen felt a tinge of guilt for enjoying the warmth of their friendship. She wanted to tell them, but if she blurted out the truth now, she'd not only embarrass herself but Rian, who would no doubt feel as if she'd made a fool of him. She'd have to tell in private later.

Much later, she thought as she nodded and smiled while Rian introduced her to the household staff.

Later, Kathleen stood in the lovely bedchamber she'd been allotted and reflected on the strange events of the day. It had only been hours since she'd met Rian, but she felt as if she'd known him for many years.

As she studied the beautiful wood furnishings and appreciated the lovely window curtains and bedcovers of blue chintz, Kathleen realized that she was caught, trapped in her growing feelings for her cousin's fiancé. Rian was attractive, warm, and giving. He'd been kind and solicitous, seeing to her needs at the inn and on the ship. And despite the somewhat unusual arrangements for their stay in Baltimore, he had been the perfect gentleman. Another man might have taken advantage of the situation, but not Rian Quaid.

Kathleen closed her eyes, and her mind filled with his image. Her heart started to beat harder, faster, at the thought of seeing him again.

She gasped. "Oh, dear. Nay!" she whispered to the empty bedchamber. "I'm smitten with the man, and I don't know what ta do about it."

For even if he did eventually come to share her feelings, she had purposely deceived him, and she feared that he'd never understand why she'd felt the need to lie.

Eight

She was upstairs in his house, looking different than she had as a young girl but no less lovely. Rian stood on a hill on his property and studied the house on the horizon. Since he'd set eyes on Meara Kathleen again, he'd been unable to get her out of his mind.

She's changed, he thought. She seemed more docile than she'd been as a young girl. Before, she'd been quick to argue with him. Now she seemed fearful. What had happened to change her?

He didn't want to be affected by her vulnerability. He didn't want a wife; he didn't need the complication. But instead of making plans to send her back to her father, he found himself wanting to spend time with her . . . to show her his plantation, his horses, cattle, and crops . . . his life.

"Rian."

Rian turned to Peterson, his head foreman.

"There's been damage to back acreage again. Somebody has hacked away at several rows of corn and tobacco."

Anger burned in Rian's belly. "How many rows?"

"Ten of each. Mayhap as high as twenty," the man said. "I haven't checked over by the river yet."

Enough to upset him without ruining him, Rian surmised. "Will you check and let me know?"

Peterson nodded. "No one's bothered the cattle."

"Good. Any sign of tampering with the stable door again?"

"Thomas said not. He and Jack have been taking turns at watch. Last night was quiet."

For weeks now, someone had been trespassing on Rian's land, vandalizing the place. Sometimes it had been to the crops, while at other times the target of the vandal had been the animals and buildings. So far it had been only mild damage, but it was destruction nevertheless. Since the incidents had started, Rian had worried about his horses, especially after finding strange marks on the stable door that suggested someone might have tried to break in.

If the person's aim was to irritate the hell out of him, Rian thought, then he—or they—had succeeded. But Rian feared that there was a far more nefarious plan behind the events of tampering. What that plan was, he had no idea.

As Peterson left with some of the men to continue checking the rest of the plantation, Rian made his way back toward the manor house. As he neared his home, he saw Meara Kathleen on the front porch, gazing out over his property.

He felt a sense of pride. Green Lawns. He wanted to share it with her. He continued toward the house to speak with her.

"Mr. Quaid! Mr. Quaid!"

Rian stopped and waited for Joseph Jones, a field hand, to reach his side. "What is it, Joseph?"

"Pete says you're go to come to the back acreage immediately."

A feeling of foreboding followed Rian as he and Joseph hurried to meet Peterson.

Peterson must have found more evidence of vandalism.

Any intention he'd had of playing host to Meara Kathleen vanished as plantation business stole his attention and concern.

Kathleen wandered outside to enjoy the evening, for she felt like an intruder in the house. Rian Quaid's home was lovely. She appreciated the care that had been taken to keep it that way. Henny was a wonder. The woman could be sharp-tongued with the servant girls at times, but Kathleen could tell that Henny's fondness for the staff was genuine. The girls' affection for the housekeeper, it appeared, was mutual.

She'd been made to feel welcome, but it was clear that her presence here wasn't needed. Perhaps she'd have felt differently if she were indeed whom Rian thought she was.

As she gazed out on the beautiful night, she was almost able to forget for a brief time that she didn't belong here, that she wasn't destined to be Rian's bride.

Almost.

She'd seen little of Rian since they'd eaten their first supper together. He had been pleasant over the meal, but he had excused himself shortly afterward to work in his office.

Alone and uncertain what to do, Kathleen had gone up to her room, where she'd proceeded to unpack some belongings from Meara's trunk. She didn't take out many clothes, hanging only a few select gowns on wall hooks in her bedchamber. She had no idea how long she'd be staying at Green Lawns. It could be a week, or it could be a day. She had to decide when to tell Rian the truth, but at present she couldn't bring herself to do it.

She heard the front door open and shut behind her, and she knew she was no longer alone.

"Do you need a wrap, Miss Dunne?" It was Henny's voice that came out of the darkness.

Kathleen spun to face her. There was just enough light from an oil lamp at a parlor window to make out the woman's features. "No, I'm fine . . . thank ya. 'Tis a lovely night." She turned back to stare up at the sky. "A magical night with a clear sky and bright moon," she added dreamily. " 'Tis a night for leprechauns and fairies, I've been thinking."

She could sense Henny's smile as the older woman joined her at the porch railing. "And do you believe in fairies and leprechauns?" she asked in her softened rough voice.

"I think 'tis wise not ta discount anything. There is so much in this world that is unexplained."

Henny didn't disagree with her. "Yes, that's true enough. I've always thought that it was God watching us . . . testing us when strange things happened." The deck boards squeaked as Henny shifted her weight. "Now you suggest that fairies and the like may be responsible—and not God."

"Aye, but then it was God who made the wee people, so both theories could be considered correct."

The two women stood on the porch, studying the sky. It should have seemed odd that the housekeeper and a houseguest were spending a quiet moment together, but it didn't seem so to Kathleen.

Not that I could see Meara enjoying Henny's company, Kathleen thought. Her cousin had always been more class-conscious. She had always enjoyed the servants but felt they were a shade beneath her. Kathleen saw things differently perhaps because of her upbringing. To her, everyone was the same; the only difference was in a person's personality, talents, and fortune.

It had been a long day, and Kathleen was beginning to feel the effects of her journeys. She yawned, unable to help herself. "I'm sorry."

"It's understandable that you're exhausted, Miss Dunne. You should be upstairs in your bed—"

"Kathleen, please . . . call me Kathleen. I insist."

"Kathleen," the housekeeper said, and Kathleen could just make out the white flash of the woman's teeth as she smiled. "You've had a long journey and a long day. Why don't you go upstairs?"

"But Mr. Quaid—Rian—What if he—" she quickly amended.

Henny's grunt interrupted her. "He'll not come out of his study until late."

Kathleen had the impression that Henny disapproved of Rian's leaving her alone her first night there. "He had a lot of work to do," Kathleen said with understanding.

"Yes," she said. "He has a lot on his mind, I'm afraid."

"Is everything all right?"

Henny suddenly seemed unwilling to talk. "You should ask Rian Quaid that question for an accurate answer. Me, I'm just the housekeeper, I am."

"Thank ya," Kathleen said, touching the woman's arm as she turned to leave.

"For what?"

"For yer company." Kathleen's lips twitched. "And yer advice. I think I will go up to bed." She wasn't sure, though, whether or not to disturb Rian to tell him good night.

Henny regarded her with soft eyes. "I'll tell Rian Quaid that you've retired for the night."

Kathleen grinned. "Thank ya again."

"For what? For using common sense?" The woman seemed embarrassed. "I'll see you in the morning, then. We usually get up at six, but lie in as long as you like."

"I'll be up with everyone else," Kathleen promised, then, taking Henny's advice, she headed up the stairs and down the hall to her bedchamber.

Kathleen saw Rian little in the days that followed. Plantation matters kept him extremely busy, and she got the sense that he was worried about something. When she asked Henny, the woman had no answers for her, although Kathleen was sure that as the foreman's wife Henny should know something.

"You'll have to ask Rian," Henny would say every time Kathleen asked.

"You've no idea?" she asked.

But Henny would only repeat the same words. "You'll have to ask Rian."

"I'd ask him if I ever get to see him again!" Kathleen murmured in frustration one morning after he hadn't appeared for another meal. For three days running, Kathleen had eaten alone. At first, there had been a place set for her in the dining room, until Kathleen's request that she eat in the kitchen so she could talk with Henny as she worked.

Although the housekeeper had objected mildly, she'd consented and seemed glad of the company as she planned and prepared the day's meals. After her first day dining at a kitchen table, it was given that Kathleen would sit in the kitchen.

While Kathleen ate and Henny worked, the two women carried on a conversation that strengthened their liking for each other. Curious, Henny asked about Kathleen's homeland. Kathleen was more than happy to tell her about Ireland and recollect the tales from her childhood that wouldn't seem strange for a woman with Meara's background. Although she wanted to, Kathleen couldn't forget the role she was playing.

In turn, Kathleen asked Henny about the early days of the plantation, about Rian and his family, about the crops and livestock and other questions she had about Green Lawns. For the most part, Henny was obliging, telling Kathleen everything she wanted to know, only refusing to answer some questions that directly related to the man Rian had become.

"He'll tell you who he is now," she'd say.

And Kathleen had no choice but to change the subject.

By the fourth day since her arrival, Kathleen still had only seen Rian Quaid that one time since their one supper together, and that had been from a distance. It was that morning when he'd been in the fields nearest the house; Rian was talking with several of the men, his attention so absorbed that Kathleen was sure he wouldn't notice her or even hear her if she yelled for him.

She wanted to see him again from closer than a distance. She wanted time with him to be better able to reveal the truth and give him Meara's dowry money. How could she tell him if there was no opportunity? How could she confess all about herself if he didn't understand the woman she really was?

And until he could spend time with her, she wondered what she could do in the meantime. Surely there was some way to be useful around the plantation. She wasn't an idle person by nature; she needed something constructive to do.

Kathleen gave a dry chuckle. If things continued as

they had, she would be able to live here indefinitely, pretending to be Meara, without confessing who she was, without worry of becoming Rian's wife.

She knew that things would change eventually. But when?

"Meara Kathleen?" His deep voice startled her. He must have approached from the opposite side of the porch. It was amazing, she thought, that she hadn't heard his footsteps. It was even more astonishing that he'd sought her out at all, considering how he'd managed to avoid her for the last four days.

"Rian! Where did you come from? I didn't hear your approach."

He smiled. "Your thoughts were elsewhere. Were you daydreaming?" He glanced out toward the view she'd been studying. "The land is something to dream about, isn't it."

She looked to see the breeze stirring the grass and treetops and the sprouting tobacco plants in the nearest field. The sound of the rustling was pleasing . . . peaceful. She could stand there forever and enjoy the view.

Rian shifted beside her, reminding her that he was there. "Would you like to see more of the plantation?" he asked.

"Aye," she breathed. "I'd love to."

"Can you still ride?"

Kathleen had ridden a few times but was no expert horsewoman. Her cousin Meara, she knew, had ridden frequently when they'd been in Ireland. "A bit."

"You used to ride all the time."

Kathleen thought quickly or an excuse. "I fell off me horse a while back. It's been just a wee while since I started ridin' again."

Rian's look of concern made her lie seem a terrible

sin. "Are you up to a ride about the plantation? I have the perfect mount for you. Rosebud is gentle but lively when you want her to be."

"Aye, I can ride." She had no intention of giving up the chance to view Green Lawns at Rian's side, through Rian's eyes. She'd been on horses enough not to shame herself.

"Fine. If you're able to go now, I'll have Thomas ready our mounts. Would you care for lunch first?"

"How about a picnic?" she suggested, then was surprised by her boldness.

He looked surprised, too, but not displeased. "A picnic it is, then. I'll tell Henny—"

"I'll be happy to speak with Henny while you talk with Thomas," Kathleen offered.

"I'll meet you here in a half-hour." he said. He eyed her morning gown critically. "Do you have something more suitable for riding?" he asked.

Kathleen thought of the trunk of her cousin's clothes. "I'm sure I can find something to wear." She was certain that Meara had brought a riding habit in the trunk that was upstairs. "If ye're sure ya have the time . . ."

"I've been a poor host. I'm making the time now."

She didn't know how to respond. "I'll—ah—all right. I'll be down as soon as I'm dressed and our picnic lunch is ready."

Nine

Rosebud was a chestnut colored mare, with a white star in the center of her forehead and the most pleasant disposition that Kathleen could have ever wanted. After a heart-thumping moment during which Rian assisted her onto the sidesaddle, she relaxed, prepared to enjoy the ride.

He started their slow pace, gesturing as he pointed out landmarks and explaining the history of Green Lawns. "My mother's grandfather settled here over fifty years ago. He wasn't a young man, but he was a determined one."

Kathleen studied the land as she tried to envision how it must have looked before his great-grandfather had come to this area to put down roots. "He chose a beautiful place ta live."

"True enough." Rian turned to flash her a smile. He looked magnificent in his white shirt and tan breeches. Her gaze fell on his black boots where they rested in the stirrups, and she felt that he looked at home in the saddle as much as he'd appeared at home at the helm of his sloop.

"The land was overgrown in those days," he continued. "My great-grandfather—Patrick James Melvin— had spent months clearing the fields with little help. It was a tough existence at first. My grandmother birthed two babes in the tiny one-room, dirt floor cabin that grandfather had built to shield them from the weather."

Kathleen could have told him that she was more than familiar with that kind of life, but if she did, he wouldn't believe her—or he'd ask how. And she still wasn't prepared to tell him the truth as to her identity. She didn't want to spoil the moment or the day. She was enjoying his company and his hospitality thoroughly.

"They had courage," she said. "It couldn't have been easy workin' the land, not knowin' what would become of it or them."

"Old Patrick understood the land and how to grow crops. But this land was different, wild and untamed. My great-grandparents worked this land by the sweat of their brows, and this plantation is the result. Green Lawns . . . Every time I ride across it, I think of my ancestors and what they left behind for me."

"A wonderful legacy," she murmured, gazing at the land with dreamy eyes. She felt him look at her and turned to face him.

"Aye," he said, holding her gaze. "Aye." He smiled, and she felt the warmth of it infuse her wholely, from her head to her toes.

Her heart began to race, and her mind filled with dreams that could never be. "Where shall we go first?" she asked in an effort to fight her feelings.

He returned his attention to the scene before him. "I know the perfect place for our picnic. Follow me."

With a click of his tongue, he urged his horse forward. Kathleen followed at a slower pace. Rian waited for her to reach his side, and then together they crossed the lawn and took the road through the tobacco fields. A meadow lay ahead, filled with wildflowers and tall grass. They rode through the meadow, through fragrant tall grass and summer blooms. The sun was warm, and the air was heady with a mixture of fragrances. Kathleen heard the sound of running water before they broke from the grass to a clearing near a bubbling stream.

"Oh, how lovely!" she exclaimed.

And he smiled at her. "Indeed. But come, there's more to be seen."

They followed the path of the stream, Rian still in the lead. He stopped and pulled up his gelding as he waited for Kathleen's mount to reach his side.

"There," he said, gesturing to the right. "The perfect spot."

Kathleen's eyes widened when she saw the carefully prepared scene. " 'Tis beautiful," she whispered, feeling suddenly breathless. She looked at the beautiful patchwork quilt that someone had thoughtfully and carefully spread on the cut grass. And there was a picnic basket with a bottle of wine chilling in the cool stream water.

"Shall we?" he asked.

Heart thumping, she nodded. "Aye," she breathed.

She didn't move, just stared at the scene, stunned that someone had gone to so much trouble for her. That Rian had arranged for the food, the scenery, and the wine.

"Who did this?" she asked. Kathleen glanced over to find Rian watching her.

"One of my men."

"At yer instructions?" she asked.

He inclined his head. "I thought it might please you."

"It does."

He smiled. "I'm glad."

Rian dismounted, then helped Kathleen from Rosebud. After hobbling the horses, he joined her on the blanket, across from her.

The sun was warm, but the breeze kept the temperature pleasant.

He tugged on the rope that was tied to the bottle chilling in the stream. "Wine?" he asked.

"Aye, thank ya." Kathleen watched as he reached into the picnic basket and withdrew two glasses.

Rian opened the wine bottle and poured the deep red liquid into a glass, which he handed to her.

She took a cursory sip from the cup as she watched him half-fill his own glass. She studied his hands as he drank. They were strong hands—a worker's hands. Not hands one would expect from a landlord or gentry. But then Rian was a man who would work as hard as his employees.

Kathleen felt her face flush as she envisioned his hands on her skin—her cheek and neck—caressing other places that would give her pleasure.

"Meara Kathleen?"

She blinked. "Did ya say something?"

Rian narrowed his gaze. "I asked if you wanted a meat pie or piece of roast chicken."

"I'll have a meat pie," she said. She set her wineglass down on the blanket beside her, accepted the pie, and took a bite. The crust was light and flaky, and the meat inside was tender and deliciously seasoned.

The sun was hot, and Kathleen felt warm in her riding habit. The wine gave her a deliciously woozy feeling, but it was Rian's company that made her head spin. It had been days since she'd seen him. He was more handsome and charming than she'd remembered. His green eyes glistened in a face that appeared relaxed and happy. There was a sensual slant to his masculine lips. His smile did odd things to Kathleen's midsection. Rian's brown hair looked thick and shiny, and Kathleen had the strongest desire to run her fingers through the golden brown locks.

He was magnificent, a man any woman would clearly want to call her own. *Why not Meara?* For the life of her, Kathleen couldn't understand why her cousin had refused to marry him.

Thoughts of her cousin gave Kathleen renewed twinges of guilt, but they passed quickly, for it was too nice a day. And she was enjoying her time with Rian too much.

"Are you settling into the house?" he asked as he took her glass from the blanket and poured her more wine.

"Aye. 'Tis a lovely place. Henny keeps it nicely. I wanted to help, but she wouldn't let me—"

"And so she shouldn't," he said.

"I'd like to do something, Rian," she said, turning pleading eyes to his. "Isn't there anything I can do to help?"

He studied her with interest. "What would you like to do?"

"Is there sewin' that needs to be done? I've a good hand with a needle . . . a loom, too."

"We've a girl for those chores." Rian raised his eyebrows as he noted her disappointment. "If you'd like to be busy, I'll see what I can do." He dug into the picnic basket and pulled out a pastry. "Sweetmeat?"

"Thank ya," she said, accepting the cake. "I'd be happy to help around the manor house, Rian."

"You're not a servant girl, Meara Kathleen. You've only been here a few days. Have you explored the library? I've a number of books you might enjoy reading."

"I'll have to look. Thank ya."

He smiled. "But you'd rather help at the house."

She grinned as she nodded. "Aye."

The horses nickered, drawing their attention. Kathleen glanced at the animals. "Ye're right about Rosebud. She's an easy mount." She studied the mare with appreciation.

"I thought you would like her." Rian studied Meara Kathleen and marveled again at how different she was from the girl he'd known. She looked appealing in her forest green riding habit. He watched as she undid the top button of her jacket, exposing a little more of her smooth white throat. Her hair was unbound, a glorious mass of long red waves. He had the strongest desire to finger the auburn strands, to see if her hair felt as silky as it looked.

She turned suddenly from her study of the horses and caught him staring at her. He was delighted by the light flush that stained her cheeks. Desire hit him hard, making him want to touch her . . . kiss her . . . take her into his arms and hold her.

He had the crazy urge to do something romantic. Without thought, he bent to pick a wildflower, which he presented to her with a flourish. "For you."

The pleased look on her face as she studied the blue blossom infused him with warmth. " 'Tis lovely, thank ya, sir." She held it to her nose to enjoy its fragrance.

"Rian," he urged.

"Rian," she repeated softly, blushing again.

"Have you forgiven me?"

She looked puzzled. "Fer what?"

"For all those things I said when we were children."

"I've forgotten those things." She looked uncomfortable.

"You're being kind now. I taunted you unmercifully when we were younger, and you rose so wonderfully to my baiting." He leaned closer to caress her cheek. "I'm glad you hold no ill will over it." He felt her tremble.

"As you said, ye were a child, Rian Quaid. We can hardly be held responsible fer our behavior as children."

His eyes twinkled as he shifted his hand to briefly finger an auburn strand. "I agree. Just as I've forgotten the time you dumped a bucket of cold water over my unsuspecting head."

"I—what?" She jerked her head back, taking the silky strand with her.

"You don't remember that, either?" He regarded her with amusement as he dropped his hand. In truth, she had done no such thing, but he'd wanted to tease her.

"No," she stammered. "I don't remember that at all. But if I did such a thing, I apologize." She looked horrified by such behavior.

"Don't apologize, Meara Kathleen. If you did such a thing, 'twas probably because I deserved it."

She looked relieved. "Could you not call me Kathleen? Meara Kathleen seems like too much of a mouthful. I feel as if I'm bein' reprimanded by me mother fer something I'd done wrong."

"If you'd like . . . Kathleen." The name, in fact, suited her more than Meara. "More wine?"

"No! No, thank ya."

"Feeling a bit inebriated?"

The flush staining her fair complexion gave her away again. "I'm fine. I'd still like to see the plantation."

"There will be plenty of time in the days to come."

"Oh, but I'd like to see more of it today!"

He was intrigued by the anxiety in her expression. "And see it you shall." He narrowed his gaze to study her. "Is there something wrong? Something you're not telling me?"

She glanced away, unable to meet his gaze. "Nay. What could be wrong?"

He sighed. "You seem upset."

"I'm not upset. I'm just befuddled," she said, sounding woebegone.

He chuckled, his mood lightened. He caught her chin to gaze into her eyes, eyes that were blue as the summer sky and as bright as the sun above . . . but they were slightly unfocused.

"You are tipsy," he whispered, smiling. "But I find it quite charming that you can admit such a thing and hold yourself so well." He stared at her lips, and his craving for her rocked him. "I'm going to kiss you, Kathleen."

Her lashes fluttered, but she didn't object as he lowered his head to capture her mouth. Her lips were soft and warm and had the sweetest taste of wine and honey. He had intended just the barest brush of his mouth against hers, but her flavor, her response, was more enjoyable than he had ever imagined.

He deepened the kiss until he heard her sharp intake of breath blend with his own rapid breathing.

When he lifted his head, he saw her dazed expression and leaned in to kiss her again.

Ten

His lips were gentle but demanding, and Kathleen clung to him, her head spinning. Beneath the dizzying whirl of sensation, she was aware of his strength, his scent, and she enjoyed all of him.

As fast as he initiated the kiss, Rian ended it. Kathleen blinked as she attempted to control her wayward heart.

"I'm not apologizing for that," he said.

"I didn't expect you to."

"We are betrothed," he said.

"Aye." But she was inwardly shaken by the kiss and the reminder of who she wasn't.

"Perhaps we should kiss again."

"I don't know if that would be wise."

"And why ever not? Didn't you enjoy it?"

She looked away without answering.

"Kathleen," he said softly. He touched her shoulder, and when she glanced back, he caught her chin with his finger and raised it to study her face. "Didn't you enjoy it?"

"Aye." Barely a whisper.

"Would it be so terrible if I kissed you again?"

"Nay," she said quietly, her eyes downcast.

"Look at me." He tapped her jaw with his finger. "Meara Kathleen, look at me," he demanded.

She raised her eyes and felt her breath slam in her

chest as she drowned in the green pool that was his gaze. His expression was tender, amused, but as she stared, the spark of desire in his eyes brightened, and she shivered.

"Rian."

"Aye" he said, the Irish brogue evident in his voice. "That's what I want to hear. Me name on yer lips. Say it again."

She blinked. "Rian."

"No. No that way. Like you said it before . . . when I was kissing you."

She flushed. "I don't know what ya mean."

He began to stroke the soft skin of her jaw, running his finger up to her ear, where he played with her lobe before trailing a path down her jaw to her throat. He cupped her neck with both hands. "Say me name, Kathleen."

"Rian—"

"Better."

"Rian." Shyly.

He stroked her neck, her throat, all the while holding her captive with his eyes. "Try again."

His tender touch made her groan and close her eyes. "Rian . . ."

"That's it," he said, sounding triumphant. "That's the way I wanted to hear it."

Her eyes shot open just in time to see him loom over her as he found her lips with his mouth. He brushed the corner of her mouth lightly. "Open for me."

She gasped, and he took full advantage as he kissed her intimately, taking her lips, then delving past with his tongue. She detected the flavor of honey and port, and she loved the taste and texture of him.

She moaned softly as he lifted away from her.

"That wasn't too terrible, was it?"

She shook her head.

"I suppose you're worried that someone might see us . . . about the impropriety of our kiss?"

Again, she shook her head.

He looked surprised. "You're not?"

"Nay."

"Why is that?"

"We've already spent a night in an inn together. A harmless kiss in full sunlight during a picnic doesn't seem out of the ordinary."

"So you've picnicked with and kissed many." Rian's expression became unreadable.

"I didn't say that—"

"What did you mean, then?"

Kathleen stared at him, then suddenly sighed. "For Paddy's sake, why are we having such a conversation? Do ya want me to feel terrible about kissin' you? Fer if ya do, then I'm sorry, but I'm not sorry. Not one bit."

"Is that so?" The darkness in his expression had left, and merriment shimmered in his eyes once again. "So the kiss was enjoyable to you."

"Didn't I just say so to ya?" she said, exasperated.

He laughed then, making her straighten up and stare at him.

"And what is it that's so funny?"

"I find it more than a little amusing that I kissed you and was worried that you'd be offended by it, and here we are arguing about whether or not you weren't sorry you enjoyed it."

Kathleen stopped, understood his words, and chuckled. "I see. Put that way, it does seem a might strange, doesn't it?"

"It does."

"So where does this all lead?"

"To the realization that you and I have kissed and we both thoroughly enjoyed it. To the knowledge that we'll kiss again . . . and no doubt enjoy it."

"I see." She gazed at his lips, unable to help herself. "But not today."

He raised an eyebrow. "If you say so."

" 'Tis getting late, and I've yet to see all of Green Lawns."

Rian stood then, and offered her his hand. "Then, by all means, we should be going. I wouldn't want to disappoint you."

She accepted his help and was lifted carefully but quickly to her feet. He pulled her against him and fastened his gaze on her mouth. "We've time for one more," he said.

And he kissed her in a way that put shame to those glorious moments earlier when she thought she'd received all the pleasure possible in a man's kiss.

"What of the basket?" Kathleen had asked as Rian helped her into the saddle.

"It will disappear the same way it appeared."

They left their picnic and rode along the stream and through fields and farmland.

As they passed Green Lawn's tobacco fields, Rian explained how the crop was planted, harvested, and readied for market.

"How many acres do you have?"

"Four hundred."

She widened her eyes. "So much? Ye must have a lot of money," she said.

He shook his head. "No more than the next man. It

takes a great deal to run this place. Most of my earnings are put back into Green Lawns."

"Ye've done nicely with it," she said.

"Thank you." He looked pleased. "I'm glad you like it."

"Aye, I do."

"As much as my kisses?"

Kathleen blushed and opened her mouth to make a tart reply.

"I'm teasing you, Meara Kathleen. You look lovely when your cheeks turn pink. And since I'm up on Jake here and can't make the heat in your cheeks rise by my kissing you, I figured I could do it by provoking you instead."

"Ye're impossible. Were you always so?"

"You used to think so. Have I changed?"

"Nay, apparently not."

"You don't like it when I tease you?"

She shrugged. "Do I have to?"

"If we're to marry, then I suppose you do."

She sniffed. "Very well, then, I like it."

Rian's short bark of laughter made her realize how ungracious she'd sounded. "Thank you for your enthusiasm."

She fluttered her eyelashes at him; and when his gaze darkened with desire, she realized that she'd been flirting with him. *Flirting!* she thought with surprise. She'd never flirted in her life, and here she was flirting with Rian Quaid.

Meara's fiancé, an inner voice taunted.

But she doesn't want him, she argued silently.

But that doesn't change the fact that he thinks you are her.

Upset, Kathleen felt the sudden need to escape with

her thoughts. "Rian, I'm tired. May we finish another day?"

He paused to look at her. "Are you all right? You look peaked."

"I feel tired suddenly. If you don't mind, I'd like to return to the house to rest." In fact, she wasn't physically tired. Her mind was too active for that. But she'd been enjoying Rian too much, forgetting, too, that she wasn't, and would never be, the woman in Rian Quaid's life.

Rian spied Peterson up ahead and waved as he steered their mounts down a different path. "Are you sure you want to go back?"

She nodded.

"I'll see you back to the house."

"No," she said. "Go ahead to your foreman. I'll find the road back. I'll be fine."

"No, I'll take you back—"

"There's Jack," she said, suddenly spotting the young man on horseback coming up the path. "Perhaps he can escort me." She gestured for young Jack to speak with them. "Jack, would ya take me back to the house, please?"

Jack glanced between his employer and Kathleen. He must have seen the agreement in Rian's eyes, because he nodded. "Aye, if Mr. Quaid wants—"

Kathleen turned pleading eyes to the man she was strongly attracted to. "Please, Rian."

"Are you certain that you'll be fine?"

"Aye."

"I'll see you for supper?"

She blinked to cover her confusion. He'd kept his distance for days, and now he seemed determined to spend time in her company. "Aye. I'll see you at supper."

"Jack, you'll take her by way of the orchards." It

seemed to Kathleen that a meaningful glance passed between Rian and his employee.

"Aye, Mr. Quaid."

"Kathleen," Rian called after she and Jack had started to ride away. "I will speak with you after supper." This time his look held meaning for her.

She shivered. What did he want to talk about? she wondered. Her strange behavior? Did he suspect something amiss?

Or could it be their marriage—his marriage to Meara?

Kathleen felt her stomach clench. She didn't want to talk about any of it. She didn't want anything to spoil the day they'd shared.

Eleven

"I still say that we shouldn't have left her." Meara felt terribly guilty for leaving her cousin on the quay. "She has no one. Only me."

Seated next to her in the carriage, Robert smiled and patted her arm. "I told you, dear, that if she doesn't go with Quaid, Biggley will bring her."

Biggley was a disreputable-looking character that Robert had hired to tote his trunk to Robert's plantation.

"But what if Biggley can't be trusted?"

"I'm sure you're concerned for nothing." His smile had slipped a bit. "I've trusted him with my belongings, haven't I?"

She nodded. " 'Tis just Kathleen's family, and I'm not wantin' anything bad to happen to her."

"And so it won't. So it won't. Now stop fretting and enjoy the ride." He chucked her affectionately under her chin. "We're almost to Abernathy."

Meara brightened. "Is Abernathy a magnificent place?"

His smile was doting. "I like to think so."

"I can hardly wait to see it." She forced her concern for Kathleen aside, convincing herself that her cousin would come later, safely escorted by George Biggley.

The carriage began to jostle a bit as it hit a patch of uneven road. Laughing, Meara enjoyed the ride and the scenery, which was far different from anything she'd ever seen in Ireland. They were traveling a dirt lane in the forest. It was only natural, she thought, that the road would be bumpy and that the trees and underbrush would grow quickly in the shade to branch out onto the trail.

She studied the passing view out of the open carriage window and wondered how far they had to go before the lane opened onto the cleared property that had once belonged to Robert's father and now belonged to Robert.

Suddenly, the vehicle hit a big bump that nearly unseated her. With a chuckle, Robert steadied her by pulling her onto his lap. "We're almost there," he cried with obvious joy, and he kissed her.

Meara clung to him, enjoying the intimacy, which she'd missed since disembarking from the ship. They'd had little time to be together alone. She kissed him, moaning softly, and became startled when his hand cupped the side of her breast. Gasping, she pulled back.

"We mustn't. We're not wed yet."

Was she mistaken, or did his gaze darken for a moment before it cleared and he finally smiled at her?

"Soon," he promised. "Mother will be happy to help with the wedding."

With an inner sigh of relief, she relaxed. " 'Tis eager to meet yer mother, I am."

Robert ran his hand down her hair, allowing it to linger a moment before helping her back to her seat. "Oh, I can assure you that she'll be more than eager to meet you."

"She couldna expect us?"

He raised his eyebrows. "How could she?" He captured her hand where it lay on her lap. "You must allow me to speak with her before making your presence known."

"What if she hears the carriage and comes out to meet us?"

He shook his head. "My mother rarely leaves the house," he explained. "She's sickly and doesn't get out as she would like to." He smiled and touched a bright red strand near her ear. "Which is why she'll be so happy to see you!"

Meara felt a sudden unease. Had she come to be married to Robert, the man she loved, or to be companion to his mother?

"You do love me, don't ya, Robert?"

His brown eyes filled with concern. "Of course, I love you. Didn't I ask you to be my wife?"

"Aye," she whispered, feeling the inexplicable pinprick of tears.

He slipped his arm about her shoulder, hugging her to him. "I love you, Meara Dunne. Don't you question that for a second."

"I love you, Robert."

He gave her shoulders a squeeze. "I love how you say my name."

"Robert?"

He grinned. "You've a delightful accent, dear. Don't ever lose it."

She shrugged. "I don't know as how I will, since I've spoken this way since the day me mother urged me to speak."

"This is your land? Your house?"

Robert smiled. "Yes, dear. Abernathy. It's a wonderful place, isn't it? I've got my work cut out for me, but it promises to be a grand plantation."

Meara stared with horror at the run-down house with

the overgrown gardens and lawn. Robert had said he was wealthy. What kind of wealth was this? What had she gotten herself into? Abernathy was a terrible place next to her father's estate back in County Clare.

You're in America. You're not in County Clare anymore, she reminded herself.

She glanced at the man by her side, who was gazing at the house with the affection one reserved for home. She loved Robert, didn't she? Then she would make the adjustment and transform this shanty into a home.

"Wait here while I speak with mother," Robert told her.

Meara remained in the carriage as Robert left the vehicle and went into the house. While she waited for him, she studied the surrounding land and outbuildings. There was a barn or stable. Its roof had been repaired recently, but the building needed a fresh coat of whitewash, for the siding looked brittle. And there was a window or two on the structure that needed fixing.

Robert was gone a long time, and Meara began to feel uncomfortable as she waited. Tired of sitting, she got down from the carriage. The horses danced a bit, but their driver calmed them.

She glanced at the house and wondered what to do. If Robert didn't make an appearance soon, she would go inside, she decided. Welcome or not, this was to be her home, and she would not stand outside until nightfall.

"I thought ya didn't need me dowry money, Robert," she grumbled as she saw a bevy of chickens run about the yard. A sleepy-eyed dog lay basking in the sun on the front porch of the farmhouse. The porch roof sagged and was in dire need of some new support posts.

"That's it!" she exclaimed. If she was to be Robert's

wife, she had no intention of playing second fiddle to her man's mother.

Scowling, she reached inside the carriage and pulled out her reticule. The sound of a closing door made her glance back to see Robert exit the house.

"Mother has just gone upstairs to rest awhile. Let's go into the house. I'll get you settled in your own room," he said as he approached.

Meara nodded and allowed him to take care of the conveyance. "How did your mother take the news?"

He seemed reluctant to answer. "Quite well, actually. I'm sure the two of you will get along famously once you get to know each other. She will love you as I do." He bent and kissed her full on the mouth. The kiss reassured Meara as nothing else had since their arrival.

Robert dismissed the driver and picked up the largest bags. With her hands filled with belongings, Meara followed him toward the house. She bit back an exclamation of disgust as she stepped over piles of dog waste and gingerly walked past a stray chicken.

Meara entered the house and studied her surroundings. The interior looked much better than the outside. The furnishings were bold and dark, but they were obviously of good quality. But the foyer could do with a bit of brightening, she thought. And so could the parlor and the rest of the house, she decided as she took a quick peek into the rooms she passed.

"Ya did say you didn't need me dowry, didn't ya?" she asked Robert as she followed him up the stairs to the second floor.

"Of course not." He seemed offended by her question. "That money is yours. But you did say you kept a portion of the sum for yourself."

"Aye. Just a wee bit. Rian Quaid will never miss what I've taken."

He led her to a door in the second-floor hallway. "Why don't you let me hold it for you? I'll lock it in the safe."

She hesitated. She was going to marry him, wasn't she? Then she had to trust him. She dug into her reticule and handed him an emerald brooch.

"Saints and heaven, I thought you had coin, Meara, but this is jewelry."

"Aye, 'twas me grandmother's."

"It's a beauty," he said. Gazing at it with awe, he absently pushed open the door and gestured her into the room.

"Aye. And worth quite a bit, I'm told. Rian Quaid knows nothing about this piece or how much I'd brought with me. I wasn't ready to part with the brooch yet, fer I was fond of me grandmother, and so I am of it." She studied the bedchamber and was disappointed. She would have thought he'd give her a grand room, but this one was dark and sparsely furnished. She would have to make some adjustments. Surely the man had money enough for that.

"I understand how this is special to you," he said with a small smile as he slipped the brooch into his pocket.

Meara wanted to utter a protest when she saw her emerald brooch disappear beneath cloth.

"I want you to be happy here, Meara," Robert said. His eyes glowed. "Come downstairs as soon as you're settled, and perhaps mother will be down and you can meet her."

Twelve

He wanted her. He'd never felt the kick of desire so hard as when he looked at her. And he'd never expected to feel this way at all.

Another complication, Rian thought.

Rian scowled as he remembered the picnic, the wildflower. Then, he'd best stop courting her. Kissing her had proved to be a pleasure beyond compare.

But that didn't mean he'd changed his mind about marrying her. He didn't want to marry. His father's unhappiness in his marriage had left him too disillusioned, too wise, to want a wife.

He couldn't send Kathleen back to Ireland. Her father and family—and his own family—would be offended. They would consider it an insult if he refused to honor the betrothal agreement. No, he couldn't tell her he couldn't marry her. He would have to find a way to make her realize that he wouldn't make her a suitable husband.

He didn't want to marry, it was true, but he wanted her in his bed. He would have to control his desire, for he couldn't shame her or her family by seducing her, either.

He cursed beneath his breath as he crossed the paddock to speak with his groom, Thomas. He had the feeling that reining in the urge to touch Kathleen would prove the hardest thing he'd ever done.

"Thomas!" he called as he drew near.

"Master Quaid!"

Rian forced away his dark thoughts. "How's Midnight?"

"Being a gent this day."

"Has Jason Foley been around to see him?"

Thomas smiled at the mention of their lively eight-year-old neighbor. "He was here bright and early this morning." The groom's gaze caressed the black stallion that pranced about, then pawed the ground. "His mother brought him."

"Lizzy did?" Rian was surprised.

The man nodded. "The boy said that she came to invite Miss Dunne to tea."

"That was nice of her." Rian remembered Lizzy's determination to befriend his fiancée, and he felt mixed emotions. While he wanted Kathleen to have a friend here in America, one would only make Kathleen's stay seem more permanent. But he couldn't very well tell Lizzy or John Foley that he had no intention of marrying his betrothed, just as he couldn't tell the woman herself. He could only hope to persuade Kathleen that her interests would lie better in another direction.

"Have you seen Miss Dunne this morning already, then?" It was barely eight o'clock. He would have thought she'd preferred to lie in. Another puzzle, he mused. As a girl, she'd been a pampered daughter, too lazy to do any chores.

Why now did she seem so intent on helping about the manor?

"I see Miss Kathleen every day," Thomas informed him. "She comes down to visit the horses each morn at seven."

Rian hid his surprise. "Has she asked to ride?" The

girl she'd been would have jumped at any chance to take one of the horses. At nine years old, Meara Kathleen had felt comfortable about her father's stables. He'd seen her riding hellbent and for leather over the grass-covered hills that made up a good deal of her father's property. He'd been taken aback when she'd seemed hesitant to ride the day of their picnic. And while she definitely held her own, he could tell it had been a while since she'd ridden. He had sensed that she was nervous as he'd helped her climb onto Rosebud's back.

It was true that she'd moved more easily into the saddle later in the day, but she clearly wasn't as comfortable on a horse as she'd been when she was a child.

"Miss Dunne has never asked for a mount," the groom was saying. "Although I thought, a time or two, she wanted to."

"You thought this?" Rian was intrigued.

"Sure enough. Perhaps she didn't because she'd forgotten to ask you if it was all right?"

"Perhaps." But Rian doubted it. Still, he would have to ask her.

He and Thomas discussed Rian's decision to breed one of his mares with John Foley's prized stallion; then Rian left to find Peterson.

As he skirted the stables and headed toward the tobacco-drying shed, he saw her instead. Kathleen.

"Hello!" she called, waving with a smile. She had somehow managed to get Henny to allow her to hang sheets on the clothesline.

"Hello yourself!" he answered. He couldn't for the life of him stop from grinning back as he approached her. "Working, I see."

Her beautiful blue eyes looked away. "I hope you're not angry with me."

"Angry? Why should I be angry?"

She met his gaze with a wariness that should have amused him, but he found it annoyed him instead. "Well, ye seemed determined to keep me from being useful."

He frowned. "Was that what I was doing? Keeping you from feeling less than you are?"

"I didn't say that," she was quick to assure him.

"But I did, didn't I." His tone was soft. "By insisting that you relax and allow others to work, but not you, I made you feel useless." She continued to amaze him. How could he resist a woman who continually surprised and pleased him?

Damn, but he had to resist her! Marriage was not in the cards for him. And it was best if she began to understand that the two of them would not be compatible as man and wife.

Kathleen stared at the handsome man at her side and felt the struggle within him. She didn't understand Rian Quaid. He could be kind and thoughtful one moment, then aloof and mysterious the next. Was that why her cousin had stayed away? Had she been afraid to trust this man with her heart? There was no doubt she could trust him with her life.

"I didn't mean to make you feel less than you are," he said gruffly.

His harsh tone made her stiffen. Who was he now? she wondered. He had come to her with a grin and a hello, but now she could feel him withdrawing from her.

"It pleases me to work, Rian Quaid," she said defensively.

"If it pleases you, then by all means work." He turned from her as if the topic had lost interest for him. Shielding his gaze against the sun with his hand, he inspected his land with a critical eye. "Just don't overdo it. It wouldn't look good for others to learn that I've been working my fiancée until she drops from exhaustion."

He lowered his hand as he turned to her once again. "You'd best ask Henny for some salve. The sun is already burning that fair skin of yours."

With a gasp, Kathleen looked down and saw that the area above the scooped neckline of her gown and the part of her arms bared beneath the sleeves had warmed to a light shade of pink. Not a serious burn but a burn nevertheless.

" 'Twas a time when the sun would make you freckle," Rian commented.

She looked up to admit that at times she still did but then remembered that it wasn't she they were discussing, but the woman he thought was Meara Kathleen. She saw that he had already turned his attention elsewhere.

"I'll be careful," she said politely, although something about his manner set her teeth on edge.

"Good," he said distractedly. "See that you do." He started to walk away, calling, "Have a good day now."

"Why I never!" she exclaimed as she watched Rian— with a different side to him—stroll away.

I could have been the hired help fer all the attention he gave me, she thought. No, that wasn't true, she realized. He was more gracious to his employees. For some reason, it was just she who had inspired such behavior.

Well, he hadn't actually been rude, had he?

"Nay," she whispered. "He was preoccupied, was all."

She would never understand Rian Quaid. He was the only man who could kiss her into wanting more. The only man who could admonish her for toiling one moment, then ignore her the next.

He'd make a strange husband indeed. One who would try a woman's patience again and again. One who would make her teeth gnash with frustration one minute and yet make her hum with pleasure the next.

She had seen the side of him that had annoyed her to the point that she wanted to scream. Why, then, couldn't she forget his good side? Why didn't it bother her that Rian Quaid was a man who had faults and thus was human, after all?

Because she loved him, blast it! She had fallen in love with him hard and fast, and there was no controlling how she felt.

Thirteen

Elizabeth Foley preceded the way into the family parlor. "Please, won't you sit down?" she invited. She was a lovely woman with hair the color of ripened wheat. Her eyes were a deep brown and a wonderful contrast to her light hair and fair complexion. She was of average height, with a figure shown to best advantage in a light blue gown with a tight-fitted bodice. Her skirts were ample but manageable and only added to the lovely picture that was the full gown. "I'll check on the tea."

"Thank you." Kathleen chose one end of the sofa, where she sat down slowly and studied the room around her. She herself felt properly outfitted in a green two-piece outfit that had belonged to her cousin. She wore a chemisette to cover the skin exposed by the V-necked jacket, and while she wore a petticoat beneath her skirt, she'd once again avoided one of those stiff ones made of horsehair.

As Kathleen made herself comfortable, her gaze wandered about the room.

The Foley home, she'd noted immediately, was smaller than the house at Green Lawns, but it was impressive nonetheless, and charming. Elizabeth clearly had a hand in the furnishing and decor.

She'd been startled when the woman came to Green Lawns yesterday morning to invite her to tea. Elizabeth had been warm and friendly, and Kathleen had been quick to accept her invitation. Afterward, she'd felt guilty, for she'd now added another to the list of those she'd deceived.

Kathleen tried to banish her guilt as she studied the porcelain figurines on the shelves flanking the fireplace. Two high-backed armchairs, one upholstered in blue and the other in gold, sat across from the sofa, which had been made with a rich royal-blue-and-gold floral fabric. Drapes of material that matched the sofa hung at the two large parlor windows and had been opened to allow in the morning light. A variety of knickknacks and framed portraits of family members added a homey touch to what was often considered a formal room.

"I hope you've a craving for sweets," Elizabeth said as she reentered the room carrying a huge silver tray. She nodded toward the table that was set between the two chairs. "Would you mind clearing that surface of those pictures? I think that table is the best one for this tray."

"I don't mind takin' tea in the kitchen," Kathleen replied as she hurried to oblige the young pretty blond woman.

"You wouldn't?" Elizabeth looked at her, and Kathleen was surprised to see her hopeful expression.

"Nay. In fact, to be truthful, I'd prefer it."

"Well, let's go into the back, then. I hate formal gatherings, don't you? I do enjoy the kitchen for taking tea."

The two women exchanged grins. "I'm glad to hear it," Kathleen said, knowing in that instant she and Elizabeth Foley would be good friends.

Kathleen followed her into the warmth of the Foley

kitchen. She immediately appreciated the herbs and baskets hanging from the ceiling beams, the clean, whitewashed walls, and the hearth. "May I call you Elizabeth?" So far she'd avoided calling her by any name except when she'd first arrived and bid hello to Mistress Foley.

"No," Elizabeth said, startling her. Then she smiled. "Call me Lizzy. Elizabeth is just as bad as Mistress Foley."

"Kathleen," she said.

"I thought your name was Meara." Lizzy waved Kathleen into a chair at a table that was clearly the site of family gatherings. A dining room, they might have, but the Foley family obviously enjoyed the intimacy and warmth of the kitchen hearth.

"Rian used to call me Meara Kathleen," she said without agreeing or disagreeing. "I told him I prefer Kathleen, and he said it suited me."

"It does," Lizzy said, smiling as her daughter toddled into the room. She opened her arms to the child, but the little girl sat on the floor instead and began to play with her doll. "Kathleen is a lovely name. It's so much softer than Meara." She gasped and clapped a hand over her mouth. "I didn't mean any offense—"

Kathleen chuckled. "None taken. I've never thought of meself as Meara, only Kathleen. I'm glad you think the same."

Lizzy looked relieved. "As I started to mention earlier, I've cakes and pastries coming out of my pantry. Do you like trifle?"

"Trifle? Aye, I love trifle, if 'tis the same I tasted while in Liverpool."

"Ireland and Liverpool and now here in Maryland," Lizzy murmured. "It must be wonderful to have visited so many places."

"I—ah— Aye, I suppose it has been." Lizzy went to another small room, and Kathleen's eyes widened when she brought out the promised trifle. "That looks wonderful."

"I decided we deserved something special. Only this isn't the best example for the children—" She stopped. "Emma, don't put Abby in Momma's kettle," Lizzy scolded. "You'll hurt her."

The child looked up and blinked at her mother with huge liquid brown eyes. Like her mother, little Emma had blond hair, but her features were entirely her own. With her short little nose and large eyes, she looked like a pixie. Emma had an impish look about her, while Lizzy's beauty was more ethereal.

"I'm sorry," Emma's mother apologized. "I didn't mean to interrupt our conversation."

Kathleen smiled. "Yer daughter is a sweetie."

"When she isn't getting into mischief," Lizzy lamented, but she gazed at the child with adoration.

"Ya have just the two? Emma and the young boy who came with you—Jason, is it?"

Lizzy seemed to hesitate before nodding. "Two is more than enough for John and me to handle."

"Aye, I'm certain it is."

"So tell me about Ireland. What part of it did you come from?"

"County Roscommon," she blurted out before she thought. Recalling who she was supposed to be, she quickly added, "Fer a time, anyway. But lately of Clare. Me family still resides there."

Kathleen and Lizzy enjoyed a lively conversation over tea. Lizzy asked and Kathleen answered questions about Ireland. Kathleen was only too eager to talk about home, for although America was beautiful, she missed her home. She missed Roscommon and its memories of her parents. She missed Uncle Sean and Aunt Shannon and her younger cousin Shamus. And she even missed her cousin Meara. Here she was in a strange land and had no family. The closest thing she had to a relative now was Rian Quaid. And that connection wouldn't be lasting long, not once she handed Rian Meara's dowry over and told him the sorry news.

She had spent a pleasurable two hours in Lizzy Foley's company. When the clock in the Foleys' foyer chimed the hour, Kathleen realized how long she'd been there and regretfully told her hostess that she had to leave.

"Poor Jack," Kathleen said. "I suspect he's tired of waitin' fer me." When Rian had gotten wind of Lizzy's invitation to tea, he had instructed Jack Peterson to take her. Not knowing how long she'd be, she had thought Jack would wait. Now she felt terrible for expecting it of him.

"Oh, Jack didn't stay, Kathleen. John told him that we would see you home. I hope that was all right."

Kathleen looked at the woman in gratitude. "Aye, 'twas more than all right."

Relieved, her hostess went to the back door and called for her son, Jason. "Tell your father that Miss Dunne is ready to go home now."

"I don't want to be a bother to ya now."

"Not a bother at all," Lizzy assured her. "John will simply send one of our young men to escort you. Most probably Michael as he is the most reliable of the bunch."

"Thank you."

"You're most welcome. Now you will take home some of these cakes, won't you?" Lizzy asked.

Besides the trifle, Lizzy had brought out cookies and finger cakes, and Kathleen had been surprised to learn that she'd made them herself.

"I enjoy baking," Lizzy had said when Kathleen had asked.

"I can see you do," Kathleen said with a grin.

The two women laughed together. "I do tend to overdo it at times."

"Well, I'm sure that Rian will be happy to take some of these fine cakes from ya any time ya'd like to send them."

"Yes, he does have a fancy for sweet treats," Lizzy said, giving Kathleen a new bit of information about the man.

So the bloke likes to eat cakes and treats, Kathleen thought. Why did that knowledge surprise her?"

And she knew, because there wasn't one ounce of him that wasn't hard muscle and sinew. She would have thought that a man who indulged often in treats would have a thickening middle or swollen jowls. And she recalled with a flush of heat that Rian Quaid most definitely had none of those.

Lizzy was right. Young Michael Storm was about nineteen, pleasant, and serious in his duties to the Foleys.

"You'll come back to visit again, Kathleen," Lizzy urged.

"Aye, I will. But first you must come to Green Lawns, where I can play hostess."

The new friends hugged before Michael helped Kathleen into the Foleys' open carriage. They waved and exchanged smiles as Michael pulled the vehicle away.

Kathleen was glad to have found a new friend. Her only regret was that she couldn't confess to Lizzy the predicament she was in. And once Lizzy found out, would she lose her friendship?

She hoped not. She was alone in the world and needed all the friends she could make.

doubt she'll be after both of us for lunch. Bring her, shortly."

She heard and then chose gone quite warm and packed ...

Fourteen

"They're small annoyances, but if they continue," Rian said, "they'll end up costing us a lot of money." The vandalism at the plantation had already cost him time in wages, repairs, and new supplies.

"I wish I knew who was behind it," Peterson said. He regarded his employer across the expanse of Rian's desk. They were in Rian's office at the manor house. It was near noon, and Rian had wanted some private time with the man to garner his opinion on the situation.

"Aye." Rian rubbed fingers over his right temple. "Could it be any of our employees?"

The foreman shook his head. "I've checked all of them. Everyone can be accounted for during the past week, yet we've found that those fields and the paddock had been tampered with."

Rian leaned back in his desk chair. "Well, there's nothing to do for it but keep watch and hope the culprit will make a mistake."

Peterson nodded and rose. "I'd best get out there."

"I don't want you neglecting your family or your health because of this, Pete."

Pete smiled. "No fear of that. Not while Henny is still with me."

Rian smiled in appreciation of the man's assessment of his wife. "I think I smell something cooking now. No doubt she'll be after both of us to come to dinner shortly."

"We'd better go, then."

The younger man waved his employee away. "You go ahead. I'll be there in a minute. I just want to check some figures," he said, and then turned his attention to his ledger book.

"Rian?" a feminine voice said hesitantly.

He glanced up and was startled to see her framed in the doorway. "Kathleen? Did you enjoy your morning with Lizzy?" His heart began to race at the sight of her.

"Aye. Lizzy is wonderful. She made me feel welcome. I like her."

Rian nodded. "Yes, she's a special lady." He looked down at his books, and although she was loath to bother him, Kathleen moved into the room.

"Can I help you with something?"

She flushed. "I—actually—I was wondering if there was somethin' I could do to help you." It was on the tip of her tongue to tell him who she was, but she trembled, wondering if she could do it.

He regarded her thoughtfully. "With?"

"Rian, somethin' is wrong. I can feel it. I saw Mr. Peterson leave here. He looked worried. Can I help?"

His expression warmed. "I appreciate the thought, but it's nothing that you need to concern yourself with."

She recalled Meara's comment that Rian Quaid was marrying her only for the dowry she could bring him.

"If you need money," she began, "there's the dowry—"

His eyes hardened, and his face became shuttered. "I've not married you yet, Meara Kathleen. I've no right to the dowry until we're wed, and besides . . . 'tis not the money."

Kathleen continued to study him after he looked away. It might not be money directly, she thought, but whatever plagued him apparently affected the plantation and its books, for no one unconcerned about funds would spend so much time over his ledger accounts.

"Shall I tell Henny you'll be comin' to dinner?" she asked softly.

He looked at her, and the irritation that had first been apparent vanished. "Aye, that would be a fine thing. You tell her so, and I'll be there quickly."

Feeling dismissed, Kathleen left Rian's office for the back of the house, where she knew she'd be welcome in Henny's kitchen.

They were already taking supper in the dining room when a messenger came.

"What's this?" Rian asked when Henny brought him a missive.

"The Joneses' boy brought it."

Simon Jones worked for the Smithfield family downriver. Rian accepted the letter and unfolded it. He read silently, then looked at Kathleen, who sat to his right. "We've been invited to a dinner party at the Smithfields' come Saturday."

"The Smithfields?" she asked.

"Aye. A pleasant family who live about two miles up the Sassafras." He set the letter down and picked up his fork. "Are you up to going?"

"Do ya think we should?"

Rian gave it considerable thought. "It would be nice for you to meet some of the neighbors."

"Will Lizzy be there?"

" 'Tis possible."

Kathleen stared at him, puzzled by something in his tone. "Lizzy is a neighbor. Is there some reason she wouldn't be invited?"

He seemed hesitant to reply. "Not all of the folks here in Kent think highly of Elizabeth Foley."

She blinked. "Why ever not?"

"Lizzy is much younger than her husband. Some think that she married John only for his money."

"But that's ridiculous!" She narrowed her gaze. "And you? You don't think this, do ya?"

"I think very highly of John's wife."

"But?"

Rian sighed. "To some, it doesn't matter whether or not Lizzy is a good wife. Only that she may have—ah—charmed him into marriage."

"And given him two children as well!" she exclaimed, outraged on Lizzy's behalf.

"Kathleen, this is not my opinion, mind you. But John used to take frequent trips to Baltimore. Then, one day, he came home with a wife—a wife and two children."

"I see." But she didn't really.

"They believe that John had been 'seeing' Lizzy each time he'd be gone for those few days in Baltimore. Many believe that Emma is John's but that young Jason is another's."

"They think she got herself with child so that he had to marry her?"

"It would seem so."

"And what if it's true? Must the poor woman suffer fer the rest of her life?"

"People have long memories here, Kathleen," he said. "I'm not saying it's right, but the fact stands that they do."

"Well, I think that's dreadful!" Kathleen exclaimed.

"Lizzy Foley is a wonderful young woman, and if society can't see that . . . well, 'tis too bad, as she is me friend."

Rian regarded her with warmth. "She is lucky to have you for a friend."

The heat in his gaze made her breath catch. "She's a good woman, is all." She set down her fork. "Will I be looked down upon as well because I've chosen Lizzy fer me friend?"

He shrugged. "Does it matter?"

"Not to me, but what of you?"

"I think you should know this about me: I care little about what polite society thinks. And besides, Lizzy will no doubt be invited. Everyone has tremendous respect for John, and as long as he is around, I would guess that no one would dare to shun his wife. And the Smithfields are kind people. It isn't like them to do so, anyway. I was merely speculating how it could be in certain social circles."

"I don't think I care to meet these people."

He looked at her mockingly. "You constantly surprise me, Meara Kathleen," he said, reminding her who she was supposed to be. "The girl that I once knew would have cared a great deal about polite society and what was expected of her."

Kathleen lifted her chin. "Well, I'm not that girl, Rian Quaid."

A half-smile curved his lips. "I can see that."

Fifteen

Kathleen was nervous. As she stood in front of the cheval mirror in the bedchamber next to hers, she viewed herself with a critical eye. This gown of Meara's that she'd picked was lovely. Of a beautiful blue taffeta, it was an evening dress that was just off the shoulder, with a wide lace collar. The sleeves were short, gathered and edged with similar but smaller lace. The center of the bodice and the skirt hem were adorned with white silk roses and ribbons. Despite the adornment, which was tasteful and had been kept to a minimum, the garment was simply but expertly handcrafted; and Kathleen liked the feel of it.

"I told ya you would look lovely in the full looking glass, miss," Lucy said. Rian had assigned Lucy to be Kathleen's lady's maid. While she needed the girl on occasion to help her dress in some of Meara's gowns, she didn't use the maid's services as Lucy had expected. The girl was pleased that Kathleen had asked for her help this evening.

"I don't know—"

"You'll be the envy of everyone's eyes, miss. And Master Quaid, he'll not see another lady in the room this night."

" 'Tis a beautiful dress," Kathleen murmured as she

eyed how it fit her snuggly. The dress could have been made for her and not Meara.

"Yes, miss. Very nice indeed. The blue matches your eyes." Lucy sighed. "I wish I could look as grand as you for my dear Jack."

Kathleen spun to look at her. "You're a lovely girl, Lucy." She smiled as she studied the girl's flushed cheeks and bright hazel eyes. "Jack? Jack Peterson, is it?"

The girl blushed. "He's a fine man."

Although he was only a few years younger than she was, Jack seemed a child next to Rian. Lucy probably was all of seventeen, a good age for the young Jack. "You could do worse than him."

"He's captured my heart, miss, but he doesn't know I'm alive."

"I think he does."

The girl looked eager. "Why do you say that, miss?"

"Fer he's been comin' around the kitchen lately, and 'tis not to eat or to see his mother."

At the mention of Jack's mother, Lucy's face fell. "Henny," she said forlornly. "I don't expect she'll approve of me for her son."

"Nonsense," Kathleen said. "Henny cares fer ya. She may snap at ya like, as a dog that's got a thorn in her paw, but she thinks you're a dear. She's said so, and I've seen the way she regards ya."

"Truth?"

Kathleen smiled. "Aye." She went out into the hall, with the maid following, and reentered her own bedchamber. "Now, I'm sure I have somethin' here that will impress young Jack."

"Excuse, miss?"

"A gown, Lucy. I'm certain I've a gown or two that

would look right good on a girl such as yourself. I've a
mind to give one to ya."

Lucy inhaled sharply. "You do?"

Nodding, Kathleen found a lovely yellow-and-blue
sprigged gown that she was sure could be made to fit
Lucy.

"Here." She held it up for the young maid's inspection.
" 'Tis nothing fancy, mind ya." It was, in fact, one of
Kathleen's own very best dresses, and she was giving it
away when she might only have two left once Rian
learned of the truth.

"Oh, miss! Truth, it is lovely!" She eyed the garment
reverently and ran a gentle finger over the shoulder and
neckline. "I've never owned a gown so grand."

Smiling, Kathleen thrust it at her. "Well, ya do now.
You may need to take a tuck or two, but I think it will
be good for you. And I'm certain, I am, that Jack Peterson will not be able to take his eyes off you when you're
in it."

"Thank ya, miss." Eyes filling with tears, Lucy gazed
at her mistress with gratitude as she clutched the treas-
ured garment to her breast.

"Take it and be welcome."

"Kathleen?" Rian's voice came from the landing at
the bottom of the stairs in the foyer.

"Oh, miss, I've kept you from being ready. Hold on
a minute!" She thrust the garment on Kathleen's bed and
ran out the door and into the hall. "She'll be down in a
wag of a dog's tail, Master Rian."

"See that she does, Miss Lucy," he called back. "See
that she does."

Lucy came back into Kathleen's bedchamber with
dreamy eyes. "He calls me Miss, did ya hear? Such a

proper gentleman, and so kind as to call me—a servant girl—Miss."

As she spoke, Lucy began to tuck in a few stray strands of Kathleen's pinned-up hair. She then picked up one of the fresh flowers sitting on Kathleen's vanity table and wove it and several of the others into Kathleen's auburn tresses.

"There," she announced. "You look like a fairy queen."

Kathleen flashed her an amused glance. "That could be good or bad depending on the fairy," she said with all the wisdom of being Irish and knowing.

"Oh, a good fairy, miss. One whose beauty can steal away your breath even as she helps ya."

"Well, 'tis all right, then. . . ." Kathleen turned and glanced in the small vanity mirror. Lucy had done a spectacular job of adorning her hair with blue-and-white blossoms. It did make her look a little like a fairy, she thought. *A red-haired fairy princess waitin' fer her handsome prince to come.*

"You'd best hurry now, miss. Master Rian is waiting for ya."

"Aye," Kathleen said, pleased by her reflection. There were twin spots of red on her cheeks, color brought on by nerves, she thought. And her lips looked pinker than usual, although Kathleen had used nothing to brighten them.

She stood at the top of the stairs, hesitant about descending. Her heart thumped. Rian would be waiting for her. Would he like what he saw? No doubt he would look grand, another look to steal away her heart.

"Go on, miss." Lucy whispered from behind her.

Kathleen glanced back to see Lucy's nod of encour-

agement. "You'll look better than all of them combined,"
Lucy said softly.

Smiling, Kathleen turned around and proceeded down
the stairs.

Rian waited impatiently in the parlor for Kathleen to
finish readying herself. Why was it that when you gave
a female more than an inordinate amount of time to pre-
pare herself, the time is never enough for her?

Leaning an elbow against the fireplace mantel, he
stared down at the ashes left in the firebox. He would
have to ask Jack to clean the fireplace for his mother,
he thought vaguely. It had been some time since they'd
burned a fire.

"Rian?"

Her soft voice drew his gaze to the doorway. One look
at her made his chest tighten and his heart leap high into
his throat. He straightened away from the mantel and
drank his fill of her.

Her dark red hair had been pinned up with flowers.
The blue gown that exposed her neck and shoulders
made the blue of her eyes appear darker and brighter.
He thought that he could look into those eyes forever
and never tire of the beautiful woman before him.

Careful, he thought. This night was to find her another,
not to become enraptured with her himself.

"Kathleen," he said huskily. "You look lovely this evening."

He heard her release a pent-up breath. "Thank ya."

She smiled, and if he didn't know better, he would
have thought she'd meant to be flirtatious, until he looked
deep into her eyes and saw that she was not just nervous
about the evening, she was terrified of it. He smiled,

pleased, because it made his planned surprise for her all the better.

Kathleen saw Rian's smile and was unable to read it. It seemed as if it could be genuine or mocking or satisfied. She just couldn't understand it. She felt her skin tingle as he crossed the room and approached her. He looked so magnificent that he stole her breath. He wore a white shirt with white cravat and navy waistcoat, jacket, and trousers. His black shoes had been polished to a high sheen. But it was the man who filled the clothes rather than the attire itself that impressed her.

"Ye're looking handsome," she said as he came to her and reached for her hand. To her amazement, he bent over her wrist and kissed it. The warm contact of his lips infused her whole body with heat. She hoped that he didn't notice as he tucked her hand about his arm and led her from the room.

He led her through the door of the manor that faced the water. He had said that the Smithfields lived downriver, but she'd thought that they'd be transported by carriage, not by boat.

Rian released her arm, stepped outside, and held out his hand to assist her down the steps. Before her lay the crystal-clear Sassafras River and a vessel smaller than the *Windslip*. She kept her eyes on the vessel as they approached. But it wasn't until they had nearly reached the water's edge that Kathleen realized that the ship didn't belong to Rian but to the Foleys, who stood on the deck. She caught sight of the named painted on the boat, *Millicent*.

"Good evening to you!" Lizzy waved, and invited them on board.

"Lizzy," Kathleen gasped, surprised and extremely pleased to see her friend.

"Elizabeth. John." Rian gave each of them a nod and a grin.

"Rian and Miss Kathleen. Good to have you with us this evening." John shook Rian's hand. "Glad to see you."

Lizzy gave her friend Kathleen a hug. "Rian thought it would be nice if we went together. Are you pleased?"

Kathleen flashed Rian a look of gratitude. "Very. Thank ya, Rian."

His green eyes glowing, he inclined his head. "I thought you ladies would want a womanly conversation while we discussed business."

"Business, humph," Lizzy muttered beneath her breath, but then she grinned as she caught Kathleen's hand. "You look marvelous, Kathleen! That gown is perfect for you!"

"You're the one for all eyes, Lizzy," Kathleen said, meaning it. Her friend looked like a fragile blond beauty. Her lavender silk gown was of the latest style and fit her perfectly, hugging her small, round breasts without being indecent. Like Kathleen's, Lizzy's gown was off the shoulder. Lizzy wore a strand of jewels that Kathleen thought could be amethysts. Kathleen's jewelry was a simple gold locket, which had been given to her by her mother, about her neck.

Lizzy moved to brush a strand hair from her face, and Kathleen caught the bright wink of the amethyst ring on her friend's wedding finger. "Such a lovely ring and necklace," she said without envy.

Lizzy glanced over with fondness at her husband. "John gave them to me before we married. He wanted to win me, you see, and although the jewels are lovely, it wasn't that about him that convinced me."

It was just the opening Kathleen needed to comment

on her observation. "You and John seem very happy together."

"You mean despite the fact that he is old enough to be my father?"

Kathleen flushed. "I'm sorry. I didn't mean anythin' by it."

"And I took no offense, Kathleen. Don't worry. John and I just found that the arrangement suited us very well. We were friends long before we became husband and wife. I love and respect John. He is the most honest, caring man that I've ever met. The only one who has come close to him is your fiancé."

"Rian?"

Lizzy smiled. "Yes. You sound surprised. Doesn't Rian treat you well?"

"Aye, he treats me well indeed. And I know he is a kind and generous man."

"Be warned," Lizzy said, her smile fading a bit. "There are many who would like to be Rian's wife. Fiancée or not, you are the enemy. Don't allow any of them to intimidate you or make you feel less than you are. Rian would be a fool to want anyone but you. Besides, I know you don't have to worry. I've seen the way Rian looks at you."

The way he looked at her? she thought. How did Rian look at her?

She hoped that Lizzy was right, that Rian liked what he saw when he glanced her way. She recalled the way he'd regarded her earlier, then kissed her hand, and her heart brightened.

"You're a dear friend fer saying so," Kathleen said.

"I wouldn't say it if I didn't think it, Kathleen Dunne," Lizzy said. "Now I'd like to see you and Rian all married and settled. Have you and he made plans yet?"

Kathleen avoided her glance. "Nay, not yet. Rian has been busy with the plantation, and well, I've been learnin' me way about as well."

"I should think he'd want to do something soon."

"Why do you think that?" Kathleen's heart began to pound. What would she do if Rian decided to push marriage? So far it had been easy pretending to be her cousin Meara, but she couldn't very well marry him in her place. That would be a deception that was unforgivable. It didn't matter that she—and not Meara—loved him with all her heart.

"Kathleen, didn't you know that your husband-to-be is an impatient man?"

She shook her head. "I don't think I've ever seen that side of him," she admitted.

But then Kathleen realized that she had seen that way about him, which made his reluctance to speak of the wedding all the more intriguing.

"You will, dear." Lizzy patted her arm as if she commiserated with her. "You will soon enough. All men are impatient. Even my dear John."

"Truth, is it?" Kathleen said, studying the kind, older man who was Lizzy's husband.

"True enough." Lizzy grinned.

The Smithfield home was a glorious sight to behold as John Foley's man steered the *Millicent* toward the dock and the dinner party.

"Would ya look at that?" Kathleen breathed. "A fine house 'tis. Every window is lit up, me thinks."

Rian came to her side to study the view with her. "Aye. 'Tis a fine sight."

"Isn't that a waste of good candles?" she asked. " 'Tis not even full dark yet."

He smiled down at her. "Probably. But Adelaide isn't

one to be bothered by it as long as she achieves the right effect."

To his dismay, Rian found the sight of her a whole lot more rewarding than a lit house on a summer's eve. He didn't want to desire her, but apparently the choice had been taken from him, for he wanted her with an urgency that frightened him. And made him all the more determined to steer her this night in another man's direction.

Still, Rian had the strongest desire to touch her arm . . . her hand. Anywhere. He shifted closer until his sleeve brushed her bare arm, and he had the satisfaction of feeling her tense and pull away ever so slightly.

She's affected by me, too, he thought.

And then he scowled. That wasn't what he wanted, so why was he happy about it?

It's a fine kettle of fish you've gotten yourself into, Quaid.

"Oh, look!" Lizzy cried, drawing everyone's attention. "Look at the fine carriages!"

"I thought this was to be a small dinner party," John commented.

"Aye," Rian said. "I thought this, too." Perhaps it would be better if it was a large party. More men for Kathleen to become acquainted with.

The men disembarked first, then assisted their ladies.

"Shall we?" Rian offered Kathleen his arm.

She smiled at him and placed her small hand on his sleeve. "I'm frightened," she confided in a quiet voice.

He saw that her smile was indeed a nervous one. "You'll be fine," he told her. "No one in the room will hold a candle to your flame." Rian realized that he meant it, and that knowledge disturbed him even while it pleased her.

The two couples made their way from the dock toward the grand entrance that faced the river. At one time this door was the main entrance, used more than the other, for travel by river was much easier than by road. If the number of vessels docked was any indication, Kathleen was told, it seemed that water travel was still the best mode of transportation.

Up close the house looked grander than it did from the water. Candles and oil lamps lit up the place with a rich golden glow, and as the door opened after Rian's knock, Kathleen could make out the wink of a crystal chandelier and the bright flash of Mrs. Smithfield's earbobs and matching necklace.

"Mr. Quaid. Mr. Foley. How lovely to see you and your ladies." The woman offered Kathleen a warm smile. "And you must be Miss Dunne. It's a pleasure to meet you. And Lizzy? A fine sight you are! I've been looking forward to seeing you again after our last visit, when your husband managed to pry from mine one of our finest horses."

"Come in!" Mr. Smithfield came up from behind his wife. "Adelaide, why are they still standing out there? Invite them in. Invite them in!"

Kathleen and Lizzy exchanged grins; and then, clutching their escorts' arms, they entered the house and were immediately enveloped by the noise made by the guests, the music, and the clink of glass and silverware.

Sixteen

He could feel her clutch his arm tighter as they entered the Smithfields' drawing room. "There must be fifty people in this house!" she gasped.

"Aye." Rian frowned. "If this is a small dinner party, I wonder what Adelaide thinks a large dinner party is." He felt her tremble beside her. "Are you all right?"

She bobbed her head, but her face looked pale.

"Shall I get you a sherry?"

"Do they have something stronger?" she asked.

He grinned. "Looking for courage?"

"Nay. I've tasted your wine, and I've drunk whiskey. I don't know if I have a taste for sherry or not."

He took her hand off his arm and patted it. "Stay where you are while I wander over to see what spirits they have."

Kathleen nodded. She released a heavy breath and stood awkwardly, waiting for him to return. She found that she was the object of several curious gazes. She shifted uncomfortably and wished herself anyplace but here.

"Kathleen." Lizzy appeared from behind her and hugged her arm. "Would you look at that gown on Mrs. Dormouse?"

Kathleen was glad to see her friend. "Which one is Mrs. Dormouse?" she asked, and then she saw an elderly

woman in an outrageous frilly gown of violet and pink.
"I see her."

Lizzy grinned. "She has an unusual taste in clothing."
She narrowed her gaze as she studied her friend. Her
face softened with concern. "Are you well?"

"Barely." Kathleen studied the room. "So many
strangers." She turned back to Lizzy. "I'd wondered
where you'd gone."

Lizzy made a face. "John's attention has been captured
by Mr. Grover. I managed to escape after three minutes
of boring discourse." She turned to regard her husband
with amusement. "Would you look at him, Kathleen.
Poor dear is being ever so polite, but I can tell that he
would give anything to get away."

"Perhaps ya should rescue him."

"I will, but I saw you standing all alone and thought
that you might need rescuing more. You looked so lost."

"Aye, you've the right of it." She smiled as her gaze
caught sight of Rian as he crossed the room toward her.

"I see that your knight in shining armor is returning."
Lizzy leaned close to whisper. "I'll be going to save my
John now."

"Was that Lizzy I saw bending your ear?" Rian said
as he handed her a small glass.

"Aye." She glanced back and chuckled when her
friend rolled her eyes at her before turning back to her
husband to tug on his arm and murmur a few words to
him.

"What's so amusing?"

"Lizzy is trying to rescue John from that man over
there."

Rian looked to where Kathleen had gestured discreetly.
"Grover," he said.

"Pardon me?"

"Ralph Grover. That's the man's name. He's a Baltimore merchant. The fellow has quite a high opinion of himself."

Kathleen's lips twitched as she shared his amusement. "I see." She glanced about, the glass she held untouched, as she observed the other guests. Rian's presence had calmed her, given her confidence. She caught one woman eyeing her with envy. She smiled, feeling pride that Rian was hers, at least for the evening.

"Aren't you going to drink your whiskey?" Rian's voice was close to her ear.

Startled, she spun her head, and their noses and mouths nearly collided, for he had bent low to speak to her. Their lips were a hairsbreadth away, and her heart fluttered. She could feel his breath whisper against her skin.

"Rian." Unwilling to destroy the sudden accidental intimacy between them, she didn't move.

Something glowed in his green gaze and then was gone as he straightened. "Your drink," he said politely.

Too politely, she thought.

She glanced down at the glass but barely noticed it. Her mind replayed those last few seconds when they'd almost brushed lips.

"Are you planning to stare at it all evening or taste it?" he mocked. "I went to considerable trouble finding that particular whiskey for you."

She blinked, and her gaze cleared. She lowered her eyelids as she studied the amber liquid. Surprised at what she saw, she held the glass up to her nose.

"Whiskey?" she asked. "Could this be true Irish whiskey?"

His lips twitched; then he grinned. "Aye, lass. Just for you. Only, I suggest you don't tell the world about it, for it seems ladies drink only wine or sherry these days."

"Oh, then perhaps I shouldn't." Crestfallen, she started to hand the glass back to him. She had come with him this night, and she wouldn't shame him.

He pressed the glass back in her hands. "Drink it, Kathleen, and be welcome. I thought to bring ya a bit of home to make things easier fer you this night."

She felt the immediate pinprick of tears. "Rian, you are a thoughtful man," she said, meaning it.

He looked taken aback by her compliment. " 'Twas nothing."

Was that a hint of red staining his cheeks?

By all that is holy, 'tis! she thought.

" 'Twas everything to me, Rian Quaid," she said. When the flush darkened, she smiled and grabbed hold of his hand.

Rian stared down at the feminine hand gripping his and felt a jolt to his midsection. He shouldn't be enjoying her company this much. It was dangerous to be with her. He should have declined the invitation and stayed home, in his office . . . and away from her.

He had thought to introduce her to a few gentlemen, a proper gentleman, someone who would impress her and make her see that he was not the ideal man for her. But he hadn't expected her to be so vulnerable and alluring. Judging from his memory of her as a young girl, he'd expected her to shine in this party crowd, to move from one person to another, smiling, charming them with her beauty and wit. But Meara Kathleen Dunne wasn't acting at all as he'd expected, and she hadn't from the day he'd met her at the *Mistress Kate.*

Meara Kathleen had grown up but seemed more vulnerable and was more lovely and generous than any woman had a right to be.

Which made it damn hard for him to ignore her.

Kathleen leaned down to take a tentative sip of her whiskey, and after swallowing it, she grinned. "Nothing so fine as a taste of good Irish whiskey."

"I was certain that Smithfield had the best."

"I wouldn't have taken him to be Irish," she said thoughtfully.

"Does one have to be Irish to enjoy our whiskey?" he asked.

She noticed that he said "our" and was pleased that he included the two of them as one. He was part British, a small bit from his mother's side, Meara had told her. In fact, it had been one of the things that her cousin had claimed to dislike about him. *A lie,* she thought, considering with whom Meara had run away.

But Kathleen didn't see that side of him, nor did she care that it existed. A man couldn't help who his ancestors were. To her, Rian was as Irish as her uncle Sean, and she could tell he felt it, too. At times, his brogue was as thick as any man who had just stepped off Ireland's shores.

Kathleen sighed. She loved Rian's voice. It was deep and masculine, and it touched her ears like fine music.

"Nay, one does not have to be Irish, but I'd not have thought it easy to get a bottle this fine if one has no connection."

"Adelaide's mother is from County Cork."

She stared at his mouth and wished she could feel his lips again, touching hers, taking hers, loving her.

Her blue eyes laughed at him. "The Irish connection," she murmured.

"Aye."

"And who is this enchanting creature?" A young man suddenly appeared before them. Kathleen thought he was handsome in a boyish kind of way, but his looks did not hold a candle to Rian's rugged, masculine features.

"Beau Radcliff," Rian said, his expression becoming unreadable. "How did you get an invitation to this event?"

The man looked slightly offended. "Now, Rian, I'm a sought-after man everywhere I go."

Kathleen suspected Rian was stifling the urge to snort derisively.

"Are we going to argue the wisdom of the Smithfields inviting me to their party, or will you introduce me to this delightful lady?"

"Kathleen, this is Beau Radcliff. Beau, this is Kathleen Dunne, my—"

"Gentleman extraordinary," Beau interrupted before Rian could finish the introduction. He smiled and bowed gallantly. "Kathleen. Such a lovely name for a beautiful woman. I would offer to get you a drink, but I can see that Rian has already taken care of it." He barely looked at Rian; his attention was on her alone.

Kathleen studied him and judged him to be harmless. She glanced at Rian and saw nothing in his face to betray his thoughts. Irritated that he didn't appear bothered by Beau Radcliff's attention to her, she gave Beau a smile that was brighter than usual.

"Would you care to dance?" Beau asked.

"We haven't eaten," she said. "Yet there is dancing?" She looked to Rian for confirmation and saw his nod.

"Adelaide wants her guests to enjoy themselves," Beau said. "No doubt she'll be calling us soon to partake of the most scrumptious food."

It was then that Kathleen heard the music she'd detected when they'd first arrived; it was coming from the other room. She glanced briefly at Rian, hoping that he would ask her to dance himself, but he remained quiet, brooding almost. She felt the need to do something to shake him from his silence.

"I would be delighted to dance with you, Mr. Radcliff." She extended her glass toward Rian. "Would you hold this fer me, please?"

He nodded, and she felt the intensity of his gaze on her back as Beau led her away. They moved into a room that had been set aside for dancing and the simple enjoyment of the music. Beau immediately swept her into a waltz. Unfamiliar with the steps, Kathleen felt awkward and inept.

"Relax," Beau urged her. "Follow my lead and you'll do fine." He paused. "You're Irish, aren't you?"

She looked up. "What gave it away—the color of me hair?"

He chuckled. "Your delightful pattern of speech."

She stumbled through a step, and he steadied her and attempted to draw her closer. She resisted, and with a sigh of regret, he allowed her the distance.

Beau began to talk of the party, their hosts, and his position in society. Kathleen smiled and listened politely, but inside she was wishing she was back in the other room with Rian. She recalled Lizzy's warning that there would be women who would be jealous of her relationship with Rian. She tensed. Would they attempt to get close to him while she was gone?

If ya only knew the truth, ladies, she thought. Rian Quaid was not hers; she had no right to him. She loved him, but except for their shared kiss at the picnic, he had shown no real affection toward her.

Where was Rian? Was he off with some beauty, smiling at her, getting her a drink, as he'd gotten hers? Her heart melted as she recalled that he'd found her that whiskey—a bit of home for her. That he wasn't bothered by the fact that she was a woman at a social event imbibing spirits usually reserved for men endeared him all the more to her.

Rian, come rescue me. I didn't want to dance with Mr. Radcliff. I wanted ya to say no so I would know that ya care fer me just a wee bit.

But the room and the doorway stood empty of Rian Quaid.

He should be happy that Beau had asked her to dance. It was what he wanted, wasn't it? To introduce her to other men so she would realize that he'd be a poor husband?

Then why was he fretting about the time they'd been gone? He wanted to march into that room, interrupt the dance, then steal Kathleen away to somewhere private.

But what he wanted to do and what he was going to do were two entirely different things. He wished only the best for Kathleen, he realized, and given his own opinion on marriage, the best would not be him.

If things had been different, if he'd thought it wise, he would have moved heaven and earth to wed her before the night—late though it was—was through.

Despite his best intentions, Rian set Kathleen's glass on a table and made his way toward the music in the other room. Just one peek to assure himself that she was having a good time.

Did he really want to see her? It would kill him to know that she was enjoying Beau Radcliff's company.

Beau Radcliff of all people! He was a successful man, it was true, and the man could provide adequately for a wife, but Beau was an idiot who was handsome to the ladies and knew it. No doubt, at this very moment, he was telling Kathleen what a wonderful catch he was.

Picturing the scene, Rian made a wry face. Would Kathleen be impressed by Beau's praises of himself?

Catching himself, he stopped in the hallway. What was he doing? Kathleen was having a good time. What right did he have to interfere?

"I was just going to check on her," he murmured.

But if you see her, you'll want her, and you'll march into that room and steal her away from Radcliff, uncaring of how it would look to the gaping audience.

Bored, Kathleen waited for the music to end so that she could escape her partner and find Rian Quaid—and award him a bitter piece of her mind.

Seventeen

"Mr. Radcliff, I believe it's my turn. After all, the lady is with me."

Kathleen's heart slammed in her chest at Rian's voice, at his words, and then again after Beau left graciously and Rian slipped his arms about her.

"I'm afraid that we don't have much time before dinner," Rian said.

She nodded, conscious of the strength of his arms and the heady mixture of scents that were his.

"Did you enjoy your dance?"

Her gaze sought and found Beau Radcliff where he stood off to one side, conversing with a young woman with dark brown hair. "He thinks a lot of himself, doesn't he?"

Rian's grin transformed his features, making Kathleen's pulse race. "Aye, that he does," he said, sounding very Irish.

She melted. How she loved this man—her cousin's fiancé!

"It's dark outside. I imagine the house would look more beautiful if we were to walk out and view it later."

Was that an invitation?

"Could we?" she asked, daring to be bold.

"Aye." His expression made her breath catch. "We could."

Kathleen wanted nothing more than to walk out in the warm, dark night with him.

Suddenly, the music stopped, and they could hear the sound of a dinner bell.

"Time to dine," he said, smiling. To her surprise, he released her but wove his fingers through hers. He gazed into her eyes and bent gallantly to kiss the back of her hand. The warm contact infused her with heat, making her want more from him.

Taking her hand and placing it through his arm, he escorted her into a huge dining room.

The array of food was magnificent. All manner of fare had been set up on the tables, and the guests were free to choose what they wanted and then find a seat where they could.

Viewing the laughing and chatting guests, Kathleen thought that the scene looked like an indoor picnic, only with more people and a tremendous amount of food.

Rian took one look at the food table and chuckled. "I should have known that Adelaide would go about this unconventionally. A very unconventional lady is Mistress Adelaide."

Catching his amused look, Kathleen grinned up at him. This was far from the proper dinner party she'd been afraid she would have to endure for the evening. She began to relax. Here there was no table to gather at, and she wouldn't have to sit self-consciously while others gawked at her or asked questions. Thus far, the only one who had approached was Beau Radcliff. And after the look Rian had given him earlier—one that made her forgive Rian entirely for allowing her to go with Beau—she didn't think Beau Radcliff would be seeking to dance or even speak with her again.

Rian and she stood in the dinner line with the rest of

the guests. When it was her turn, Kathleen stared at all the food and wondered how to make choices.

"I suggest you try the vanilla cream if nothing else," Rian whispered in her ear.

Kathleen nodded and then remembered Lizzy's statement that Rian had a love for treats. "What about that cake?"

"I believe it's lemon cake." She glanced back at him as he reached to serve her and himself the dessert.

"You will eat more than pastries, won't you?" she asked, astonished to see him pile on several sweets without trying any of the main dishes.

"Aye." He gave her a boyish grin. "But I prefer to eat the best first, then the meal. I'd hate to think that I'd fill up with stuffed goose eggs."

She wrinkled her nose at the thought. "Stuffed goose—" she began, then stopped when she saw the glint of humor in his eyes. "I see." She nodded, pretending to take him seriously. "I should try eatin' the same way this night. Let's see. Vanilla cream. And what is that?"

"Compote of apples. Tasty, but not as good as those fresh strawberries over there with biscuits and sweetened cream."

She decided to try some of both. "And that?"

"Sponge cake. Probably flavored with extract of almond."

Kathleen looked at him and smiled, for he was already sampling one of the desserts. "I know ya don't always eat like this—"

"No. Only on occasions such as this." He popped a fresh strawberry into his mouth, chewed, and swallowed with a sigh of enjoyment. Catching her look, he grinned. "Henny won't let me."

"Nay," she said, returning his grin. "I didn't suppose she would."

As she took his lead and continued to fill her plate with desserts, Rian looked pleased. "A woman after my own heart," he said.

Her stomach fluttered. *Am I, Rian? Am I?*

Kathleen ate her dinner as if in a dream. Everything tasted wonderful. She and Rian had found two chairs together in the drawing room, and they chatted amicably while they ate. They discussed the food, the other guests, and Green Lawns. When they were done, to Kathleen's delight, Rian suggested they take their walk outside.

He escorted her outside and asked her if she was chilly.

"Nay, 'tis a beautiful night," she said, looking up at the sky, which was star-studded and glorious. But even as she studied it, it was Rian who had her attention. She tingled with awareness of the man beside her.

"Aye, there is much that is beautiful this evening," he said softly.

Something in his tone had her glancing at him quickly. His features were highlighted in the golden glow emanating from the manor house. Rian's green eyes seem to devour her, making her insides warm and her head spin.

He thinks I'm beautiful, she thought, and the evening seemed perfect.

"We'll be staying the night," Rian said, bringing her out of her trance. "The evening is late, and Adelaide has prepared rooms for her guests."

"But I've brought nothing with me."

"Earlier I had Lucy gather some clothes and personal items for you." He smiled as he touched her cheek, running his fingers along her skin, making her breath quicken. "It was part of the surprise."

"But how can she house so many?"

They continued to walk, wandering away from the house and past the gardens, farther into the dark of night.

"I'll be staying on the boat with John. You may have to share a room with another. Probably Lizzy."

She nodded. She'd enjoy sharing a room with her new friend. "Will we leave tomorrow, then?"

"Aye," he said. "I've much to do at Green Lawns. Do you mind?"

"Nay. I never expected to stay. I can be ready to go whenever ya want me."

Want her? Rian thought, staring down into her beautiful blue eyes. Hell, yes, he wanted her. The moonlit night had darkened the blue of her gaze to a shiny sapphire. He stared into those eyes and felt ensnared, enraptured. He had the sudden desperate urge to take her into his arms and kiss her until she was breathless.

"Rian?" Her voice trembled as she gazed up at him.

He controlled himself, realizing that his expression was fierce. "It's getting late. I don't know why Adelaide chooses to hold her parties at such an advanced hour—"

Kathleen had seen the look in his eyes, and although it was gone, she had difficulty controlling her skittering nerves and pounding heart. Had she been mistaken about his intent, or had he wanted to do more than kiss her?

"We should get back to the house," he said. "Adelaide will be assigning rooms. I wouldn't want you to be put in with Mistress Dormouse or Amanda Trent." He started to head toward the house.

"Rian—" She stopped him.

She had no idea who Amanda Trent was; nor did she care. She didn't want to go back inside. She wanted to stay outdoors with Rian, to recapture that moment of danger when she'd felt his desire.

He froze, and she could feel the tension emanating from his lithe frame. "I think it's best if we return inside *now*," he said, sounding stiff.

"But me clothes," she said, feeling helpless. An inner excitement had started to build. "Did ya not say that they were still on the *Millicent*?"

She felt his shudder. "Aye."

"Then can't we get them?"

He didn't immediately answer. The silence seemed deafening. "I don't know if that would be wise at this point," he admitted in a husky voice.

"I could hurry on board and retrieve them," she suggested.

She didn't want him to feel uncomfortable, but she needed her belongings. If he was reluctant to go, then she would find her own clothing on John Foley's boat.

Still, Rian didn't move. They stood in the shadows cast by a copse of trees that bordered the sizable Smithfield gardens.

"Rian?"

Suddenly, he looked down at her with a smile that seemed strained. He sighed as if he were resigned to giving in. "We'll go to the *Millicent* together."

"Thank ya."

He nodded, and it somehow didn't seem strange or unnatural when his fingers recaptured hers. They walked down to the dock and the waiting *Millicent* hand in hand.

"Hallo, there!" Rian called as they neared the vessel that belonged to the vessel. "John? William?"

William, Kathleen knew, was John Foley's man; he had captained the vessel for them. John, she was sure, remained at the house enjoying the festivities with his wife.

Rian released her hand, and she felt the loss of his

warmth keenly. "I didn't expect John to be here, but I thought that William might be—"

"Perhaps William and the other crewmen are enjoyin' a party of their own," Kathleen suggested.

"It would seem."

And Rian didn't seem happy about it, she realized.

"If ya would tell me where 'tis—"

"I'll get it," he said.

She shuddered. "And leave me standin' here alone in the dark?"

"Afraid?" he taunted.

Hurt by his tone, she inclined his head. "I'm sorry if I am and have disappointed ya, but this is all new and strange to me. What if someone comes along to hurt me?"

His eyes flashed in the moonlight, as if the thought of an injury to her disturbed him greatly. "Come on board, then." He held out his hand to her, and she was more than happy to feel the warmth of his touch again. "Watch your step," he warned.

She felt the strength of his grip as he assisted her onto the *Millicent*'s upper deck. They stood for a moment and listened. The quiet was almost eerie. Kathleen could hear the pulse pounding in her head and the wild beating of her heart in simultaneous rhythm.

"Where are me things?" she asked, feeling impelled to whisper.

"Down below," he admitted. "Come. Let's find them."

She sighed, glad that he hadn't asked her to wait above, for she wanted to remain close to him.

The cabin area belowdecks was pitch-black, for no one had left a lantern burning. The threat of fire on an unattended vessel was too great.

Rian mumbled beneath his breath as he led the way

into the darkness. Kathleen held on to his hand tightly and followed him.

"Do ya have any idea where 'tis?" she asked in a whisper. The darkness seemed to demand that she keep her voice low.

"Aye, but it will take me a bit to get my bearings in the dark."

"I'm sorry to put you through this trouble."

"You've been trouble since the first day I set eyes on you, Kathleen Dunne," he said.

Stung, she tried to withdraw her hand, but he tightened his hold on it. "I didn't realize I was such a bother and a nuisance to ya, Rian Quad," she said stiffly.

" 'Tis not a bother ya are to me, darlin'. Nor a nuisance."

She heard a thump and then his mild curse. He released her hand as he turned, but then he grabbed her shoulders. She gasped.

"Don't ya know that ya've been an ache clawin' at me until I want to satisfy it?" he growled.

"I don't mean to be." It was barely a whisper. She was trembling, and she didn't know how to stop it.

"Ah, now, Meara Kathleen. I've a hankerin' to kiss ya now," he said. "Should I do it? Or should I allow better judgment to take hold of me and deny meself?"

He wanted to kiss her! *Do it,* she thought. *Kiss me!*

"Ya must do what ya think is best, Rian Quaid. You're a grown man, and I'm not the one controllin' your decision or yer thoughts."

"Wrong, lass," he said as he drew her near. "You've done nothin' but control me thoughts since the first time we kissed. Aye, I'm a thinkin' that I should try it again to see if the magic is still there. The heat . . ."

Then she felt the urgency of his lips, the warmth of

his embrace, and she moaned and gave herself up to him. The world spun, then shifted, and she thought she would fall if he released her.

"I want to touch ya, Kathleen. Ye're like a breath of sweet air, and I want to inhale all of ya."

She shivered as his words and his hands, which were running the length of her arms, pleasured her in a way she'd never before experienced.

She wanted it, too. But this was her cousin's fiancé, and he thought she would one day be his bride.

The magic dissipated, and she started to pull away.

"Have I scared ya, now?"

She nodded, then realized that he couldn't see her. "Aye," she breathed.

"No need to be afraid. Have I hurt ya before?"

"Nay."

"Will ya let me kiss ya again?"

"Nay." She caught her breath and changed her mind. "Aye."

"Would ya kiss me?"

She swallowed hard. "Aye, if ya want."

"Oh, I want, Kathleen. I want."

Tentatively, in the darkness, she searched for and found his shoulders, then she sought his lips with her own.

"I can feel your breath, Kathleen."

"Aye."

"Kiss me."

She reached up and kissed him, and he allowed the contact to be gentle . . . sweet.

"Now again," he instructed.

She obeyed him, brushing his mouth with her lips. This time, he cradled her head and deepened the kiss until the contact was a tangle of lips, teeth, and tongues and she was gasping and spinning in a whirlwind of pure pleasure.

"Let me touch ya, Kathleen."

She caught herself nodding again. Smiling, she grabbed his hand and gave it a squeeze before releasing it.

With a groan, he kissed her again, and she was swept away in a vortex of sensation so strong that she felt her knees threaten to give way.

And then she was falling back, back, until she felt the soft cushion of the bunk beneath her and the warm, solid weight of the man above.

Eighteen

She'd never been with a man, but the weight of Rian didn't frighten her, nor did his lips against her cheek . . . her throat.

"Kathleen, don't be afraid," he whispered against her neck.

Her answer was to run her fingers through his silky hair while he nuzzled the exposed area above the neckline of her gown. She lay still, breathing heavily as he trailed his lips to her shoulder, kissing the curve before tugging the edge of her sleeve down and following the bared skin with his tongue.

She gasped and moved beneath him. He lifted his weight and shifted to the side, and she wished she could see him—to gaze into his eyes and read what he was thinking.

"You're so soft, so smooth," he said with reverence. "I'm not going to shame you. I just want to hold and kiss you just a little while longer."

She released a shuddering breath as he cupped her shoulder, then transferred his attention to the opposite arm.

"Can I touch you?" she asked, feeling unsure.

"Ah, darlin', you can touch me all that ya like, but have a care now, fer I'm only a flesh-and-blood man and not made of iron."

She found his chest, then slipped her hands beneath his waistcoat to his shirt, which held the heat of his body. She moved her fingers until she could feel the heavy pounding of his heart. *He wants me,* she thought. Now if only she could get him to care.

She leaned up and kissed his chin. "You've a strong jaw, Rian Quaid."

"No stronger than the next man."

"Nay, 'tis stronger than most. And ya have a good face. . . . I only wish that I could but see it."

She couldn't see him, but she could sense his smile. "I don't know why a woman wouldn't want to marry ya," she murmured, thinking of Meara.

He hesitated, and she could feel the sudden shift of mood in him. "Perhaps I'm not good enough to be a husband."

He was withdrawing from her, and she didn't want him to. Rian was her cousin's betrothed, but Meara had rejected him. She knew it was foolish to want the man when all she'd done since meeting him was deceive him, but she wanted and loved him all the same.

Just fer this moment, she thought. She would have him just for this moment.

"Kathleen—" he began, and she could feel him pulling away.

"Nay!" she cried, and grabbed hold of him to tug him closer. She kissed him, putting all of her pent-up feelings for him into that kiss, whimpering with pleasure when he responded.

She was heat and sweetness, Rian thought as he gave in to her warmth. Her rose fragrance enveloped him, incited him, and he found that he'd never enjoyed the scent of roses this much.

He felt the softness of her breasts pushing against his

hard chest. Desire slammed him in the gut hard, and he couldn't prevent his lips from trailing along her throat or his fingers from settling on her breast.

He felt as if he'd been given a gift when she arched up into his hand with a moan of pleasure. Urged on, he lowered his head to the neckline of her gown bodice and trailed his lips over the upper swells of those soft, feminine mounds.

She was unlike anything he'd ever known before. Her innocence . . . her spirit . . . her response to his touch. How in God's name was he to hold back? He knew he had to stop so he wouldn't shame her, for although she was his betrothed, she would not be his bride.

He drew back slightly, "Kathleen," he said huskily.

"Nay, Rian, don't think of the consequences," she whispered. "Think only of this." She grabbed him by the hair and brought him down to her, clutching his head to her breast. With a groan of surrender, he nudged aside the fabric of her gown to kiss the soft feminine swell farther down. Then he tugged the bodice and chemise aside until her breasts were bared to his touch.

He heard her harsh rasp of breath as he kissed one fleshy mound, felt her shudder when he captured her nipple. He drew the tiny bud between his lips, and he felt himself losing himself in her . . . losing control. . . .

No, he thought. He shouldn't do this. *Nay!*

She stiffened, and he realized that he must have cried out loud.

"We mustn't do this, Kathleen."

She didn't say anything, but he could feel the heat of her embarrassment encompass him in thick waves. "You're a beautiful, desirable woman, and I want nothing more than to have you, but it wouldn't be right."

Kathleen felt humiliated as she waited for him to leave

her. She heard him shift and felt him rise. With heat staining her cheeks, which she was glad he couldn't see, she sat up and attempted to put herself to rights. She had wanted to see him, now she was glad that it was too dark. She could barely make out his outline.

"Kathleen." His voice came from across the cabin. "I'm sorry, I didn't mean to—"

"Nay!" she gasped. "Don't say it, Rian Quaid. I understand what you're doing, and I can only honor your good intentions. Ya said you wouldn't shame me this night, and ya didn't. 'Tis meself who would have shamed me if ya hadn't stopped when ya did."

"I'm no hero." His words were thick, harsh.

"Did I say ya were a hero? Nay, I didn't say that. Don't ya be thinking so." She heard a rustling in the cabin. "Rian?" She felt a flicker of alarm.

"I've found your belongings," he said in a voice filled with irony.

"Then 'tis best if I collect them and go . . . before John Foley or his man comes back to find us here."

Tears filled her eyes as she realized how shameless she'd acted. She loved the man, truth, but she had no idea of his feelings. A man could desire without love, and she had almost been reminded of the fact the hard way.

"Can you find yourself topside?" he asked when silence reigned in the cabin, making the moment between them more awkward.

She would find her way without help or die trying. "Aye, I'll be up to follow ya."

"I'll wait for ya onshore."

He didn't say it, but it was probably in his thoughts, as it was in hers, that it would look less improper if she was seen to be leaving the boat alone. "I'll leave your bag at the base of the ladder. Be careful that ya don't trip on it."

"I will be careful."

She didn't hear a sound and could sense his hesitation. Finally, he spoke. "I'm sorry—"

"You've nothing to apologize for," she assured him. It was she, only she, who had reason to apologize that day, but she couldn't bring herself to utter those words. She was afraid she'd burst into tears as she did so. Her heart was breaking, and her throat felt tight.

She heard him leave and struggled in the dark to straighten her appearance. How would she fix her gown and her hair when she couldn't see? It seemed that she struggled for a long while. Whenever she moved, she bumped into something in the cabin.

As if he'd read her mind, Kathleen saw a light on the stairs, and Rian was back carrying a lantern.

"I found this above and had a crew member from another vessel light it for me. I thought you might need . . ." His voice trailed off as he looked at her.

She stared back at him, her heart thundering, her mouth turning dry at what she saw in his green gaze.

She glanced down at herself, saw what he did, and her face heated even as she responded to his flaming desire.

"Kathleen," he said in a strangled voice. He quickly turned from her. "I'll wait for you topside."

Then he abruptly left her.

Hands shaking, Kathleen pulled her chemise up higher over her now-tingling breasts, then tugged up her gown so that she was properly covered.

"Where are Kathleen and Rian?" Lizzy asked her husband.

"The last that I saw them they were walking about, enjoying the night air."

Lizzy nodded, looking pleased. "Has Rian mentioned their upcoming marriage?"

John shook his head. "I'm sure they'll tell us in their own time."

"Seems strange, doesn't it? That Rian hasn't hurried her to the altar. I'm sure he's smitten with her."

"You're a romantic, Lizzy Foley," he said, his eyes warm.

"Me?"

His expression sobered; regret shimmered in his eyes. "I should have left you alone. I'm a selfish old man, and you're a young, beautiful woman. You deserve better than me."

Lizzy turned to him and slipped her arms about his waist, leaning close in an embrace that was affectionate more than passionate. "You're a good man and a wonderful husband and father. I don't regret our marriage for a minute. Why should I when I've got you, Emma, and Jason? I'm a lucky woman indeed."

John's eyes filled with tears. "You're a special woman, Beth. A wonderful wife."

"Aren't we just too wonderful together, then?" Smiling, she reached up and patted his cheek. "Now let's mingle together before Adelaide sees us and presses us upon Mr. Grover or Mr. and Mrs. Dormouse."

Rian stood topside, leaning against the rail, perspiration on his brow and about his neck as he fought the temptation to go below. Dear heavens, he'd been unprepared for what he'd found when he went down with the lantern. He didn't know what he'd expected, but it hadn't been the pure jolt of lust he felt when he'd seen her with her eyes slumberous, a portion of her breast bared and her hair askew.

How was she to fix her hair? Many of the pins must have been worked free while they'd kissed. He recalled putting his hands on it, enjoying its silky length as he breathed in the fragrance of her hair and the flowers.

He closed his eyes, envisioning how she'd looked with her lips reddened from his kisses, the gleam in her eyes that could have been tears.

"Rian?"

He heard her voice from below and realized that she needed help climbing the ladder with the lantern and her belongings. He cursed himself for not grabbing her things when he'd come above. He'd been in too much of a hurry to leave her—before all his good intentions vanished and he went to her again.

"Aye, Kathleen," he said. "I'm here. Hold on a minute."

He descended the ladder and faced her. Her blue eyes were swimming with tears, and he felt a tenderness for her that made him reach out to touch her shoulder. "Turn about," he told her. "I'll help you with your hair."

With a small, shuddering breath, she obeyed him. "I think 'tis a lost cause."

"To have it pinned up, perhaps, but we can take out the pins and flowers. You have lovely hair. You've no need to wear it tucked back or pinned up." As he spoke, he began to carefully pull out each pin.

Kathleen closed her eyes as she felt his touch and fought the tears that threatened to escape at his gentleness.

"I'm sorry to be such a bother," she whispered.

His hand stilled on her hair. "What nonsense is this? 'Twas your fault that you've mussed up your hair?"

"What if John returns? How will me hair look to him and the others?"

"I'll hurry, and we'll be finished long before John Foley says good night to his wife." He had finished with the hairpins and was now combing her red hair with his fingers. The lantern, which sat on the floor only a few feet away, shone on the auburn tresses, enhancing their beauty.

"There, now," he said thickly. "All done."

Embarrassed by the attention and moved by his touch, she turned to look for her bag.

"I'll get that," he said as they both started to reach for it at the same time.

They brushed hands, and Kathleen withdrew hers quickly, her fingers tingling. "I'll get the light, then."

"Nay," he said. "Hold on." With a deft twist of motion, he tossed her bag up to the deck above. "I'll get it." He retrieved the light. "You go first. I'll follow with the light." He held up the lantern. "Have you enough light to see?"

"Aye."

"Go ahead, then,"

Kathleen climbed up the ladder, pausing once to shift her skirts. As she climbed up into the night and the fresh air, she was grateful that she hadn't worn crinolines, for her way down and up the ladder had been made easier for it.

She waited, feeling self-conscious, as Rian climbed up the ladder behind her.

"Do I look all right, do ya think?" she asked. She had to know. She would have to face the other guests before she could escape to whatever bedchamber the Smith-fields had assigned her.

He held up the light and inspected her with glowing eyes.

"Aye. You'll do." Just then a breeze blew up, making the lamp flicker, tugging at their clothes and hair.

He grinned. "You can say the wind took hold of your pins and you decided to take it down."

She reeled under the impact of that delighted grin. "Aye."

"Are you ready to go back?" When she gave him a nod, he took a moment to extinguish the lamp. "Let's go, then."

Then they headed toward the manor house. Walking silently with Rian by her side, Kathleen felt her throat tighten as she longed for something that would never be.

Nineteen

Rian closed the ledger book on his desk and rubbed his tired eyes. He'd been working on math figures for hours, but he'd made little progress. He had trouble concentrating, so he'd decided to tackle the chore again later, when there was a chance that he'd be more clearheaded.

As he leaned back in his chair, eyes shut, he had a mental image of her. He couldn't sleep, could barely think, because of Kathleen.

Since the night at the Smithfields' when he and Kathleen had lost their heads a bit on the *Millicent*, Rian had been unable to get her out of his mind. Her vulnerability, her beauty, and her loyalty for those she cared about only increased his desire for her. He couldn't forget how she'd come to his office, believing Green Lawns was in financial trouble and offering her dowry to him. She was a puzzle, she was, Meara Kathleen Dunne. She was a mystery he wanted to unravel, a woman he wanted to distraction.

Perhaps they should marry, he thought. Much to his own surprise, he'd found himself entertaining the idea more and more with each passing day. After all, they were betrothed. Why not go through with the marriage? Kathleen was not Priscilla, his stepmother. She was kind and lovely, whereas Priscilla was hateful, with a beauty that Rian had judged cunning and evil from the first. His own mother and father had been happy. Perhaps he shouldn't allow his father's disastrous second marriage to influence his future.

Lately, the incidents of vandalism against Green Lawns had stopped. He still had no idea who was responsible, and he could only hope that whoever it was had gone. Until they recurred again, he would have no way of knowing.

This would be a good time to talk with Kathleen about marriage, perhaps set a date. And her dowry would be useful, although it wasn't the money that was urging him to marry her.

As he thought of Kathleen, he wondered how she would react. She hadn't brought up the subject of their marriage, although she had mentioned giving her dowry to him. Had that been a hint that she was ready to wed?

Rian sat forward and stared at the door. He remembered the girl that she'd been and found the woman she'd become so different. It was as if a fairy had sprinkled fairy dust on her, transforming her from the spoiled, feisty child to an enchanting woman. Not that Kathleen had lost her spirit. He'd seen it on occasion, when her blue eyes had sparked with anger when she'd been challenged or her hot Irish tongue had gotten the best of her. For the most part, however, she'd managed to control it.

Once they were married, he would enjoy provoking her, he thought, making her let loose her tongue a time or two. But not too often. He'd rather enjoy her fire in the marriage bed when they made love. He smiled. Kathleen had grown up, and he liked who she was now.

He had teased her as a child, delighting to rouse her ire, and while he'd liked her enough, he had to admit that the thought of marrying had seemed a bit daunting. But he'd been prepared to do so because his family had wished it—until his father's remarriage, to Priscilla. And Rian had forced his own betrothal from his mind.

How does one go about bringing up the subject of marriage?

He thought of their picnic together, of the time on the *Millicent*, and felt it would be best to woo her a bit so that she'd agree that a date should be set quickly.

He rose from his desk and went to the window, studying the green lawns that his grandfather had planted and which he, as a boy, had enjoyed running free over.

Another picnic? Or should he take her out on the *Windslip*? Perhaps a day on the boat alone would be the ideal thing to do.

But then, who would captain the ship so that he could spend time with her? He had no intention of bringing another along on this occasion.

A skiff? He could take her for a short boat ride, go ashore in a private spot on his property along the Sassafras, and there they could be alone to . . .

The warmth of her skin . . . the sweet taste of her mouth moving beneath his . . . her blue eyes glistening, glowing . . . the soft sounds of her whimpers as he touched her, pleasured her.

Rian cursed as he felt himself harden beneath his breeches.

He wanted Meara Kathleen Dunne, and he would marry her to have her. He only hoped that when the passion died, he wouldn't regret life with his new wife.

He closed his eyes, saw her face, her sweet smile, and shook his head. He would have her—any way he could get her. Since he'd thought long and hard on the subject and found no way to take her to bed without shaming her, himself, or their families, then he would simply

marry her. And marry her soon, before he shamed them
all with his lack of control over his lustful body.

"Miss Kathleen, you don't have to be helping out here
in the kitchen," Henny said from near the stove.

"But I like helpin', Henny." Kathleen picked up a
green bean and snapped off both ends before putting it
in a pot.

The two women were working on the evening's supper.
Henny was making a thick stew, and Kathleen was fixing
the vegetables for her. Earlier, she had cut up a head of
cabbage and yellow and green squash. After she was
done with the long green beans, she had tomatoes and
onions to slice and chop up.

Kathleen watched Henny stir the simmering meat and
broth. The housekeeper might seem a gruff old soul, but
Kathleen loved her. Henny had shown only kindness toward her, and she welcomed Kathleen in her kitchen . . .
and in her heart. Kathleen could only ask now for anything, and it was granted her. Knowing the background
of Meara Kathleen Dunne, Henny had been surprised by
Kathleen's desire to help, but Kathleen had proved herself an eager and capable assistant. And now Henny and
the other girls were more than grateful for her help.

"You should be out picnicking with your betrothed,"
Henny said as she added some salt and other seasons to
the beef stock.

"Rian is busy with his plantation work. I'm content
to assist here."

"Well, I should have a talk with the boy, then, for
you're a young woman and should have some fun in your
life other than house and kitchen work."

Kathleen looked up as she grabbed a handful of beans

from the pile. "Please, Henny, don't ya be sayin' a word to Rian. He has enough worries on his mind."

Henny stiffened as she turned. "What have you heard?"

Frowning, Kathleen snapped another bean. "Nothing, only . . ." She met the housekeeper's gaze with a look of concern. "I saw your husband and Rian talking earnestly. I think something is wrong, but I don't think he'd be happy if I asked or interfered."

"Don't concern yourself, Kathleen," the woman said, her expression softening.

"That's what Rian said the first time I inquired about it." She shook her head and went back to her chore. "I'm not such a foolish child that I can't listen and perhaps help."

Henny came to the worktable, and Kathleen looked up at her. "You're a sweet child, Kathleen. Rian, he'll tell you things in time."

"I don't think so, Henny. I think he wishes I'd leave. I think I'm a distraction to him. One he doesn't care to have about."

"Nonsense. Rian Quaid is glad you're here. And he'll tell you himself once he gets around to it. You see, men are strange creatures. They know what is good for them, yet they resist it like they did their mother's remedy for a bellyache when they were young. They know the remedy will make them well, but they say no because it was their mother—a woman—who suggested it."

Kathleen grinned. "Perhaps I should fix Rian some of me elixir fer bellyaches." She finished the one pile of beans and reached for the remainder.

Henny chuckled. "Perhaps you should, Kathleen. It would be one way to get the man's attention."

"Miss?"

"Aye, Lucy?"

The maid glanced at Henny before switching her gaze back to Kathleen. "Master Rian, he asked me to get you. He wants to see you outside. He's in the garden. The one with all the flowers and herbs in it."

Kathleen set down her last bean and rose. "Henny—"

"Go, child. Lucy will help me, won't ya, girl?"

Lucy nodded. "Yes, ma'am, I'll be happy to help." The girl sat in the seat that Kathleen vacated and began to snap the last of the remaining beans.

In the end, when he thought of her, he decided somewhere with flowers, and he chose a place that was close and familiar, and safe. He waited for her in the garden, where the scent of roses was strong but pleasant. He paced the stone walk, thinking of her, nervous, wondering what she would say, eager to see her.

He sensed her coming before she broke through the border of trees. He watched her approach as she stopped to sniff a flower. She wore a green-and-white-striped satin dress. Her hair was unpinned, flowing in a glorious red cloud about her neck and shoulders. He felt his chest tighten as she plucked off a blossom and tucked it into her hair, wedging it behind her ear.

He moved forward to meet her.

"Kathleen."

Her smile was tentative. "Rian."

"Thank you for meeting me here."

Concern flickered in her expression. "Is something wrong?"

He could feel emotion building within him. He wanted her, and each time he saw her, he was bowled over by how beautiful she was, how enchanting.

"Nay." The Irish brogue was thick in his voice again. "I wanted to talk with ya. Will ya walk with me?"

She studied his face and nodded.

He reached for her hand and felt her surprise as he took it, but she didn't pull away. "Kathleen, about that night . . . on the *Millicent*."

She was silent, and he turned to find her flushing with embarrassment. "Rian, I'd prefer to forget that night—"

"I wouldn't." he said huskily. "I wanted ya that night, and I want ya now."

He heard her make a little gasp. "Rian . . ."

He stopped, turned her to face him, and gazed down at her with longing. "Kathleen, marry me. Marry me today. Tomorrow. As soon as it can be arranged."

Her eyes widened, and her features grew pale. "Rian, I don't know what to say."

He had to stifle a surge of disappointment. "Say, 'Aye, Rian, I'll marry ya.' "

"But there are things ya don't know about me,"

"As there are things you don't know about me." He tilted his head as he gazed at her mouth. He wanted to kiss those lips, to hold her and caress her until she whimpered with desire for him.

"We'll have our whole lives together to learn of each other's faults and foibles . . . as well as our talents, our habits, and our good sides."

"Rian, I—"

"We are betrothed, Kathleen. Why are ya hesitatin'? Isn't our betrothal the reason ya came to America?"

She bit her lip before answering. "Aye."

"And you find me attractive enough, don't ya? You've told me a time or two, I believe."

She nodded, her cheeks warming to a bright crimson.

"Then just say what I want to hear. Tell me that you'll

marry me. Ya can choose the day and time. Whatever ya want is fine by me just as long as ya don't make me wait much longer."

He put his arms around her, pulled her toward him slowly, and then lowered his head until his lips were almost touching hers. "Say it, Kathleen," he whispered urgently.

"I don't want to anger or disappoint ya."

"You couldn't disappoint me unless ya tell me that ya don't want to marry me." He lifted his head a fraction higher. "Ya do want to marry me now, don't ya?"

She raised her chin and looked him steadily in the eye. "Aye, Rian Quaid, I want to marry ya. Nothin' would make me happier than to be your wife."

Her words rang true, and for a moment he was startled. Then he smiled and felt a great burden lift from his shoulders.

"Ah, Kathleen, you've made me a happy man this day." He took her lips, kissing her tenderly. When she responded with fervent passion, he deepened the kiss. "A very happy man," he murmured against her mouth.

She slipped her arms about his waist and called his name in a raspy voice that begged for him to do more than kiss her.

He set her back. "We'll talk after supper and make plans," he said.

"Aye." She looked happy but dazed as she started to turn back to the house.

"Kathleen?"

She whirled around, her blue eyes glistening. "Aye?"

"Here," he said. He chose the prettiest rose and plucked off the thorns before giving the blossom to her. "A rose for an Irish rose." He lowered his head again and sipped from her lips, unable to keep from kissing or touching her as they stood there in the garden.

She felt his chest swell with pride and happiness. And it gave her immense joy. "Thank ya, Rian Quaid."

"You're very welcome, Miss Kathleen . . . soon to be Mrs. Quaid." To his delight, it felt wonderful knowing that she would soon be his.

Twenty

"The gown's going to be lovely, miss," Lucy said. "You'll be the most beautiful bride."

"You're going to look like a dream, Kathleen," Lizzy agreed.

Kathleen looked down to examine the garment as she stood for the fitting. " 'Tis a lovely fabric." Rian had commissioned a gown from a woman from Baltimore, and Mrs. Elton was on her knees, taking tucks and pinning up the hem. The gown had been made with Irish lace. She recognized the quality of the material and appreciated it all the more, for she knew the work that went into its creation.

The wedding preparations were moving along at a fast pace. Kathleen felt as if she'd been caught up in a storm of activity, unable to stop or control the whirlwind's raging fury.

She would be getting married in one week. One week—to a man who was her cousin's betrothed, not hers. Yet she didn't know how to stop it. She loved Rian Quaid, and while she didn't want to continue to deceive him, she hadn't had the opportunity, or the desire, to tell him the truth.

I should have told him that night after supper, she thought. But he'd seemed so pleased with her acceptance that she hadn't had the heart then, was afraid that he'd hate her just as he had begun to care for her. . . .

I will have to tell him soon. It doesn't matter if he sends me away. I'll have to tell him.

She felt a sharp shaft of pain at the thought of leaving him. She wanted to marry him more than anything, but how could she under these circumstances?

"Kathleen?"

"Aye?" Her friend eyed her with concern.

Lizzy said nothing for a moment. "Mrs. Elton is done. Lucy, can you get Miss Dunne and me a pot of tea?"

"Yes, miss." The maid dipped a curtsy and was gone. With Mrs. Elton's and Lizzy's help, Kathleen stepped from the pinned wedding gown.

"I'll have this ready for you in three days," the woman said in a businesslike tone.

Kathleen nodded. "Thank you, Mrs. Elton." She forced a smile to her lips. "The gown is lovely. Thank ya 'gain."

When everyone had left, Lizzy grabbed Kathleen's hand and led her to the upholstered chair in Kathleen's bedchamber.

"You look pale," Lizzy said softly. She pressed Kathleen to sit down. "What's wrong, Kathleen?"

Kathleen averted her glance. She opened her mouth to confess, then snapped it shut again.

"Kathleen? What's wrong? Tell me. I swear I won't tell anyone."

The desire to tell her friend was strong. "This is happening very fast, Lizzy."

Moving another chair to sit before her, Lizzy sat and patted Kathleen's hand. "Kathleen, do you love Rian Quaid?"

Kathleen was startled by the question, and her gaze

flew to her friend's face. Lizzy's expression was gentle with understanding. "Aye. Aye, I love him. More than anything."

"You're going to marry the man you love. Why are you worried?"

"There is something he doesn't know about me," she replied. "Something ya don't know. . . ." Her eyes filled with tears as she looked down at their joined hands and clutched her friend's fingers. "I've done a terrible thing, and I don't know how to unravel it."

She could feel her friend's curiosity, but mostly her concern. "In Ireland or here?" Lizzy asked.

"Here." Kathleen whispered.

Lizzy smiled. "You've been here how long? A month? What could you have done in a month's time that's so terrible it's got you fretting so?"

Kathleen had to tell someone, and Lizzy was the one person she trusted above all others—except Rian. And she hadn't found the courage to tell him yet. "You won't tell a soul?"

The other woman nodded, her eyes warm, her expression compassionate.

Kathleen hesitated, for she didn't want to see the shock, the horror, in her friend's gaze. She didn't want to lose her only friend.

"I'm not Rian's betrothed. Meara Kathleen Dunne is me cousin. I'm Kathleen Maguire, and now I'm to marry me cousin's fiancé, and I don't know how to stop it! I don't want to stop it, God help me! Oh, Lizzy, tell me what to do!"

"Your mother doesn't like me," Meara complained. "I can see it in her gaze. She hates me."

"She doesn't hate you," Robert said. He looked annoyed. "She's not an affectionate woman, that's all."

"Affectionate? By all the saints that are holy, Robert, the woman is a stone-cold fish. She watches me like I'm an eel that's slipped into her home and wrapped itself about her baby."

"You must have patience with her!" Robert snapped. "She's my mother. We all live here. You must learn to get along with her. To love her."

Love her? Meara thought. Mrs. Widham was unlovable in her opinion, but she would give it more time, have more patience. For Robert. The man she loved.

"I'll try to do better with her, Robert," she said, touching his sleeve, trying to coax a smile from him.

She hated to be at odds with Robert. He was so handsome, and he made her heart flutter as no man before. It hurt her when he was upset with her. She wanted their life to be perfect. And if this house, this estate, wasn't Ireland or the grand picture that Robert had painted for her, it was livable and would improve with a little hard work and a great deal of care.

She frowned. If only Mother Widham would allow her to tackle the job; if only the woman would accept her as the one who would be Robert's wife.

"Robert," she said softly. "I love you, and I love your mother." *Just a wee lie,* she thought, and promised to ask for God's forgiveness later. She would grow to love the woman, she vowed. Somehow she would crack the layer of bitterness and grief that had hung like a haze about the woman since the death of her husband three years before.

To her relief, Robert's expression softened as he turned her to face him and pulled her into his arms. "That's my girl," he said, bending to kiss her.

His kiss was filled with passion but was all too short, and it left Meara wanting.

"Robert, can you get away for a little while? May we have an outin' together? Perhaps a picnic?" She was dying to be alone with him. It seemed that they were rarely allowed time alone together.

He gazed down at her with an affectionate smile on his lips. "I'll see what I can do."

"Please, Robert." She ran her hands up his chest and then higher, tangling her fingers in the hair that brushed his collar.

Although he was basically a farmer, he rarely wore anything but trousers, shirts, fancy waistcoats, and jackets—all very proper attire for business but not for working the soil with your hands or running about the farm doing other tasks.

Still, his dress, his perfection, titillated her. She wanted to tug off his jacket and waistcoat, slip her fingers under his white shirt and then down into his trousers. She could hardly wait until they were married so she could have him all proper, without shaming herself.

Boldly, uncaring of how it would look to any workers who passed by, Meara pulled his head down to kiss him. She nibbled his lips, then opened her mouth and touched him with her tongue. She could feel him tense, heard his groan of desire, and she deepened the kiss and slipped her hands between their pressed bodies, delving fingers beneath his waistcoat to rub his nipples through his shirt.

He was overcome with the heat that built between them, and Meara knew that she lived for the moment when she could be his wife and his lover.

Robert lifted his head and reluctantly pushed her away. "Meara."

"Please, Robert. Just a picnic. We'll be out-of-doors,

enjoyin' the sun together. I'm sure I can find some food to take with us."

He stared down at her, his dark eyes glowing, his breath labored, his expression grim.

"I love you, Robert." Her eyes pleaded.

He released a shuddering breath. "You'll have your picnic. After I meet with Hackney."

Meara nodded, pleased. Hackney, the foreman, was a slimy, slippery little man, but Robert seemed to trust him. All the same, she was glad he was going to check up on him. "I'll make us some sandwiches."

"And some of that chocolate cake you made yesterday?" he said, his eyes bright with a little boy's anticipation.

She laughed, feeling happy. "Aye, Robert, me love. I'll cut two huge slices of that chocolate cake fer ya and one tiny one fer me."

Twenty-one

"Oh, Kathleen . . ." Lizzy regarded her with dismay.

"What am I to do, Lizzy? What am I to do?"

"You love him, don't you?"

"Aye. More than anythin'."

"How did this happen?"

And Kathleen explained how she accompanied her cousin to America, how her cousin had fallen in love with another man and refused to consider honoring the betrothal agreement.

"I can't tell you what to do, Kathleen," Lizzy said when Kathleen had finished her explanation. "You must do what's in your heart."

"I know what's in me heart and what is right. I just don't know how to tell him. I truly want to marry him, but once he learns the truth, he'll hate me . . . send me away.

"You don't know that."

Kathleen shook her head. "Aye, that I do. Rian needs Meara's dowry money, and I've got it here for him. But I don't think he'll take it without the bride."

Lizzy gazed at Kathleen with warm compassion.

"You're not angry with me?" Kathleen was astonished. "You're still me friend?"

"Of course I'm your friend," Lizzy said.

"You must think me a terrible person."

"No," she said. "I don't think that at all."

"But how can you feel that when your marriage is so good. So perfect. How do you think John would feel if ya'd deceived him the way I've deceived Rian."

"My marriage is not what you think it is," Lizzy admitted. "My relationship with John is wonderful, but it's not what you would call a real marriage."

Kathleen gaped at her, surprised by her friend's words. "I don't understand . . ."

"This secret, as well as yours, will stay in this room forever?" Lizzy looked worried.

"Aye," she whispered.

"John and I are husband and wife in name only," Lizzy confessed. "We share a house and a family, but we don't share the marriage bed."

"No, surely . . ."

"It's true, Kathleen." Lizzy gave her a crooked smile. "I married John because he needed a mother for his daughter and I needed a father for my brother, Jason."

Kathleen was shocked. "Emma and Jason are not your children?"

"No. My parents died, leaving Jason in my care, and I was struggling to provide for us when John asked me to marry him. I refused at first, but, well . . ." A tender smile curved her pink lips. "John Foley can be quite persuasive. He's really a dear, and I don't regret our marriage one bit. Only sometimes . . ."

She sighed and glanced at Kathleen's bedchamber window. "It's not important," Lizzy continued. "The important think is that I've got a family—a wonderful husband, two children, who I think of as my own—and now I have you, Kathleen Maguire, for my friend."

Tears filled Kathleen's eyes, making it difficult for her to see. "Thank ya for sayin' that."

"It's the truth." Lizzy smiled. "Somehow you will get through this. If I can help, if you need me, know that I'll be here for you."

"I've got to tell him," she said, "but I'm frightened."

"You think about what to do long and hard; then you decide what's best for Rian . . . *and* for you."

Lizzy grabbed Kathleen's hand and squeezed it. "He cares for you, Kathleen. I can see it in his expression every time he looks at you. I never thought he would marry. His father made a terrible mistake the second time around. Rian and his stepmother never got on. Priscilla couldn't stand the fact that Rian was the only heir to Green Lawns and first in Michael Quaid's affections. Priscilla had two children by her first marriage, and she felt it was their due that they each inherit one third of Green Lawns . . . but Michael . . . he saw things differently. Green Lawns was a legacy built by Rian's grandfather meant for Rian and his heirs."

"You've met Rian's father?"

"No," Lizzy admitted. "But John knew Rian's father, and he told me about Michael's relationship with Priscilla. Priscilla made not only Michael but also Rian miserable. When Michael died, Priscilla got nothing, and so she left—with her two offspring. Bitter and angry, she hasn't been back to Green Lawns since."

"That's good, isn't it?"

Lizzy shrugged. "Yes, one would think. He never mentions her, but I wonder if Rian trusts her to stay away. She'd been gone for three years now, but she made such an impression on him that even John thought Rian would never marry." She grabbed a pastry and studied it. "We were startled to hear that he had a fiancée . . . that he had you."

Kathleen smiled sadly. "Meara."

Lizzy looked up and set the pastry back on her plate. "But he cares for you, not Meara."

"And so what are ya sayin'? That I should keep me secret and go on to wed him?"

Lizzy picked up her teacup and took a sip, giving herself time to consider Kathleen's question. "I'm saying that you should weigh everything that's involved, then make the decision you think is best. I'll be on your side whatever you decide. And you can trust me to hold your secret forever, if necessary."

Later, much later, when the household had retired for the night and she was alone in her bed, Kathleen thought of Lizzy's words. Was her friend giving her advice?

"And you can trust me to hold your secret forever."

Was she telling her to hold her tongue, to keep her secret and marry the man she loved but had deceived?

Could she live with herself if she continued to deceive him?

She tossed and turned in bed, unable to sleep until the early hours of dawn, when exhaustion took over, and Kathleen fell asleep for an hour or so, before the morning sun woke her. She climbed out from between the sheets to face another day's struggle of deciding what to do.

There was the crack and the sound of splintering wood, then a man's pain-filled cry.

"Pete!" His heart thumping with alarm, Rian ran inside the barn, saw what had happened, then hurried to his foreman's side to check his injuries.

Peterson had been in the barn below the hayloft when the loft above had given way, sending wood and hay raining down on the man beneath. Pete's leg was pinned by a wooden beam. From his head injury, Rian realized that a broken chunk of wood had bounced off his head; he saw where it lay within a foot of Pete.

Rian knelt by the man's side, his stomach tightening as he saw the blood on Pete's forehead. His gaze carefully sized up Pete's condition. The open wound on Pete's head was minor. His attention lowered to the overseer's leg.

Pete's right calf needed medical attention, but first it had to be freed from beneath the beam that pinned it to the barn's dirt floor.

"Thomas! Martin!" he called. But no one was around to help. Rian tried to move the beam, but it wouldn't budge.

Hearing sound behind him, he glanced back and inhaled sharply when he saw Pete's son. "Jack, where's Thomas?" he asked.

The young man looked shaken by the sight of his injured father. "In the stables."

"Find him. And find Martin and Jacobs the worker as well. We've got to move this beam off your father's leg, and now."

Jack stood frozen, staring at his bleeding and pale father.

"Now, Jack!" Rian ordered sharply. "Hurry!"

The boy flashed him a distressed look, then took off running to find the hired hands.

While waiting for Jack and the men to return, Rian tried to make Peterson comfortable. He again checked Pete's head wound. While he was sure the loss of blood wasn't serious, he was worried about broken bones and what the knock to the man's head had done to his brain.

"Can I help?" The voice was deep, Irish, and unfamiliar.

Startled, Rian turned and narrowed his gaze at the sight of the stranger. *"Who the hell are you?"*

The man didn't flinch, but held Rian's gaze steadily. "Conor," he said. "Conor McDermott. Newly come from Ireland. I'm lookin' for work, and I was told that the owner of Green Lawns might be hirin'. Might ye be him?"

"Aye," Rian said. "But I don't know where you've heard such a tale, for I haven't sent out a notice of looking to hire."

The man shrugged. "Looks like you can use the help at present."

Rian glanced up at him suspiciously. "You wouldn't know anything about falling lofts now, would ya?" he challenged.

Anger flashed in the man's blue eyes. "Nay, I wouldn't."

He had eyes of bright azure—much like Kathleen's, Rian thought. And the man was Irish. He shifted his gaze to gauge the man further and felt the wariness leave him. Conor McDermott didn't appear to be a threat. Perhaps he'd been too quick to judge the man.

"Can you help here to raise this beam, Mr. McDermott?"

"Aye." Conor McDermott crouched at the opposite end of the beam from Rian. "We must go easy," the man said. "If she drops back into place, we're liable to crush the man's leg or slice his calf. 'Tis certain that he'll be needing his leg again, and soon."

Locking gazes with the Irishman for a long pause, Rian nodded. Conor McDermott was a man of size, with muscles that had seen work and with the strength of two of his hired hands. "I've sent for help."

Conor shook his head. "Nay. We shouldn't wait for help. We should do it, and quickly. Too many men are liable to stumble and fall. I can hold up me end," he said. His look challenged him. "Can you?"

Rian's expression was grim. "Aye." He repositioned his big hands around the beam. "On the count of three."

Footsteps could be heard as Jack ran back before the others. "Master Rian—"

"Shh, Jack! I've got help. Stand back and let McDermott and me free your father."

"One," Rian began. "Two. Three. Lift!"

Rian strained but managed to raise his end. Conor hefted his side with little effort, and they moved the large piece of splintered wood beam where no one would be harmed by it.

"Pete," Rian said when he saw that the overseer had his eyes open and was looking at him. "Are ya all right?"

Pete regarded him through a haze of pain. "Don't tell my Henny about this. She's going to have my head. She wanted me to repair a kitchen cupboard for her, and I insisted on checking on old Pamela first."

At Conor's questioning look, Rian explained. "Pamela is one of our milk cows."

"Can you stand, Pete?" Rian asked gently.

"Sure, I can—" He started to rise then fell back, gasping.

"I'll carry him," McDermott offered.

Before anyone could object, McDermott had lifted the man gently, effortlessly, and stood holding Pete as if he weighed no more than a child. "Where would you like me to take him?"

"To the main house," Rian said. Henny was there and would want to tend to her husband immediately. He followed McDermott across the yard, impressed with the Irishman's gentle strength, considering. Perhaps he could use another hired hand. With Pete down, he could use a new worker.

McDermott carried his burden to the house and up-stairs to the second story, where he was instructed by his wife to set Pete on a bed in one of the guest rooms. When he was done, the Irishman quietly went down the stairs and out the door without waiting for praise or thanks.

Rian, noticing the man had gone, hurried downstairs to find him. He saw him leaving, walking down the hill toward the dirt road, a broad-shouldered, dark-haired man with a pack slung over his shoulder.

"McDermott!" he called. "Wait!"

The man froze and turned then waited until Rian caught up with him.

Rian was slightly winded by the time he reached the man's side. "I'd like you to stay, Conor McDermott. I'll need a another hand while Peterson is down, and I'd like you to be that man."

The Irishman looked surprised by his offer. "But ya don't know me. Nor do ya know if I've the experience."

Rian examined the man intently and found that he liked what he saw. And he felt he could trust him. "I know you're a man who helped when we needed it, yet expected nothing in return. You didn't wait for a thing. Ya just went on your way."

"Ya said there was no work here—"

"Nay, I said I hadn't put the word out that I was hiring. And now I don't have to, for I have you." He stuck out his hand. "Welcome to Green Lawns. I'm Rian Quaid. And it's happy, I am, to meet ya."

Conor McDermott took a moment to take Rian's mea-sure. Eyeing Rian's extended, calloused hand, he sud-denly grinned. "Pleased I am to meet ya, Master Quaid."

"Rian, Conor McDermott. Rian will do."

"McDermott," he said. "I've rarely been called by me given name."

"McDermott, it is, then." He smiled. "Are ya staying on?"

The man nodded.

"Good. Ya can eat up at the house, but you'll bunk in the rooms above the stables with the others."

The Irishman inclined his head.

"I'll pay you once a month," and he named a figure that made McDermott's blue eyes widen slightly. Rian smiled. "If ya give me a good day's work, I'll give ya a good wage. I ask only for that, and for your loyalty, while you're working here."

"Aye. 'Tis to be expected that if I work for you, ya'll get the best that I've got to give."

Rian grinned, pleased. "Now you'll want to come to the house. You've not met Henny, my housekeeper and cook. Peterson, the man you helped, is her husband. I'd say that it's best to get on her good side, but I believe you've already done that by taking such good care of her man as you carried him inside."

"Henny," McDermott repeated. "Can she cook?"

"Aye, that she can. She can cook up a dream and then top it off with a touch of heaven for dessert." Rian turned, and McDermott fell into step beside him. "And then there's Meara Kathleen. She and I are to be married soon. She's a quiet thing, but she can be full of Irish fire when angered. The fine thing is that I've rarely seen her mad. She's from County Clare." He paused. "What county did ya say you were from?"

McDermott gazed at him with bright blue eyes. "I didn't." He smiled. "But 'tis County Roscommon I'm from."

"County Roscommon," Rian murmured. "We'll have to talk, you and I. 'Tis been a long time since I've been to Ireland. I'd like to hear it from a man's view. . . ."

And the two headed toward the house, employer and new employee. Their respect for each other was firmly cemented.

Twenty-two

"Fire! Fire!"

Kathleen shot up in bed and climbed out to hurry to the window. "All saints a'mighty," she whispered as she saw the flames. The barn was ablaze, and she could make out workers scurrying from the nearby stables, running to get buckets and help.

She threw on a dressing gown and ran down the stairs. The main door had been left wide open, a testament to the alarm of the inhabitants of the house.

"You will not be leaving that bed, James Peterson!" Henny's scolding voice came from down the hall.

Kathleen headed toward the sound. She found the housekeeper's husband looking waxen as he leaned on the worktable and struggled to slip his boots on. His wife stood but a few feet away, distressed and angry.

Henny turned, saw Kathleen, and her eyes were filled with fear as she pleaded with Kathleen to help her. "You agree with me, don't you, Miss Kathleen?"

"Aye." She moved forward to grab the man's arm and helped to lower him into a chair his wife had quickly brought for him. "You'll do the rest of the men no good out there, Mr. Peterson. Leave the barn to Rian and that new man, Conor McDermott. They'll see that the fire is put out." She had yet to meet McDermott, but from what Rian had told her, she assumed he was capable.

Peterson glanced up, his brow creased with worry, his expression torn.

"Please, Pete," Henny said softly. "Don't you be taking years off my life by doing such a foolish thing as going out there and getting yourself killed."

"Who said I'd be getting myself killed?" Pete answered gruffly. "I feel so helpless here. I should be out there helping them!"

"You're in no condition to assist, Mr. Peterson. Ya can barely stand, let alone walk. Just you rest and let the men do what they have to do."

Pete rose, then fell back, gasping. "Will you look and see how they're doing? Would you, miss?"

"Aye, I was about to go out there when I heard you and Henny here in the kitchen." Her gaze met a grateful Henny and she nodded, trying to smile but failing. "I'll be back when I have something to tell ya, and not before, Mr. Peterson."

He grabbed her hand as she was moving to leave. "Bless you, Miss Kathleen."

Kathleen patted the fingers that held hers. "I'd best go," she said, her heart hammering with fear for what was occurring outside. She had, in truth, hoped that it was Rian she would find. But now that she hadn't, she knew where to look for him, as she should have known before. He was in the thick of things, working to put out the fire.

"Thomas, grab this bucket! Jack, get out of the way, lad, before ya get trampled by the animals." Conor McDermott sized up the situation and acted quickly. He barked out orders left and right, and to his relief, the others obeyed them.

He hadn't been sure that they'd listen, as he was the new man. But in situations of emergency, others were only too happy to follow someone else's lead.

"McDermott!" It was Rian Quaid. "Get the rest of the animals out!"

He spied his employer leaving the burning building, tugging a cow and a goat behind him.

"Aye!" he shouted. "I'll get the animals." The scent of burning wood and straw was strong. If they didn't get control of the fire soon, the blaze could spread to one of the other outbuildings . . . and farther still to the house.

He ran into the blazing inferno, grateful to see a path that wasn't blocked by the blaze.

A keening bellow drew his attention toward a stall to the right, and he hurried to find a frightened milk cow, Pamela.

"Come on, Pamela! Come to Conor," he coaxed. The animal's eyes were wide with fear as he reached out to pat her hide. Carefully, he eased past her to the back of the stall and gave her a little push. But the animal wouldn't move until Conor shoved her harder.

Still, she didn't want to budge, her pitiful lowing rising to accompany the crackle and pop of burning embers and fresh wood.

"Pigheaded piece of leather! Get ya sorry hide moving, Pamela!" With a grunt, Conor shoved her again. This time the animal started to move. The Irishman kept pushing, shoving, coaxing her, until Pamela was moving toward the open door and fresh air. The cow began to run. She must have gotten a whiff of the air, for suddenly she was racing from Conor, away from the fire and into the night.

"Anyone else ya got in here, Miss Pamela?" he muttered as he went on to search the other stalls. The air was thickening with dark smoke. Conor felt his lungs sting as he tried not to inhale deeply. Covering his nose and mouth with his shirtsleeve, he reached the last stall, coughed, and then looked inside.

He uttered a mild curse. There in the stall was a mother cat with her passel of baby kittens. Mother and babies were mewling pitifully. Conor stared at the mother, valued the length of his bare arms that she was certain to claw, then made a decision to save them anyway. He bent down to pick up the four babies first before their mother. To Conor's relief, the mother cat seemed to trust him, for she made no move to sink her claws into any of his body parts. Cradling the crying cats in his arms, he battled through the smoke-filled barn as he hurried to the outside.

The air suddenly cleared as he broke free. Eyes stinging and shut, he paused to draw deep breaths of air. Then he blinked to clear his vision, and he saw her. The woman. She stood with her flowing red hair, wearing a dressing gown and indoor slippers.

Quaid's woman, he thought. He stared at her a long moment, gave her a nod; then, setting the cats down, he hurried back to help put out the fire, her image firmly secured in the back of his mind.

Kathleen stared at the dark-haired man and recognized a healthy, strapping Irishman, a big brute of a man with thick arms, a strong face, and a head of dark ringlets that most women would die for.

Conor McDermott. So this was the new farmhand.

McDermott was a huge man but a gentle one, she

thought. She watched how carefully he cradled the kittens as if still protecting them from the fire.

As Kathleen stared at the man, the Irishman gazed back. His eyes, of the brightest blue, were unreadable, his features grim. He inclined his head in greeting, and she found herself nodding back.

Heart beating wildly, she watched him run back to the fire. Then all thoughts of Conor McDermott vanished when she heard Rian's voice. Immediately, she spun toward the sound. Rian was near the bucket brigade that had been organized to put out the fire.

"Rian!" she gasped, rushing to his side. The men continued to fill and pass and dump buckets of water in their efforts to battle the fire. Kathleen stared at the burning building in horror. Despite the men hard at work, the fire seemed to be winning. The buckets of water being dumped had done little to tamp down the blaze.

Oh, Rian, she thought. *Poor Rian. Please, God, spare Rian's farm.*

Rian looked up as she hurried forward. His green eyes flickered brightly with emotion, then went dim. His hair was tousled, his face dark with filth. Yet despite the black cloud of thunder on his face, he was alive, and she rejoiced in it.

"Kathleen," he said. "Go back to the house! 'Tis no place for a woman."

"I want to help."

He eyed her dressing gown, and she was stung by his look of derision. "You go in, Kathleen. Leave this to the men. What do ya think ya can do?"

Anger stirred within her breast. She recognized and understood Peterson's frustration as her own. However, unlike Peterson, she was healthy, willing, and able to assist.

"I can pass a bucket as well as any man," she snapped.

Despite his objections, she marched over, pushed into the middle of the line, and grabbed a full bucket of water from the man before she handed it to another.

She could feel Rian's angry gaze, but she didn't care. Her arms strained under the weight, but she wouldn't stop. She could and would help, whether or not Rian Quaid gave his say-so.

"Here, miss," one man said. "Let me take that from you." The young field hand stood before her, ready to relieve her of her burden and take her place in line.

"Nay," she said sharply, sorry when she saw him flinch. "Please," she said, softening her tone. "I want to help where I can. I'm sure there's a place elsewhere that Rian Quaid can use you."

The man seemed startled by her decision to stay. "But, miss, your gown. What if it catches fire?"

"I'm away enough from the fire," she told him. "I'll be fine. Go! Find another place! This one is mine."

"Martin, do what the lady says and find Quaid. He's at the back of the barn. He'll be looking for men."

It was Conor McDermott who'd spoken. Kathleen stared at the man, expecting him to step in where Martin had left off. She glared at him, daring him to stop her. To her surprise, she saw a glimmer of amusement in his blue eyes as he dipped his head in acknowledgment, then left.

He's not goin' to turn down me help, she thought, amazed.

Then all thoughts other than putting out the fire vanished as she worked with the men to douse the flame that was slowly, methodically, consuming Green Lawns's barn.

Twenty-three

"It's a loss," Rian complained as he entered his office, with McDermott following. "A complete loss."

"We can rebuild," the Irishman said.

"We'll have to rebuild. We need that barn." He went behind his desk and pulled out his chair. " 'Twill be difficult and risky. There have been strange things here that have taken my profits lately."

"Strange things?" McDermott asked.

"Aye." Sighing, he sat down behind his desk and waved the Irishman into another chair. He began to explain about the other incidents, the vandalism, and his suspicion that someone was now trying to do more than just annoy him.

Was the fire the work of an arsonist? Had the man's intent been not to irritate him but to destroy everything he possessed? He had no suspects. It was just a suspicion.

He needed to learn the truth soon, before something darker, more devious, happened or someone got killed.

"Do ya think that Peterson's accident was a true accident?" McDermott asked.

Rian scowled. "I don't know. I think not. The loft was built to last a hundred years. Someone must have tampered with that main support beam. I don't know who or when they would have the opportunity, but someone did."

"And now they've covered up the evidence before ya could call in the authorities to investigate it."

"Aye, it could be so!" Rian considered it, wide-eyed. "I hadn't thought—" He sat back in his chair and closed his eyes. The headache he'd begun to experience more and more recently had cropped up again, tightening his temples, hammering behind his eyes.

"We'll find the bastards," Conor McDermott said. "If the culprits are out there, we'll find them and make them pay restitution."

A small smile played about Rian's lips at McDermott's vehemence. "When ya give loyalty to a body, ya mean it, Conor McDermott," he said.

McDermott raised a dark eyebrow. "Of course. Did ya think I wouldn't?"

"No, I knew you would, but I'm glad to see that my gut instinct about ya was right."

"And that is?"

"That you're a good man to have on one's side . . . and, Conor McDermott, as long as you want to stay, I'll want to have you. I didn't thank ya for helping us douse the fire. You not only kept the men to the task; you rescued the animals."

"One cow and a passel of kittens." He grinned. "And I haven't even the scratches to prove it."

Rian's lips curved in response. "Well, we're partial to what is ours, whatever they are, be it a cow or horse . . . or kittens or chickens."

"If you're thankin' me, then be welcome."

"I am."

"So I've proven to be a worthy foreman?"

"Aye."

"And Peterson, what will he say of that?"

"He'll welcome the help when he gets back. I'll not be taking away your title or your pay, McDermott. You and Peterson will share the responsibility. In fact, I hope that you'd jump in to keep the old man from doing what he shouldn't be doing."

The Irishman smiled. "Without his knowin', of course."

"Aye."

"Will do, Rian Quaid. Will do."

And despite the tragedy of the burning barn, their aching, bruised, and tired bodies, the two men grinned at each other. Trust was a precious thing, and each found that one could trust the other.

Rian could detect her scent before he saw her. He'd requested her presence and knew he shouldn't be surprised that she'd come, but the sight of her nevertheless startled him. Although it had only been hours since he last saw her, he had forgotten how beautiful she was, how alive he felt just by having her there.

But he hadn't forgotten that she had disobeyed him and put herself at risk at the fire scene.

"Kathleen."

"Rian." She nodded and eyed him warily as she entered his office. He had picked his office for their meeting, for he wanted to maintain some distance from her. A distance, it appeared, he was having a hard time keeping.

As he gazed into her glistening blue eyes, he wanted to go to her, take her into his arms, and kiss her breathless.

"Please . . . have a seat."

She sat primly, arranging her calico skirts carefully about her. Then, with hands in her lap, she straightened and stared at him.

"You disobeyed me tonight." A muscle ticked along his jaw.

"Aye," she said politely. "So?"

His green eyes flashed with fury that she could be so casual about it. "You could have been hurt or worse."

"I didn't go into the burnin' buildin'. I stood outside, yards away, with the others, passin' buckets of water. How could I have hurt meself? I was hardly in any danger! Were ya afraid I'd drop the bucket on me toes?"

In actuality, she had hurt her hands. She had the blisters and sores on her fingers and palms to prove that she'd worked that day. But she was happy about it. She had done something worthwhile. And she'd been able to keep an eye on Rian . . . to see for herself that he was all right instead of worrying about him constantly from inside the house.

"You could have been hurt, damn it!"

His sharp tone made her raise her eyebrows. "So, now I've made ya angry enough to swear, have I?" she said.

He stood, his eyes glowing, with a look of intent on his face that made her tremble and her breath still.

"Rian—" She rose and backed away from the chair.

"Ya should have listened to me, Kathleen!"

"I couldn't," she whispered urgently. "I needed to see . . . to help."

He skirted the chair and grabbed her shoulders. Giving her a gentle squeeze, he pulled her close. "I was worried that somethin' terrible would happen to ya," he said, his brogue thick and evident in his voice.

"I'm sorry. I was worried, too."

His gaze flamed. "About me?"

PLACE
STAMP
HERE

‖‖‖‖‖‖‖‖‖‖‖‖‖‖‖‖‖‖‖‖‖‖‖‖‖‖‖‖

KENSINGTON CHOICE
Zebra Home Subscription Service, Inc.
P.O. Box 5214
Clifton NJ 07015-5214

She nodded.

"The barn is gone," he said.

"Aye, I know."

"Ya could have been gone, too."

She disagreed. "Nay, I was never that close."

" 'Tis a damn good thing," he said. And then he kissed her, a wild, desperate mating of mouths that startled her as much as it delighted her.

His lips seduced and pleasured her, and she embraced him, loving the strength and feel of him.

She whimpered, aware of the sound that came from deep in her throat. He had bathed. His hair and face were still slightly damp from the washing, and there was no evidence of soot or ash on his skin. But together with the fragrance of soap was the scent of smoke and the night air that lingered on his clothing.

The memory of him near the fire was all too real and disturbing to Kathleen. She held him, clutching him by the shoulders, arching to press into his kiss.

"Kathleen," he said thickly as he pulled back to gaze into her eyes. "What am I do to with ya?"

"Ya were doing a good job of things a second ago," she quipped.

He chuckled, and the amusement in his features was heartwarming. He'd worn a strained and worried expression since he'd learned of the fire. And when she'd come in, she could tell there was something pressing on his mind, something else beside the loss of his barn.

She had made him laugh and smile. The knowledge made her heady. She loved him, and was happy to ease some of his distress.

"Rian," she said, stroking his jaw . . . his chin. "I'm glad ya weren't injured."

His gaze darkened. "And you." He gave her waist an

affectionate squeeze before he set her away from him. "Sit down. I've something to discuss with you."

She obeyed him, disappointed at the distance between them. The tone of his voice scared her.

What did he have to say that he needed for her to sit down? Was it such bad news that she couldn't stand? What played on his mind that changed his mood so quickly?

"About our wedding," he began.

There was a fluttering beneath her breast. "Aye?"

"The fire . . . the barn . . . we're going to have put off our wedding plans for a time." His look pleaded for her understanding. "You can see why, can't ya?"

She nodded, and the wild surge of feeling within was relief. She had yet to tell Rian the truth. Now she had more time to find the right moment to make her confession.

She breathed a silent sigh of relief. She had a chance to turn things around and pray that he would care enough to marry her, anyway . . . to wed her for herself . . . Kathleen Mary Maguire . . . and not because he was bound by some betrothal agreement to Meara Kathleen Dunne.

"I don't know how long it will be until we make plans again," he said.

And she felt an unexpected thump of fear.

"The animals will need temporary shelter. We'll have to rebuild the barn." He cradled the back of his neck with his hand, and seeing pain on his face, Kathleen wanted to rub it for him.

"The building shouldn't take but two weeks," Rian continued. "Once we get the supplies and the help . . . I'll know more after the barn is started."

"I understand."

"Do you?"

"Aye."

He turned away. "Fine." He went to stare out the window at the property that was his. "I understand that the invitations have already gone out."

"It doesn't matter," she assured. "Word will be out soon about the fire, and with it, the change in plans. People will understand."

"And you truly do?" He spun back and gazed at her intently. "You will not feel slighted because there is plantation business that will take up my time and attention?"

Kathleen was puzzled. "Green Lawns is your property . . . your life. Why should I feel slighted?"

He smiled. "Two weeks. Maybe three. A month at the most."

Her spirits brightening, she grinned back at him. "Fine."

"Good." He sat down at his desk and took out his account ledger. "Henny says she has you to thank for keeping Pete from the fire." At her nod, he said, "Thank you."

She shrugged. "He's an injured man. It would have been foolish for him to fight the fire. I merely managed to help Henny to convince him to stay."

He studied her hair, her lips, then lowered his eyes to her breasts. She saw his gaze wander and felt the heat of his desire reach out to scorch her. She gasped, shaken, and looked away.

"Henny will be wantin' me in the kitchen," she said breathlessly. She went to leave.

"Kathleen?"

She froze and slowly turned.

"There is one thing I regret about all of this business."

"Aye?"

"That come Sunday I'll not have ya as me wife and in me bed where I can make wild, sweet love to you."

Her face flushed with heat, and she quivered with longing for him. The images he painted were crystal-clear and shattering to her equilibrium. "Rian, I—"

"Soon," he promised, his green eyes glowing. "Soon."

Breath hitching, Kathleen spun from his passion for her and hurriedly left the room.

Twenty-four

Kathleen was putting the finishing touches on a handkerchief she'd been embroidering when Lucy knocked, then burst into her bedchamber.

"Miss, there's a woman downstairs. 'Tis Master Rian's cousin."

"Cousin?" Kathleen set aside her handiwork. "A woman, did you say?"

"Yes, miss. Miss Nancy Sparks, her name is. A distant cousin on his mother's side. Lottie said she's come before, but I wasn't with Green Lawns yet, miss."

Nancy Sparks, Kathleen thought. She rose, looked into the mirror to see that she looked presentable, then left the room and descended the stairs.

Tingles of nerves skittered across her skin as she made her way to the parlor. Rian's cousin. Here was a member of Rian's family.

She heard voices before she entered the room. A young woman was seated on the sofa, scolding a servant for serving her lukewarm tea.

"Take this away," she demanded. "And bring me a fresh pot. I wanted hot tea, not warm water."

"Yes, miss. Sorry, miss." Lottie, a kitchen maid, grabbed the teapot from the tea table and, flashing Kathleen a glance as she passed, headed back toward the kitchen.

"It's Miss Sparks to you, servant girl!" the woman called after her.

Frowning, Kathleen stepped into the open archway. The woman, she thought, had been insufferably rude. She straightened her spine. She wasn't sure she was going to like Rian's cousin. "Can I help you?" she asked stiffly.

Miss Sparks threw her a glance. "Who are *you?* Don't tell me. Let me guess. You're the seamstress?"

Kathleen's temper burned at the woman's condescending tone. "Nay, *Miss Sparks.* Me name is Kathleen." She stuck out her hand. "I'm Rian's betrothed."

"His—" Her eyes widened. Her mouth quivered. "Rian's not getting married."

Startled by her response, she stared at the woman.

"Aye, Miss Sparks. I can assure you he is, and soon.

"Kathleen Dunne, Nancy Sparks." Henny made the introductions as she entered the room. It seemed to Kathleen that the housekeeper had taken great delight in imparting the news. "Miss Sparks is Master Rian's cousin."

Nancy Sparks waved a hand. "Far too distant a relationship to claim actual kinship, I assure you."

"Then why do you come claiming to be family?" Henny grated beneath her breath, for only Kathleen's ear.

"Will ya be stayin' long, Miss Sparks?" Kathleen asked sweetly.

She rose from the sofa, a cool blonde in a green silk traveling gown. "Where is he? Where's Rian?" She looked the perfect example of a society woman at her best.

"He's busy," Kathleen told her. "With the plantation. Is there somethin' I can do fer you?"

"When will he be in?"

Kathleen shrugged. "For supper, perhaps. It's hard to

say. We had a barn fire, and there is work to be done. Rian is workin'."

"Will you tell him I'm here?"

"You can tell him yerself if you'd like. No doubt he's with the cows and pigs, seein' to their temporary quarters."

"Cows and pigs?" Nancy looked horrified. "No. I won't disturb him. I'll come back in a day or two. Please tell Rian that I stopped by."

"I'll do that." Kathleen's lips tightened as the woman dismissed her and left without drinking the hot tea she'd demanded.

"She's a nasty one, isn't she?" Kathleen said conversationally.

Henny grinned at her. "Yes, she is. I never did like her, but don't tell a soul that I've told you."

"Me?" Kathleen said, her expression sweet, her gaze innocent. "We all love the woman dearly. 'Tis her manners we can't stand."

The sound of giggling behind them had them turning to find Lucy and Lottie, their heads bent low over the trays they were carrying.

"The barn can be built in less than a week once we have the lumber," Rian said. "John Foley has offered his men to help us."

McDermott nodded. "I sent Martin to Baltimore to check on the supplies ya ordered. All is as we'd expected."

"Good." Rian was pleased with his new hire. Conor McDermott seemed a fair and honest man. If it hadn't been for Peterson's injury, he might have lost the chance of a good employee, for he would have sent the dark-haired Irishman away.

"How is Mr. Peterson?" McDermott asked.

"He's doing well. He's over the knock to his head. His leg is mending, but it will take a while for him to be up and about." Rian grinned. "Henny has been having her way with him. She fusses over him like a mother hen. Although he grumbles, 'tis clear to me that he's enjoying the attention."

The Irishman grinned. "Especially her cookin'." He had a thing for Henny's cooking. Rian had been right. Henrietta Peterson could cook like a dream, and he was grateful that she'd taken a liking to him. She always had some snack for him to munch on whenever he came inside. She claimed a man of his size needed food to fuel him.

"Aye, her cooking. Speaking of which"—Rian looked at the position of the morning sun—"should be about time for the midday meal."

"Aye, that it is. Wonder what Henny has prepared for us."

Rian shut the paddock gate, and the two men headed toward the manor house. "Whatever it is, I hope it comes with pie."

"The heaven that comes later," McDermott murmured.

They were within a hundred yards of the house when the front door opened and Kathleen stepped out onto the porch.

She spied them immediately and waved. "Food is on the table!" she called.

"That's a might pretty lass you've got, Quaid," McDermott said gruffly.

"You've the right of it. Fact is, I'm eager to marry her."

"So what's stoppin' ya?"

"There's much to do. I want to take her away on a proper wedding trip. What with the barn and the repairs . . ."

McDermott made a sound of disbelief. "If I were you, I would not let a barn or anythin' else come between me and me bride-to-be."

"But the barn—"

"The animals have a place, don't they? Things are goin' along well enough, considerin' that you've lost the buildin'. Ya shouldn't wait for the woman you love. Ya should marry her today. Soon, at least. Only a fool waits to touch when a jewel has been placed within reach."

He looked at the man and felt a little jolt of recognition, as if he'd known McDermott a long time. Had he met him in his youth, perhaps?

"You're right," he said. "You're absolutely right." He grinned, for it felt as if a burden had been lifted off his shoulder. "I'll tell her this afternoon . . . Nay, tonight. I'll want to be alone with her."

"Now you've got the right of it," McDermott said. "With that settled, then, let's find us some food."

Twenty-five

Despite her promise to come back days later, Nancy Sparks returned that afternoon. Kathleen saw the woman on horseback approach the house and had a sinking sensation that it would be an unpleasant evening as well as a horrid afternoon.

She remained at the window even after she'd watched Rian's cousin hand over the reins of her mount to Thomas, long after Nancy Sparks entered the house. Kathleen could hear voices in the foyer and knew one of them was Nancy's and the other Rian's.

Her chest tightened. She had to go down sometime, but she didn't want to.

"Kathleen?"

It was Rian's voice calling up the stairs for her, his tones warm. "We've a guest. Would you come down?"

"I'll be right there!" she answered; then she scowled into the mirror. She didn't like Nancy Sparks. She wondered if Rian's cousin was sweet and simpering around Rian or whether or not she showed her true colors.

She'd already glimpsed how Nancy behaved with the house servants.

Drawing a deep breath, Kathleen left the room and descended the stairs. Rian stood at the bottom landing, waiting for her. The smile on his face warmed her, making her pulse beat faster, her skin flush. He had changed clothes, she saw, for he had worn a white shirt and knee breeches at lunch. His hair was wet, and she realized that he'd bathed. In his navy jacket, cream-colored shirt, and fawn linen slacks, he made her mouth water. He stood with his hand on the banister, that crooked, tender smile on his face, and she knew she was in love forever.

Anticipating the evening meal, Kathleen had changed her gown. Her two-piece dress was for afternoon or evening. Of lawn green, it was a perfect foil for her red hair, and she enjoyed the way it fit her waist snuggly. The only thing she regretted was the corset she had put on. It was hot and uncomfortable, but she wouldn't show it. She wouldn't give Nancy Sparks any cause for comment. She was eager to see how the dear lady held herself in Rian's company. It might be a long evening, but it could be an entertaining one as well.

"Nancy has come for supper," Rian said as he held out his arm to her. "She said the two of you met this morning."

Heart pumping, she placed her hand on his sleeve. "Aye, we spoke briefly. She wanted to see ya, and I told her where ya could be found."

She had spoken softly and, she hoped, without giving her thoughts away.

"She's in the parlor," he whispered as he leaned in close to her neck. "She's really quite irritating."

She jerked. Not only because she'd felt his lips on her cheek, she told herself, even though she enjoyed having Rian press close to her, but also because he apparently didn't care for his cousin, either.

"Ya don't like her?" she asked, studying his face. He was so handsome. The sun had warmed his skin to a golden bronze. Tiny lines were visible at the corner of each eye. She knew they were laugh lines, for she'd seen the crinkles there when he'd relaxed enough to chuckle.

"I wouldn't exactly say that I don't like her. I said that she can be annoying, and she can."

Kathleen blinked back at him. "Irritatin', ya said. Ya said she was irritatin'."

He grinned and gave her a quick kiss on her mouth. "All right, then, irritating." He touched her cheek. "Unlike you." He patted her hand and tucked it into the crook of his arm. "Shall we greet our guest?"

Our, she thought, liking the sound of that. "Aye."

"Any idea what Henny has made for dinner?"

Bemused, she said, "Confess. You're thinkin' of only your stomach now."

"Nay," he said seriously. "I'm thinking of McDermott's belly, too." His eyes twinkled. "He'll be joining us."

She was delighted by his good humor. "Roast fowl with buttered potatoes and fresh lima beans from the garden."

His eyes glowed. "And dessert?"

"Boiled rice puddin' with fresh strawberry jam."

"Hmmm . . ."

"And raspberry tartlets."

"No chocolate?"

Her lips twitched. "Not unless you want chocolate syrup over the tartlets or the vanilla cake I baked early this mornin'."

His expression was hopeful. "Cake? Vanilla cake, did ya say? With syrup?"

"Aye." She gave him a playful nudge. " 'Tis a wonder how you manage to stay so thin and hard instead of soft and flabby with all the sweets you love to eat."

"I told you that Henny doesn't allow me to—"

She shook her head. "Ya've got Henny in the palm of your hand, Rian Quaid, and ya know it. Henny thinks the world of Master Rian. She'd give ya the moon and the stars if ya asked it of her. A bit of dessert she wouldn't think to deny ya."

The air rumbled with his laughter. "So you have me." He reached with his other hand to trace her jaw. She gazed at him, trembling. And she would have remained unaffected if he hadn't smiled at her so tenderly and traced the curve of her lips.

"Rian—"

"I want to talk with you later, Kathleen. Just the two of us. In the garden, if the bugs are not bothersome. If they are, we'll use the morning room. No one uses it in the evening."

The morning room was adjacent to the kitchen in the back of the house, but it wasn't a workroom. Unlike the one at the front end of the house, it was a cozy, comfortable family parlor.

"Will ya walk with me?" he asked.

As if she could deny him anything. She was as bad as Henny, she thought. "Aye."

"Good." His teeth flashed. "I gather we can't be putting off meeting the woman any longer." He sighed. "Ah, well, after supper I'm sure she'll be gone." When Kathleen just looked at him, he explained. "Apparently she's a guest at the Hadleys' place across the river."

"Where did she get—"

"Her mount?" He looked a bit annoyed. "She came earlier and begged one off of Thomas. My groom wouldn't dare say no, for he's earned the lash of the woman's tongue before and has no desire to receive such a verbal whipping again."

"I see." She tried to control her smile. "I shouldn't be askin' to ride, then."

"Nonsense!" he said. "You're welcome to ride anytime you'd like." His features hardened, and Kathleen drew back, surprised by the change in him. "Take someone with you, Kathleen. There've been strange things happening here on Green Lawns. I don't want you riding about alone."

"Strange—"

"Promise me that you'll tell me when you're going. If I can't get away, I'll have one of the men go with you."

"But Rian—"

He placed his hand on hers, holding them firmly, drawing her in with his gaze. "Promise me." His tone was urgent.

"I promise," she said. It was little enough to give him, and her reward was a look of relief that came over his face, and a smile.

"Thank ya." He kissed her again, and for a moment she thought of turning to grab his shoulders, of deepening the kiss so that he wouldn't want to let go.

But she didn't; she stood quietly as his head lifted. He smiled, and she smiled back, then he led her to the other room, where Nancy Sparks waited impatiently.

"He was spectacular when he played," Nancy said, her hazel eyes filled with excitement, her face warm with affection for the man beside her. "I've never seen such a chess player as Rian."

"I wasn't so good as that," Rian replied dryly. "But I enjoy the game and found Walter Smithers a worthy opponent."

Kathleen had to bite her tongue to keep from screaming. For the past two hours, she'd endured Nancy's constant fawning over Rian, her telling of his past exploits and accomplishments, while she purred like a kitten and implied in a sweet voice that their relationship was closer than anything that Kathleen and Rian had or could ever have.

Kathleen knew that Rian was wonderful, but to have Nancy Sparks extol his virtues as if she knew him better than her . . . more intimately . . .

It didn't matter if it was true. It irritated her, and she was eager to see the woman gone.

"Will ya be stayin' in the area long?" Kathleen asked when there was lull in the conversation.

Nancy pinched her lips. "Why do you ask?"

"I just wondered." She avoided looking at Rian. Did he think she was incredibly rude for asking? How could she help it if she felt threatened—yes, threatened, she realized—by someone as pretty, if condescending, as Nancy. Especially when Nancy could claim a family connection and she could not even claim to be his true fiancée.

Ya wouldn't want him to be family, she reminded herself. *You want him to be something more . . . a friend, a lover . . . a husband . . . the father of your children.*

Finally, Nancy Sparks left, leaving Rian and Kathleen alone. As they watched the Hadleys' carriage take Nancy away, Rian turned to her.

"Shall we walk in the garden?" he asked.

She nodded.

They went to the kitchen first, where they raided the pantry for the cookies that Henny had baked the day before. Like two small children, they then slipped out the back kitchen door with a cookie in one hand, the other hands clasped.

The moon was a full orb that brightened the walkway and splashed a kaleidoscope of light and darkness through the shrubbery. The air was rich with summer scents.

"That was an exhausting evening," Rian said quietly. "Nancy can be trying."

"Is she your cousin? Henny says she is, but Nancy claims the relationship is so distant as to be nonexistent."

"She's a third cousin on my mother's side. Nancy lives in Philadelphia. Every couple of years she comes down to visit the Hadleys, friends of her family." He sighed. "And when she does . . ." He squeezed her hand. "She comes here to irritate me and annoy my guests."

"Nay, you're teasing."

His teeth flashed as he grinned. "Perhaps."

He led her to a stone garden bench, where he sat and pulled her down beside him. There they sat side by side and finished their cookies, enjoying the night and the star-studded sky.

"Kathleen." His hand found hers where it lay on the stone bench between them. "About the wedding—"

Her heart gave a thump. *Oh, no,* she thought. "What about the weddin'?" she asked, her voice low.

"I've been thinking, and I see no reason why we cannot marry before the barn is complete."

Rian began to play with her fingers, and she tingled as he stroked the sensitive inner area of her wrist as he held her hand.

"But what of the work?" she asked.

Rian faced her, and she melted when she saw the urgency in his expression, the warmth and the heat in his eyes. "The work . . . the plantation . . . My men can handle it. I want to marry you. Soon. Tomorrow." He grinned at her astonished look. "All right, come Saturday."

Six days, she thought. He wanted her in six days. "I don't understand—"

He released her fingers and cradled her face with both hands. "I don't want to live another day without you."

"You're not without me—"

His eyes glowed. "I want to wed you. I want to wed you and bed you . . . and see you bear my children."

"Oh, Rian." She broke away and rose, walking to the other side of a small clearing where the scent of honeysuckle was strong in the night air.

She heard him come up behind her, felt the warmth of his breath against her neck, and she shivered with pleasure. She loved this man, and he wanted her for his wife. She should be happy. It should be the happiest day of her life. But she was living a lie. How could she go on living a lie?

Tell him, her conscience urged. *Tell him before it's too late.*

"Rian, I don't—"

His hands settled on her shoulders. He turned her to face him, and gently used his finger to raise her chin.

"Do you love me, Kathleen?" he whispered, his green eyes glowing. The moonlight bathed his features, highlighting the rugged planes of his face. "Do you?"

"Aye," she whispered, her throat tightening.

His smile was quick and filled with tenderness. "Good. Then 'tis all set between us. Come Saturday, we'll be man and wife." He tenderly stroked her cheek. "I want to take you on a wedding trip, Kathleen. A place where it will be just the two of us."

Tell him. Tell him. Those words echoed in Kathleen's mind, haunting her, taunting her.

"Rian," she breathed. Her throat was tight with unshed tears. She could see herself confessing who she was . . . see the warm softness in his green gaze darken . . . harden. "Do ya care for me?"

"Care for ya?" he asked, stunned. He released her as if not only surprised but also angered by the question. "Of course I care for you! I love you. Do ya think I would ask ya to marry me if I didn't?"

"But the betrothal agreement . . ."

"That damn betrothal agreement," he muttered. He looked deep into her eyes, and what she saw astonished her . . . thrilled her.

"This has nothing to do with the betrothal agreement, Kathleen. This is between you and me. 'Tis nice that we fell in with our family's plans for us, but—"

"You love me?" Tears filled her eyes as her heart swelled with hope, with happiness. "Truly?"

She knew she must sound like a little girl seeking reassurance, but she had to know. It could make a difference, she realized. A big difference.

His expression softened as he pulled her to him once again. He cupped her face, studied her hair, her forehead . . . her eyes . . . her nose, as if finding pleasure in every feature.

"Aye, Kathleen. I love you. You're as dear to me heart as this land that surrounds us."

Her tears overflowed. *"Oh, Rian."*

She sniffed, then moaned softly as he captured her lips with his mouth. She reached to hold on to him.

She loved him. He loved her. It was best if they were together. *The best thing,* she thought. *The very best thing.* Lizzy had told her to do what was best.

The kiss was a gentle, loving mating of mouths . . . lips touching, nipping . . . hearts singing and beating as one. She felt a surge of disappointment when he lifted his head.

"Will ya, Kathleen? Will ya marry me come Saturday?"

Kathleen knew that she wouldn't—couldn't—deny him.

"Aye, Rian Quaid. I'll marry ya and be your bride."

The look of joy on his face created a starburst of happiness within her.

He is going ta marry me. Me! Not Meara Kathleen!

Twenty-six

Lightning flashed, followed by a savage crash of thunder. Startled awake from a dream, Kathleen sat up in bed, gasping, her hands pressed to her chest.

Another flash . . . a deep rumble that shook the house . . . and she was running to the window to peer out at the raging storm.

A streak of light zigzagged across the sky and bolted toward the earth. Kathleen looked at the yard. After having cleared away the burned debris, the workers had started to build a new frame in the same spot as the old one.

A spark of flame. A loud bang. Her heart thrumming wildly, she moved away from the window, praying that the lightning wouldn't hit, that the building and outbuildings, but mostly the people she cared about, would survive the storm unscathed.

Hands shaking, she sat on a chair away from the window, on the far side of the room. She drew up her legs and curled, huddled, in her nightdress, her eyes on the window . . . on the storm.

Was God punishing them all for what she'd done? Had she, by her decision, by her actions, brought on the wrath of God, ensuring that others would pay as she would? Rian? Henny? Peterson? Lucy?

If lightning struck the stables, then McDermott, the

stable help, and some of the field hands could be injured or killed, for their quarters were inside, on the main level, and above, on the second.

Please, Lord, forgive me. I love him. I do. I didn't want to lie or deceive. But I can't lose him. Not now . . . not ever.

Her bedchamber door crashed open at the same time thunder snapped with a series of bright bursts of light.

Kathleen screamed.

And then she saw him. Rian. He stood in the open doorway with the flash of lightning highlighting his face and half-naked form, and she gaped at him. He looked like some avenging god. *Dear God, no,* she thought. *He's found out. Somehow he knows!*

Then he entered the room, emerged from the blinding burst of light to approach where she sat, shivering and hugging herself with her arms.

"Kathleen?" His tone was soft and tender.

The pitch of his voice got through to her, and the horror that blinded her subsided. She could see his face as he bent to help her rise.

"Kathleen," he murmured soothingly. " 'Tis all right, lass. 'Tis only a summer storm."

"Rian?"

His was a loving smile. Her chest tightened until she could hardly breathe. *He doesn't know. He doesn't know!*

"Don't shake so, lass. I'm here. And the storm won't hurt you—"

"I heard a crash! It woke me. Then there was the lightning. 'Tis fierce, Rian. Unlike any I've ever seen or heard before."

"Aye, storms can be vicious here in Kent County. 'Tis a wonder that we haven't seen one sooner."

Kathleen's eyes widened with horror. "Ya get storms like this often?"

He smiled. "Only in the summer."

A clap of thunder made her gasp and rush into his arms.

"I don't know if I like your summer storms," she mumbled against his chest.

As she burrowed against him, he stroked her hair. "You'll get used to them in time. You'll even learn to appreciate them."

"Appreciate them?" It didn't seem possible to her.

His chest vibrated against her cheek as he chuckled. "Aye, Kathleen. Appreciate them. For the water it brings our crops."

"But not the lightning—"

"The lightning can make a pretty display for us."

"And it can kill."

"True enough. Ya must be wary of it indeed. But from the safety of the house, ya can watch the grand show nature gives us . . . hear the accompanying thunder that startles one awake."

His voice, his tone, had Kathleen leaning back to look at him. There was life in his expression, fire in his eyes. He looked as if he were one with the storm. There was something inside him that was raging. When he met her gaze, she inhaled sharply, for she knew what it was.

"Rian." Desire curled in her belly and spiraled upward. Sensation shot to tingle in the tips of her breasts, and she felt a yearning, a burning, for something unnamed but understood. It was Rian, she thought. Only Rian.

"Kathleen." His gaze darkened as he reached out to touch her face. "I thought you'd be frightened. I don't remember a time such as this when I lived in Ireland."

It wasn't the storm that frightened her now. It was Rian and the way he made her feel. It was Rian and the fear that justice would win and she would lose what she had with him.

"Are ya all right now?" he rasped.

She shook her head. She wasn't all right. She felt as if she would die if he didn't kiss her. She wanted so badly for him to kiss her.

He must have seen it in her face, for she heard his sharp inhalation of breath, felt it shudder out as he released it. He slipped his hands about her waist and drew her close.

"This is madness." he gasped. But then he captured her mouth. His kiss was anything but gentle. It raged like the summer storm, the intimacy and the intensity devastating to Kathleen's senses . . . her body . . . her heart.

Her breasts swelled against the thin fabric of her nightdress. Her palms warmed against his naked, overheated flesh. A surge of passion overwhelmed her, and she ran her hands wildly over his bare chest, moaning, gasping, as his fingers found hers.

Rian was caught, trapped in a desperate, dizzying pool of lust and love that told him he had to have her, and have her immediately.

"Kathleen." He shuddered as she touched him, played with his nipples, groaned when she put her mouth to the buds and suckled. "Kathleen!" It was a deep-seated cry begging for control.

"Let me touch you," he gasped. "I have to touch ya or go mad." He swung her into his arms and turned toward the bed. Lightning flashed and thunder boomed as he walked the few yards to the bed and laid her onto the mattress, then lowered himself down.

"You're so beautiful," he said. "I've never wanted anything as much as I want you. You're my wife, do ya hear? In my heart, you're my wife . . . and I love you." As he spoke, he slipped his fingers under the hem of her nightdress, raising it slowly, inch by inch. His breath hitched as each smooth, silken inch of her was revealed.

She wore nothing beneath the nightdress. He gazed down at the curly red hair at the apex of her thighs and felt a fresh jolt to his midsection . . . the sudden rush of blood to his engorged member.

He experienced such a wealth of love as he placed his hand over her stomach, felt how the muscles jumped under the weight of his fingers. As he began to explore the white skin above and below her belly button, every inch of his body tightened as his desire for her strengthened.

"Kathleen. You're so lovely. I want to kiss ya. Nay, not on your lips but here." He bent his head and placed his mouth just above her navel. He closed his eyes, enjoying her warmth and her clean floral scent. She smelled of roses and summer blooms. She was fragrant and dewy, and he wanted to sink himself into her perfume, lose himself in her softness.

The shock of Rian's mouth on her belly left Kathleen reeling. Shuddering with an onslaught of new shocking feelings, she wove her fingers into his hair and held on to him for dear life. And as his mouth traveled higher to her tingling, throbbing breasts, she arched up in wanton invitation. The force of her love for him was a dazzling display of color and bright lights, while the depth of her raging desire mirrored the intensity of the storm. Quick bursts of blinding lightning . . . deafening claps of thunder . . . the wind howling with delight as the rain fell in passionate torrents.

It seemed somehow right that she offer herself up to

him during the thunderstorm. The feelings between them had been reined in so long that it seemed as if the only way they could be released was in an explosion of such a force.

When Rian rose up, she whimpered with protest. Their eyes met, green orbs flaming, burning against blue eyes wild with innocent passion and a desire no less raging than his.

He stared at her, and she gazed back. His attention locked on her mouth, and she responded by moving beneath him, wanting him . . . loving him . . . inviting him . . . ready to surrender.

They came together, their mouths joined, their tongues mating savagely. The storm raging inside the bedchamber was as wild as the one taking place outside.

They caressed, stroked, fondled each other, shivering when one touched the other just right. Until the two were upon each other naked.

"Kathleen." He wouldn't be shaming her, for in his mind, his heart, she was already his wife.

"Aye." In her mind, her heart, he was already her husband.

He rose up to stroke her entire body from her throat to her ankle and back. His hands shook as he forced the control that would allow each of them to savor each agonizing but delicious moment.

"I'm going to take you, Kathleen."

"Aye," she breathed. "Do it, Rian. Do it!"

He slid down, opened her legs with his knee, and rose up to ease into her, when an explosion of light roared inside the room, making Kathleen shriek and him rise off her with a bellow.

The sound had been so loud that there was a ringing in their ears. Shocked, fearful, they raced to the window and stared out into the night. And saw the flames engulfing the tobacco-drying shed. They stood in stunned disbelief.

"My God!" Rian rasped.

"Oh, help us! 'Tis another one of your outbuildings!" Kathleen cried.

Their gazes met, flashed down to their nakedness, and then, with regret, pulled away as they grabbed their clothes to dress.

"Fire! Fire!"

They ran down the stairs, Rian first, with Kathleen following, and heard the loud hammering on the front entrance door.

"Fire! The shed's on fire!"

Rian threw open the door and shouted for the messenger to stay away from the scene, as he was only a child, either eleven or twelve years old, one of the field hands' boys.

He rushed out the door, pausing to throw Kathleen a look over his shoulder. "Stay here," he said. "Promise me, Kathleen, you'll not leave the house. I couldn't bear to worry about ya. Will ya do it? Promise me?"

There was such pain, such horror, in his face that she could only obey him.

"Go!" she told him. "I'll stay. I promise."

He nodded, his face grim, but she could see the relief in his eyes, and she gave him a look meant to convey all her feelings for him.

And then he was gone into the stormy night, while she stayed behind, scared to death that something else bad would happen and that she would lose him.

And thus lose everything.

Twenty-seven

Saturday morning dawned bright and clear, a full six days after the raging storm that nearly consumed her, and Rian, as it did more than half of the drying shed.

Kathleen stood in her bedchamber as Lucy and Lottie dressed her and fixed her hair. She felt giddy, strange. Today was her wedding day, and trouble or not, everyone at Green Lawns and about had been invited. Kathleen had been sure that with the second fire Rian would want to postpone their plans once again, but he would hear none of it. He wanted to marry her, and he wasn't going to wait another day.

"I love you, Kathleen," he'd said. "Aye, this will put a bit of a hardship on Green Lawns, but we'll get by. With you by my side, I'll get by."

And she'd felt such love for him that tears had filled her eyes as she'd reached up to kiss him.

Now she was dressed in the gown that had been made especially for her by Mrs. Elton. Her stomach was a flutter of butterflies. She felt dryness in her throat and the thrill of anticipation that soon she would be Rian's bride.

But under all the excitement, the joy, she was terrified. What if he learned the truth? What if he learned that she wasn't her cousin Meara? Would he turn against her with hate?

It was too late to tell him. Besides, he needed Meara's

dowry money, and Kathleen now knew that he wouldn't touch it without marrying the bride. And since Meara had vanished with no intention of marrying him, that left only her to ensure that he received it.

He loves me. She kept repeating those words over and over in the hope that what she was doing would feel right . . . be right.

He'd told her that they weren't marrying because of the betrothal agreement. After hearing that, she had almost told him the truth then and there. If she had, she would have risked losing the one thing she wanted more than anything in this world—his love. She had deceived him, and now she must go on deceiving him for the rest of her life. She'd be taking a chance at happiness, at the risk of losing it all, should he find out the truth.

"There you go, miss." Lucy stepped back to eye her handiwork. She had made a wreath of fresh summer flowers, which she had placed gently upon Kathleen's pinned-up curls. Kathleen's hair had been washed and brushed, and it was thick and shiny.

There was a knock on the chamber door. "Kathleen?"

"Come in, Lizzy. The door is open."

Elizabeth Foley stepped into the room, looking no less lovely in a lilac gown, her hair in ringlets at each side of her face. The rest of her blond tresses had been pinned up to form a tight little knot at the back of her head.

"Oh, Kathleen . . ." Lizzy's eyes filled with tears as she eyed her friend. "You look wonderful. The gown fits you like magic, and that wreath . . . You truly look like a vision . . . a princess on her way to wed her prince."

Kathleen's gaze met Lizzy's across the room. "Lucy. Lottie. Thank ya for your help. I'd like a few minutes alone with Mrs. Foley."

"Yes, miss," they said in unison. They curtsied and left the room.

As soon as they were gone, Kathleen turned to her friend. "I'm scared, Lizzy," she said. Her hand shook as she lifted the gold locket that had been her mother's, fingering the oval until the metal warmed beneath her touch.

"You love him. I know you do."

"Aye, and he says he loves me. That this has nothing to do with the agreement between our grandfathers, but . . ." Tears brightened her blue eyes. " 'Tis a dream, Lizzy. A lovely, wonderful dream. I love him so much that it hurts. I'm so scared that I'll have him, only to lose him. And if I lose him . . ." She inhaled deeply and released the breath on a shudder. "Me life won't be worth a halfpenny."

Lizzy's eyes widened with concern as she grabbed hold of Kathleen's hand. "You love him. He loves you. And although you've kept this secret from him, it will work out. Because true love deserves its place in the world. Your love will thrive and prosper, and you'll have children—boys and a girl, I think. All with your red hair and Rian's green eyes."

"You're a dear friend, Lizzy Foley."

Lizzy preened. "And don't ya forget it, now," she said, mimicking Kathleen's Irish accent.

"Kathleen! Lizzy! It's time!" It was John, waiting patiently for his wife to rejoin him.

"Are you ready?" Lizzy asked. Kathleen nodded. "Go forward. Don't look back. He needs you. You're just what he needs to make his life completely happy."

"Lizzy?" John's voice was still gentle and patient.

"Coming!" Kathleen called back. She held her friend's gaze for an extra heartbeat. "Let's go," she said.

And Kathleen closed her eyes, said a silent prayer for God's assistance, then left to attend her wedding.

The small church was filled to overflowing with neighbors and friends. Kathleen, in a carriage driven by Conor McDermott, gazed at the chapel, her heart thudding hard.

"You've got quite a crowd come to see ya wed, Miss Kathleen," McDermott said.

Staring, unable to take her gaze from the gathering on the church steps, she felt herself begin to panic.

"I don't know if I can." The world began to shift, then spin beneath her.

"Kathleen. Kathleen!"

She blinked, then stared up with horror into the grim face of Rian's farmhand. "I'm sorry. I must have— No, I couldn't have!" she said. She'd never fainted in her entire life!

His gaze was sharp, his expression unreadable. "Ya fainted," he said, as if his saying it would make it so.

She realized that she was all but sprawled across the man's lap. Flustered, she started to rise. "I . . . I don't know what came over me."

"Don't ya?" The man's tone was sharp.

She flashed him a glance. "I said I was sorry."

He viewed her from beneath lowered eyelids. "Just tell me one thing, Miss Dunne. Do ya love Rian Quaid, or don't ya?"

Her face reddened with a fit of temper. "I love him!" How could he dare suggest that she wasn't in love with the most wonderful man on earth?

He stared at her for a long time. She refused to wither

under his bracing glare. "I love Rian Quaid. I can swear it on a stack of Bibles if need be."

Suddenly, McDermott's face creased with humor. "Well, then, Rian Quaid is a lucky man, he is. I can tell that ya love him." His hand lifted as if he would touch her face, but then he dropped it as if he'd suddenly realized that it wasn't proper.

"Your man is waitin' in that church over here," he said, his voice rough. "Are ya goin' to keep him waitin'? Or are ya goin' to go inside and tell the man that ya love that you'll wed him . . . that ya want his life and yours to be joined forever."

She didn't answer him. But he must have read it in her expression, for he urged the horses on. After he pulled the carriage to the church door, he helped her alight from the vehicle.

"May the Lord bless ya both this fine day," McDermott said, surprising her with his sincere wishes. Before this day, Conor McDermott had kept his distance and had been quiet and reserved when in her company. Only with Rian did he seem at ease.

She held his glance and smiled. "Why, thank ya, Mr. McDermott."

Something about him made her confident, happy that she was walking the path she'd chosen. The man simply gave her a silent nod in answer before he left her to see to the carriage as she stopped on the church steps to be greeted and embraced by Henny, Lizzy, and others who knew her well.

The church filled with music, and Kathleen knew that it was time . . . time to forever change her life . . . to join herself to the one person who mattered above all else . . . to wed the man of her dreams. Rian Quaid.

The walk down the aisle on John's arm was a blur.

So, too, was the actual wedding ceremony, as she had eyes only for Rian. It didn't matter what they said or how they said it. The promises they were making to each other were there in their locked hands . . . in their loving gazes and beating hearts.

". . . Rian Quaid," the priest said, "you may now kiss your wife."

Kathleen cried tears of happiness as Rian took her into his arms and pressed a tender, sweet kiss on her lips. She could feel the tension in him, knew that he wanted her. The day would not pass fast enough until the two of them could be alone.

"I love you, Mrs. Quaid." he said, his green eyes bright with joy and love.

Kathleen was so overwhelmed with love for him that there was a second's pause before she could answer him.

"I love you, Rian Quaid," she said huskily, her throat clogged with tears. "More than anythin' . . . more than life."

And he slipped his arm about her shoulders and pulled her to his side as they accepted the well-wishes from their friends and neighbors. They were hugged, kissed, and patted on their backs. Finally, after making their way through the crowd, they climbed into the carriage that would take them back to Green Lawns. There a celebration dinner was waiting for the newlyweds and guests.

Twenty-eight

It seemed like forever before the guests had gone, the food was put away, and Kathleen and he were alone. Rian waited in his office to give his new wife time to ready herself. That afternoon, he had instructed Henny to move Kathleen's things with his into the master bedroom. He had shown her the room earlier. He'd had it redecorated for this night, a plan he'd put into motion weeks ago, when he'd first asked her to marry him.

And now she was his . . . soon to be in most every way. It seemed as though he'd wanted her forever. Last Sunday, when they'd nearly come together during the storm, he'd had a taste of heaven, only to have been thrust into hell when the lightning had stuck the drying shed, adding to the recent disasters at Green Lawns.

The destruction of the drying shed had changed things dramatically. Rebuilding both the barn and shed would set him back financially. Things would be difficult for a while. He'd have to watch his funds, at least until the crop came in and he could recoup some of the money.

Kathleen's dowry would help, he realized. But there was something inside him that regretted having to take it, to touch even a penny of it. He wouldn't sell the jewelry. He would use the coin and make due.

He remembered Kathleen that day when she'd come into his office, offering him her dowry before he'd asked her to marry him, before they'd set a date. They had been betrothed, yes; but there had been too many questions, too many doubts in his mind. The travesty of his father's marriage to Priscilla had blinded him to the happiness a man could find with a wife. He hadn't realized then that he'd loved Kathleen, that he'd wanted her in his life always.

He finished his sip of whiskey and set down his glass. Then he picked up the oil lamp burning on his desk and headed for the stairs . . . toward Kathleen.

The house was quiet. The glow from the oil lamp lit his way as he climbed the stairs and moved silently down the hall.

They were alone in the house. The servants were spending the night elsewhere. The arrangements were made to give the newlyweds privacy. Rian was grateful for the solitary quiet as he paused outside their bedchamber door. He wanted to make love to his wife without an audience, to have her cry out loud with the pleasure he planned to give her. His Kathleen would be loud, he thought. She would be unable to hold back the sweet cries of pleasure.

He turned down the lamp until the light was extinguished. As his hand settled on the doorknob, he felt a wild thrill of anticipation, a niggling of desire.

He drew a shuddering breath as his fingers turned the knob. He was eager to be with his new wife. He was anxious to be her husband.

Kathleen waited near the window, studying the night outside through the glass. She was in a different bedchamber than the one she'd been given when she'd first arrived. The master bedroom. *Our chamber,* she thought with a shiver. And she was waiting for Rian, her new husband.

Husband. Rian Quaid was her husband. She hugged herself, stared at her reflection in the glass, and grinned. She had married the man she loved, and now she was waiting for him to join her.

She moved from the window toward the dressing table to peer into the mirror for one last check of her appearance. Lighted candles sat on the top of the dressing table, the night table, and the round table near the window, illuminating the room with a soft pearly glow.

She stood near the foot of the bed and examined the room. It was an impressive bedchamber. Rian had done a wonderful job having it redecorated for her.

The room could use more signs of their married life together, she thought, but that would come in time. It had been Rian's grandfather's room, she'd been told. And then Rian's since he'd taken charge. But now it was theirs, and she would add a few feminine touches. Flowers, perhaps, although this night it seemed perfect.

She sat on the bed, thought about the coming night, and wasn't afraid or nervous. Since her time with him six nights ago, she had longed for this occasion, this night, and she was eager to be with him.

She had donned her best nightdress. Not Meara's but her own. When she went to her husband the first time, she would go as Kathleen Maguire Quaid. Not Meara Kathleen Dunne but herself, in her garments, surrendering to the man she loved.

A turn of the doorknob and the squeak of an open door heralded his return. Kathleen rose from the bed to greet him.

"Kathleen," he murmured, setting the oil lamp he carried on the nearest table.

"I thought you would never get here," she admitted.

Fire flashed in his green eyes. 'I've an eager bride. I love that."

"I love you," she whispered, itching to touch him, to lie beneath him and become his in more than name.

For a quick second, she thought of Lizzy and felt bad for her friend. Lizzy had the affection of her husband and family, she didn't have this . . . would never have this.

Rian approached her, reached out to pull her into his arms, and kissed her until she was breathless and clinging to him. "You're wearing too many clothes."

She blushed. How could she blush when she wanted this as much as she did?

"Aye," he said with a grin. "Too many clothes."

As his fingers sought the ribbons at her neck, her hands went to his shirt, then slipped down toward the hem and tugged it from his trousers.

She felt a rush of pleasure as her hands pushed up fabric and skimmed across bare skin. She heard his deep male groan and was rewarded with a look on his face that mirrored the wild desire throbbing in her heart and her body.

"Aye, Kathleen, darlin' . . ." He caught hold of her hands and pressed them to her side. "I want to touch ya first. Let me touch you."

He placed his lips to her throat. She sighed with pleasure and arched back her head, exposing more of her neck for him. She gasped as he moved his mouth lower, as he pushed aside satin ribbons and cloth to dip below her nightdress to the sensitive skin along the top and between the soft upper swells of her breasts.

Rian cupped a soft, full mound in his hand and saw the immediate response in her lowered lashes, her short, tiny intake of breath. She filled his hand, warm and silken, her nipple pebbling as he worried the tip through the fabric.

He wanted to see all of her. Excitement built as he raised the hem of her garment, tugged it over her head, and then feasted his eyes on her beauty.

Candlelight played beautifully across her shoulders, dipping to caress the rosy tips of her breasts, her smooth belly, and her milky thighs. She was perfection in the form of female, and he wanted her. She was his, and he would have her. She was his wife, and he wanted to love her until she cried out with sweet passion.

Kathleen felt the brush of air on her bare skin. Her nipples were hard, and she tingled from head to toe. The heat of his burning gaze warmed her as he swung her into his arms and carried her to the bed.

She felt the cool brush of the sheets as she lay down. She shivered but was quickly warmed when Rian lowered his weight beside her and slipped his arms around. Then he was kissing her, fondling her, making her cry out with need . . . and she was spinning . . . whirling . . . whimpering . . .

Rian paused only a second to tear off his shirt and kick out of his trousers. Then he stood, gazing down at his new wife, feeling such love, such desire for her, that he thought he would surely expire from the heat if he didn't touch all of her.

His manhood was thick and throbbing. He eased down on her gently. Understanding she was a virgin, he wanted to go slow. It would be difficult for her at first, but by the time the night was through, he would see that she was pleasured, that she would want more and more of him until neither of them would want to leave the bed-chamber come dawn.

He took his time loving her, touching her, enjoying her gasps and little cries of pleasure. Then, when he thought she was ready, he took her, easing himself inside her, sighing at the feeling of coming home.

"Rian." She gazed up at him with big eyes.

"Shhh," he whispered. "Relax . . . I'll be gentle. I love you and want only to make you happy."

And then he did just that, setting a slow rhythm of give and take, thrust and withdraw. When she responded, joining the dance, Rian groaned as he started to slip over the edge. He gritted his teeth until he saw that she had one glorious orgasm first. Then he brought her up again until she soared, panting, toward the sun. There he joined her, and their cries of release echoed throughout the room.

Afterward, Kathleen lay winded and looking stunned. Tired but pleased, Rian grinned down at her.

"Happy wedding night, wife."

She smiled and touched his cheek. "Aye, Mr. Quaid. 'Tis a happy night and one I hope will be repeated day after day, year after year. . . ."

"Vixen," he teased. Rian sipped from her pink lips, slightly swollen from his kisses. "The night isn't over, Kathleen, my love. 'Tis just begun."

And he began to nibble his way from her ear to her belly.

"Rian!"

"Aye, love . . . I'm almost through. . . ."

But it turned out he wasn't done; he had only begun, much to her immense satisfaction.

Twenty-nine

Rian and Kathleen decided to postpone their wedding trip. The reconstruction of the barn and tobacco-drying shed meant weeks of work, and Rian wanted to be on hand until it was completed.

Kathleen didn't mind. She was so in love that she didn't care where they were or how they lived. As long as Rian was near, she had found her heaven on earth.

While he was busy with business during the day, the nights belonged to her, and Kathleen thought she could never be happier than she was at that moment. Which made the secret she kept inside all the more frightening. She had never expected to be this happy in life, and she was terrified that one day Rian would learn the truth before she herself could tell him and all the happiness in her life would be stolen away from her.

Rian put the dowry money to good use. Kathleen, in that regard, was satisfied that he'd received what he deserved. And if he was grateful for her bringing it to him, the deception made her uncomfortable with his gratitude.

The barn was completed first, a big building that stood out, looking new against the other older outbuildings, although those structures were in good repair. The day they moved Pamela and the other livestock from the one area of the stables and the paddock into the new structure was an event for celebration by both the owner and employees of Green Lawns.

With the barn finished, they began work on the new drying shed, for they wanted it to be completed before the tobacco harvest. Then they'd need the structure to hang the tobacco leaves. The crop would dry there for a period of time until it was ready to be packed into casks for shipment to market.

"Mistress Kathleen!" Little Georgie, Martin's youngest son, ran into the kitchen, where Kathleen and Henny were preparing for the picnic that would celebrate the completion of the new tobacco shed.

She smiled at the little boy. "What is it, George?"

"Mama said she'd make fresh blueberry pie for the picnic if it was all right. Is it all right, Mistress Kathleen? If not, I'll tell her so. She can make something else, like johnnycakes. I like johnnycakes, don't you?"

She patted a chair near the worktable, and with a gesture of her hand, she instructed the boy to climb up. With a wave to Lucy, she gave a sign to the maid.

Understanding, Lucy got out the cookie jar. This was a ritual they'd shared before when Georgie had come to the kitchen with one excuse or another, visiting Kathleen, earning him her affection and some sweet treats.

"Well, Master Georgie," Kathleen said as Lucy opened the lid of the cookie jar. "You tell your mother that she can make whatever she likes, because there will be lots of guests to eat our food. Tell her it's best to be her choice." She reached into the sweet jar and withdrew a sugar cookie. " I guess since you like johnnycakes so much, you wouldn't like one of these?"

The boy gazed at the cookie with big eyes. "I like cookies."

She pulled the cookie just out of his reach. "But you said johnnycakes are your favorites."

"So are cookies!" the boy insisted.

"Oh, 'tis true?"

He bobbed his head, sending his blond curls dancing.

"Well, then, I guess 'tis fine if I give ya one to sample." She lowered the cookie to within his range, and he grabbed it.

"Thank you, mistress." He took a bite. "Can I have some tea?"

"No, you may not, George Martin Jr.!" Henny scolded. She softened her voice. "But ya may have a glass of milk if you'd like." She withdrew a glass from the cupboard and set it before the young boy. "Would ya like a glass of milk?"

"Yes, mistress," he said respectfully.

Henny grinned. "Good boy."

"Well, what do we have here?" Rian entered the kitchen from the front end of the house. "Is that Georgie, the cookie man, I see in my kitchen?"

The boy gulped a swig of milk and set his glass down, grinning at Rian. The child's upper lip was white with cream.

"Want one?" the boy offered, extending to him one of the three other cookies that Kathleen had set on the plate before him.

Rian's green eyes met his wife's over the head of Georgie Martin. He smiled at her, and Kathleen's heart went kerplunk.

"I think I will have one, Master George." He accepted the boy's cookie offering and took a bite. "Thank you, kind sir."

The boy giggled. "I'm not sir. I'm not old 'nough. Mama says so."

Rian looked thoughtful as he studied the boy. "Well, you seem man enough to me," he said.

"Really?"

Snatching another cookie, Rian nodded. "Only men don't eat cookies. Especially sugar cookies."

"But you're a man and you're eating sugar cookies!"

"Oh, well, then, must be I get them because I own this house and get special dispensation from the laws that affect most men."

Georgie dropped his half-eaten cookie on his plate. "Oh." He looked crestfallen as he climbed down from his chair and eyed his plate longingly.

"But Georgie," Rian said, "you may have cake, because all men are allowed cake."

The child's eyes brightened. "Cake? Chocolate cake?"

"Aye, George, me man. Chocolate cake with sweet cream icing."

Then Rian pulled up a chair, waved the boy into the seat he'd vacated, and they waited for the women in the kitchen to serve them real "men's food."

Kathleen watched her husband and the boy, their heads bent low together as they chatted and ate their cake. She felt soft and mushy inside. Rian was wonderful with children.

He'd make a good father, she thought. She was so overcome with a warm swell of love for him that her eyes filled with tears.

Quickly following, she knew a niggling fear that Rian and her life with him would all be taken away from her. She turned away from watching them, riddled with guilt.

She didn't deserve such happiness. She'd kept her secret when she should have told him.

Her stomach started to clench, and she felt cold and clammy. *I must tell him,* she thought.

She didn't know when; she didn't know how. But she would have to suffer in constant fear of losing him if she didn't tell him, and tell him soon.

Once told, would he continue to love her?

She shivered and hugged herself with her arms.

What if he doesn't love me? What if he only wants me in his bed?

What they shared in the marriage bed was wonderful, special. Did all couples have what they have? Did every woman cry out with pleasure at her husband's touch? Or did she and Rian have something more?

He'd said he loved her. She hoped he did. For if he didn't, once he learned who she was, the truth would destroy their marriage, wedge itself between them, as it had in her worse nightmares, as it did in her most private fears.

Rian looked from his cake and grinned at her sheepishly as he handed her his empty dessert plate. She took it with a half-smile and spun quickly to set it in the washbasin with the other dirty dishes.

He frowned. Kathleen looked pale, ill.

He rose from his seat, went to her, where she had started to wash his plate, and placed his hands on her shoulders. She leaned back against him, trembling.

Concerned, he turned her, took the wet dish from her hand, and carefully placed it back in the water. "What's wrong, Kathleen?"

He saw her swallow. Her eyes downcast, she shook her head. " 'Tis nothing of concern."

Unconvinced, he raised her chin with his finger and examined her taut features. "Kathleen, tell me. Something's bothering you. What is it?"

Pulling from his grip, she turned her head. "I'm all right."

Alarm ran its icy fingers along his spine. "Kathleen, I can see that you're not well." He touched her hair. "Tell me. What is it? What's got ya so upset that you're barely able to glance me way?"

She sniffed, turned to face him, and the look in her blue eyes had him sighing and pulling her into his arms. "I love you," she said, and he smiled.

"I love you," he answered. "So tell me now. What is it?"

"I . . . 'Tis nothing. Just a woman's unhappy mood, is all."

Understanding eased the cold tug of fear that had settled beneath his breast. "Your courses?" he asked softly, for her ears only.

She blinked up at him with watery blue eyes. "Aye."

He touched her lips. "Why don't ya go up and lie down if you're not feeling well?" He caressed her jaw, smiled when she pressed her cheek into his hand.

"I'm all right—"

"Nonsense," he said. "Come." He turned to Henny as he grabbed Kathleen's hand. "Henny, my wife and I will be upstairs in our bedchamber. We're not to be disturbed. I imagine ya can do without her for a bit?"

Henny started to smile until she took one look at Kathleen's waxen face, then nodded soberly. "You don't look well, Mistress Kathleen."

Kathleen sighed as she met her worried gaze. "Henny, won't you call me Kathleen? Mistress is too formal between us."

Rian nodded, and Henny smiled. "Why don't you lie down for a while, Kathleen?" the housekeeper suggested.

"Aye," Kathleen said. She closed her eyes briefly until her husband slipped his arm about her shoulder and led her from the kitchen to the stairs.

"What's the matter with Mistress Kathleen?" Rian heard Georgie Martin say as they left.

"She's fine. She and Master Rian have things to do, is all, and I think Mistress Kathleen is tired. She's been working very hard lately, baking cakes and cookies and other treats for the household and little boys like you."

Rian smiled as he helped Kathleen climb the steps to the second floor. In their bedchamber, he closed the drapes and pulled back the bedcovers. Kathleen stood, unmoving, in the center of the room. She looked tired, lost; moved to tenderness, Rian went to her.

"Come on, love. Let me help you with your gown."

She stood like a child while he unhooked the back of her gown. As he undid each tiny hook, the gown parted, and he saw the corset underneath. He scowled. "No wonder ya don't feel well! Ya don't need this contraption, Kathleen."

With a few pulls and tugs, he'd freed her from both the gown and her corset. When she was clad only in her shift and stockings, he sat her on the edge of the bed, and hunkering down before her, he began to roll down her stockings.

She seemed to come alive suddenly, as if she just realized where she was and that he was crouched on the floor before her. "Nay, Rian, ya don't have to—"

"I want to do this." His voice was husky. "Let me do this."

She gasped, for he'd caressed her leg as he slipped the fabric from her thigh . . . her calf.

When he was done and her feet were bare, he turned her on the bed, pressed her to lie down, and then opened the ribbons of her chemise so that she would lie more comfortably.

She lay trustingly before him, relaxed, her gaze shimmering with longing. "Rian . . ."

He sat on the edge of the bed and kissed her. The sweet taste of her teased him, tempted him to do more than simply touch her, but he held himself back, allowing himself only to stroke her hair back from her face . . . and to love her with his eyes.

"You need your rest." He started to rise.

"Rian?"

He froze. He needed to leave quickly. The desire to lie with her had begun to gnaw at his belly and snake through his system.

"Aye?" he said.

"Won't ya lie down with me for a bit? For just a wee while?" Her eyes swam with tears. "I need to be held. I need you."

With a silent groan, he went back to the bed and removed his boots. Then he slipped under the covers next to her.

"You've got too many clothes on," she said drowsily.

He tensed, realizing that she'd said it in innocence. She had no idea that he was hot and hard for her . . . that it was killing him just to lie there and do nothing.

He lay as stiff as a board, his eyes on the ceiling as she snuggled against him and he encircled her with his arm.

"Rian?"

Please stop moving, he thought.

"Ya don't seem comfortable." She sounded tired. "Am I keeping ya from something important?"

" 'Tis nothing that can't wait," he said gallantly.

"Truth?"

He clenched his teeth. "Aye."

She sighed and burrowed closer, slipping her arms

about his waist, laying her head on his chest, and he could feel her sweet breasts, soft and full, against his side. What he wouldn't give to slip his hand down to her breast, to caress her, to feel her stir and hear her come alive.

He was tempted, oh, so tempted. But he kept his hand where it lay and fought desire as he closed his eyes.

He was enveloped in her scent, wrapped within her warmth. He lay with his eyes shut and his wife at his side and felt himself become drowsy. Need slipped away but not love. . . .

It had become pleasant for him to lie there, with the gentle sound of her soft breathing, the smooth tickle of her hair against his arm as she shifted in sleep.

And he drifted on the edge of dreams, allowing himself the peace of the afternoon and the pleasure of napping with the woman he loved cuddled against his side.

Thirty

People came from miles—from Baltimore, surrounding plantations, and nearby towns. Everyone had gathered at Green Lawns for the picnic to celebrate the completion of the new outbuildings.

The day was a lazy summer's Sunday. The sky was clear, and the sun was on its best behavior, hot without being unbearable. The breeze was balmy and cooling without being destructive to the table settings of food.

Setting a plate of roasted chicken on the end of the long food table that had been set up for the afternoon, Kathleen admired the new drying shed. Like the barn, it was a wondrous site. Rian had decided to expand it. His tobacco crops had been increasing yearly, and this year's was clearly thriving. With Meara's dowry money and other coin he'd raised by selling some of his livestock, he had not only managed to improve the appearance of Green Lawns; he had also increased the profits. Conor McDermott was one of the main reasons for the higher earnings, Rian had told her. The field hand, it seemed, had a head for business, suggesting ways to increase crop yield per acreage, helping Pete manage the workers in such a way that every man gave his best.

And the man knew about horses. How that man knew about horses! At Conor's suggestion, Rian had been considering the breeding and selling of horses at Green

Lawns. Folks in Kent County needed workhorses, riding horses, and racing horses. And while it would take time to establish the owner of Green Lawns as a horse breeder, Rian was convinced that it was worth the gamble and that the venture would pay off.

And all because of a dark-haired stranger from Ireland.

Kathleen turned from the table and moved toward the house to bring out more food. She smiled as she passed a woman with her baby, another scolding her dirty-faced little boy. As she approached the back door to the kitchen, she turned her head slightly and saw her husband leaning against the house, deep in conversation with John Foley and another man she'd never seen before.

Spying her approach, Rian straightened from the wall and grinned in her direction. With a shy smile, she nodded at him, then at the others, before continuing past them to enter the house. She found the kitchen empty. Henny had gone outside with the others. The servants had been expected to join in the festivities, their work of food preparation having been completed the day before. Earlier, when Kathleen had been outside, directing the men on the setting up of the tables, Henny had been inside, checking and rechecking that there'd be enough food for the hoards of people they were expecting. Some of the bedchambers had been readied for guests earlier in the week. After Henny had checked on the food, she'd gone upstairs to examine those guest rooms to ensure that the servants had done their job and that everything was clean and tidy for the Quaids' overnight guests. Henny would have kept working and worrying if Kathleen hadn't ordered her from the kitchen and the house.

Kathleen smiled as she recalled where she'd last seen Henny Peterson, seated on a wooden bench, her husband not far from her side, talking with the housekeeper from the Foley place. They'd been smiling as they'd sipped at their iced fruit punch, and Kathleen had never seen a more pleasing sight than Henny relaxing, enjoying herself.

And it was all Rian's doing. He had insisted that the servants deserved the day of fun. Kathleen wanted to go to her husband now, put her arms around him, and kiss him long and eagerly in thanks for his thoughtfulness. But she stayed inside, where she could avoid the temptation to do such a thing and thus start something that neither of them could finish. She would have to wait until later, when they were alone in their bedchamber and she could show her appreciation properly.

She thought of the company they would have in the house this night and wondered how she could thank Rian properly and be at all quiet about it. She shrugged. She would find a way. There were always ways to be creative. The sudden images she'd envisioned made her smile, then grin. She was learning each time they came together how to make love to her husband slowly, devastating his senses, enjoying his deep, rasping pleas and full-throated groans.

Aye, she would find a way to show her thanks and increase Rian's pleasure as she did so.

She thought of the people who would stay, which rooms they'd be occupying.

Most of the overnight guests would be from Baltimore. Rian had invited some of the businessmen who had been helpful in the reconstruction. The neighbors who attended the picnic would have plenty of time to return that evening to their own homes.

It wouldn't be too terrible, she realized. There would be four families at most, and she'd managed to put them at the opposite end of the manor house.

Kathleen went to the pantry, pulled out two cakes that she'd baked yesterday and today, set the treats on the worktable, then went to the dining room to see about finding more napkins and plates. They would have a mountain of dirty dishes by the time they were through, she realized as she dug out some white linen napkins. Nice ones, by the look of them. She returned to the kitchen with napkins in one hand and a short stack of small plates in the other. Then, eyeing the plates and remembering the children, she changed her mind and went back to the dining room to put the dishes back in the safe haven of the china cupboard.

She was thinking about which table to place the cakes as she entered the kitchen, so she didn't immediately see him standing inside the pantry door.

"Kathleen."

Startled, she froze and stared. "Rian! You frightened me! I didn't expect to see ya here. The last thing I saw was you talking with John and that other man. The one I don't recognize."

"Smithfield," he said with some amusement. "Of the Smithfields? Remember we attended a dinner party and the Smithfields were our hosts?"

Her mind had been so active with mental scenes left by her imagination of their impending night together that it was a minute before she could answer. "Smithfield?"

"Aye." He came to her side, lifted her chin, and kissed her soundly on her unsuspecting mouth. She moaned and leaned into him.

He raised his head. "That's for looking far too delectable." He bent to nip at her ear and to whisper. "I'm longing for the time when we can be alone and in bed . . . I'm eager, my love. Very eager . . ."

Heat shot to her nerve endings and settled in her lower abdomen. Hadn't she just been thinking the same thing?

"Behave yourself, Rian Quaid," she scolded, but her eyes told him of her delight in his attention. "We've guests." She paused. "And we'll have guests spending the night."

"At the other side of the house, I hope."

She blushed as she'd been thinking the same thing again. "Aye."

He caressed her cheek. "Good."

"Rian?"

He glanced toward the door, saw Conor McDermott, then, with a flash of regret, stepped back from his wife.

"I didn't mean to intrude, but we need a moment of your time."

"We?" Rian asked.

"Pete and I," the Irishman explained. His gaze fell on Kathleen. "I'm sorry, mistress. I didn't mean to interrupt." There was amusement glimmering in the bright blue eyes.

Kathleen felt mildly irritated. "You were not interrupting a thing, Mr. McDermott."

Why did this man have the power to irk her? He seemed to be everything that Rian said he was and more, yet there was something about him. She scolded herself for being uncharitable. She was Irish, and so was he. They should have found some kind of connection, but she could find none between them.

"I'll be back to kiss ya again later, love," Rian whispered.

Roses bloomed on her cheeks. "Go away with ya now, Mr. Quaid. I've got things to do, and you're standing here keeping me from me tasks."

He frowned. "You're to enjoy yourself, Mrs. Quaid.

I'll have none of this working, woman. Go outside and have some fun. Find Lizzy and spend the day with her."

She sniffed but promised she would do so. Kathleen nodded at McDermott before the two men took their leave.

The dizzying spiral of desire that her husband had begun just by his simple kiss made Kathleen feel like a schoolgirl. Deciding that Rian was quite right in insisting that she enjoy the day, she ignored the cakes left out on the table and went outside to find Lizzy. In her search, she came up behind a trio of unsuspecting ladies having a conversation. Kathleen didn't mean to eavesdrop on their discussion, but they weren't making an effort to control their tone or their words.

"I tell you, Margaret," a woman with black hair in a yellow dress was saying. "Lizzy Foley is a trollop and a smart one. She somehow managed to seduce John into marrying her, and now he's gotten himself a little family. And how quaint they all look together. But I'll wager you that it won't last. Dear John will figure it out eventually. He'll see Miss Lizzy for what she is, and then she'll be out in the cold. Her and those two adorable brats of hers."

"I don't know, Justine. I think you're being harsh. John and Elizabeth Foley seem quite happy together."

Justine snorted. "Do you think either of them would appear differently in public?"

A third woman, a blonde in pink who until now had been silent, suddenly piped in on the conversation. "I think you're both jealous. Lizzy Foley is a lovely woman. So what if she's found a way to ensnare one of the wealthiest men in all of Maryland? She's married him, and she is apparently a good wife if what my Bradley says is true. He says that John Foley is quite smitten with his bride. And how long have they been married? Four years?"

Kathleen's temper began to heat as she listened to the women's conversation. How dare they! she thought. They were on her property talking nastily about her friend. They had no right!

Her fists clenched, and her face reddened. She took two big calming breaths before she stepped forward, her face composed, her anger controlled enough for her to be civil.

"Good afternoon, ladies. I'm so glad you could come today. Did I hear you talking about me dear friend Lizzy?"

Margaret and the blonde flushed with embarrassment. Only Justine seemed rudely unaffected. "And if we have?" the brunette challenged.

"Well, I'm a Quaid now. And as long as you're here at Green Lawns, a Quaid's land, I'll ask that you hold your tongue if you can't control its meanness. I don't think much of a vicious fishwife who takes untold delight in demeaning good people."

Kathleen's voice rose slightly, but she managed to control the urge to yell. "And Lizzy Foley is good people. If I learn that you've been gossiping about her again during me picnic, on me land, I'll personally call one of our men to haul you up off of your pretty arses and throw you off Green Lawns and into the Sassafras River!"

Ignoring the horrified gasps, she spun from the women, her temper simmering, her hands unclenching and fisting, and caught sight of Conor McDermott standing only a few feet away, watching her without expression.

She was just mad enough to stomp up to him and

poke him in his broad, muscled chest. "Have ya got something to say there, McDermott, for say it if you please. I've got enough in me to tangle with a bear. Even one as big as yourself, and I can tell ya that I'll turn out the winner!"

The Irishman's lips twitched, and then he grinned. "There's nothing better than the fine temper of a red-headed Irishwoman," he said.

Then he dipped a bow to her and left her standing there, gaping, stunned by his words and his smile.

Thirty-one

Abernathy, Cecil County, Maryland

"She's *who?*"

"Rian Quaid's betrothed, Mother." Robert grinned. "Well, she was, but she's mine now."

"Why didn't you tell me?" The woman leaned back in her upholstered chair, her gray eyes speculative. Hair that had once been blond was gray. Skin that had once been smooth was like wrinkled parchment. Her gray eyes were sharp, her mouth turned downward in a perpetual pout. The bloom of beauty that she'd possessed during her youth was now only a distant memory. Her one leg gave her trouble, and she needed help moving about.

"How?" she asked. "How on earth did you discover that she's Quaid's fiancée?"

"I overheard them talking . . . Meara and her cousin. When I realized the connection, I knew I had to do something. I thought you'd be pleased."

Robert pouted. He'd been more than pleased with himself at what he'd learned on board the *Mistress Kate*. Startled to meet the one person he hadn't known existed or had ever expected to meet, Robert had to work fast to woo her. It had been pure chance that they'd both been on the same ship. He'd been returning from a visit to his grandfather in London, where he'd asked for financial assistance for Abernathy and been given a paltry sum. Furious with his relations, who, he thought, should have been more understanding and generous, he'd been walking the upper deck when he'd happened across Meara. When he'd realized who she was, his spirits had greatly improved. He'd believed that fate had put him on the *Mistress Kate.* . . . Fate had smiled on him with opportunity.

"I always thought you wanted to get even with Rian for turning us out," he told his mother. "You don't seem pleased."

"I am pleased." Her eyes gleamed. "And I do want revenge. I swore I'd find a way to ruin him." She rose awkwardly and, on unsteady feet, patted his cheek before lowering herself back into the chair. "Dear boy, you've made your mother proud."

"I love her, Mother," he said.

"You what!" She gazed at him as if he were daft.

"I didn't expect to be drawn to her, but although she's a bit of a peasant, she's a delightful creature, really."

Mother tensed. "Peasant? Has she no dowry, then?"

"She has one."

"Excellent. How much? Have you seen it?"

Robert reached into his trousers' pocket and withdrew the emerald brooch that Meara had given to him for safekeeping. "I've got this."

"Hmmm." Her eyes gleamed with greed. "It's a fine piece, but—"

"There is more. But she gave it to her cousin." His lips curled. "For Rian Quaid."

"For Rian! Although she isn't marrying him?"

"Yes. I'm afraid so. She wants me." And he was pleased by that fact. "She'll marry me tomorrow if I wish. But she and Rian were betrothed as children. She left him the money so she could feel free to marry me."

"You must convince her to get back that money," his mother said. "As long as Rian has it, he'll be solvent. If we don't find a way to ruin him, we'll never have Green Lawns. A third of that property should have been yours . . . and a third to your dear sister. But Rian's got everything."

"Sisters don't inherit," he said with irritation.

"They can, and she should have."

Robert sighed. "Mother, Abernathy is a fine place. I'm quite happy here."

His mother scoffed. "Look around you, Robert. Look at it! It's falling down around us! We need funds to refurbish this place."

Robert shifted uncomfortably beneath his mother's piercing gaze. "What do you want me to do?"

"Convince that sweet fiancée of yours that we need her dowry money—"

"But I already told her that we didn't!"

"Fool! Why would you do a thing like that?"

He blushed. "Because I didn't think we did. I assumed we could make do with what my father left me."

"Gone!" she shrieked. "All gone!"

He turned pale. "Gone?"

Priscilla Widham Quaid nodded. "There were debts." She firmed her lips. She didn't tell him that she had spent most of the money on frivolous things to attract Michael Quaid, like ball gowns and hair ornaments and other gewgaws. She'd had plans to win the wealthy owner of Green Lawns. She clamped tight on her jaw. Win she did, but in the end she'd gotten nothing. Nothing! And the fact of that still rubbed her raw. "You must speak with Meara. You will do that, won't you, dear?"

Her son nodded but looked slightly pained. "Yes, Mother. I'll tell her."

"Good boy." She smiled. The boy would understand why it was necessary. He would know in the end when they got everything they deserved and more. Pleased with him, she was feeling generous. "Your Meara, she's a decent girl, isn't she?"

Robert's expression cleared. "Yes," he whispered. "Yes, she is."

"I'll have to have a talk with her. Make her feel welcome."

"That would be nice, Mother. She doesn't think you like her."

"Of course I like her. And I appreciate even more the fact that she comes from a wealthy sire and with a hefty dowry."

"She'll be happy to know that."

"And the fact that she was Rian Quaid's fiancée just makes it all the better."

"I thought you'd like that."

"I do."

"I love you, Mother."

"You're a good boy, Robert."

Meara eased back from the doorway, her heart beating wildly, her stomach roiling. "Oh, Robert." She hadn't meant to overhear the last bit of his conversation with his mother, but she'd heard her name and she'd been curious. Now she wished she'd never known, never heard.

Sire indeed! As if her father were a horse and she a prized mare!

And Robert knew Rian. How? Why hadn't he mentioned it? Was Rian the reason that Robert had taken an interest in her?

She hurried down the hall to exit out the back of the house. There were tears in her eyes as she wandered outside and toward the back field.

The figure slipped, unseen, through the night, past Rian Quaid's new barn and tobacco shed, and headed toward the stables. He paused outside the stable door, listening, waiting. Voices rose from within the building, and he realized that the workers inside were playing cards. He stayed for a time, his ear pressed against the wall to hear.

He heard the bantering between the men. When there was an argument between two of them, he grinned, satisfied.

And disappeared into the night.

"I'm done, lads." Conor McDermott threw his cards on the table and stood.

"But McDermott, we've only begun to win back our money."

"Sorry. But I've got work to do. 'Tis late and I'm eager for me bed, but there's no rest for the working man till he's finished what needs to be done."

"No reason for a man to seek his bed until there's a woman to warm it, McDermott, and no woman would take on the likes of you!"

"Aye, McDermott! You're a big brute of a man. And your ugly face frightens the ladies. What's your hurry? Don't you know that money is sweeter and more titillating to the senses than the warm scent of a woman?"

He took the good-natured ribbing from George Martin and Geoff Burns. "Depends on the woman, I imagine, Burns. I've seen yours. Next time, groom Rosebud before ya try to ride her!"

The group of men roared with laughter at McDermott's remark, all but the man called Burns, who stared at the Irishman in red-faced anger.

"You wouldn't think yourself so high and mighty if it wasn't for the fact that the boss is Irish!" He all but snarled. "Scum," he spat. "The whole lot of them."

"Enough, Burns!" McDermott grabbed the man by the collar and hefted him up from his chair. " 'Tis not a good thing to speak of the master so. You'd best apologize to the man." Gurgling sounds escaped from the man's throat until McDermott released him.

"Ya say something, Burns?"

"Quaid isn't here," the man rasped as he rubbed his sore throat.

"Well, then, 'tis a shame, for now you'll have to go up to the manor house to speak with him."

Burns's eyes widened, and he looked scared. "No, I didn't mean anything by it. I was just having a bit of fun, is all."

"Is that so?" Conor narrowly eyed the red-faced man. "Well, then, I guess 'tis all right. Have a care tomorrow, Burns. We wouldn't want to have another misunderstanding."

"I've got no quarrel with you," he said, shaking his head.

"Good."

Swiping Burns's money from the table before him, Conor ignored the man's outrage and strode from the room. Burns was a liar and a cheat, but he knew his tobacco, so he wouldn't have him fired. But the man bore watching.

As he stepped out into the night, McDermott felt the back of his neck prickle. He froze, listening. But he heard only the sounds of a summer night. He checked the exterior of the building, the shed house, and then went to examine the barn area. There was no sign of anyone.

He wondered what was so wrong that he'd be getting jumpy over nothing. He headed back toward the stables, where he wanted to check on Rosebud, the pregnant mare. He opened the door, raised his light, and that's when he felt it. The sensation that someone had been here, someone who didn't belong. There was an evil feel about the place.

He went for his rifle and returned to take up residence to keep watch for the night.

As he sat in the corner, crouched near the door, McDermott thought of the warm comfort of his make-shift bed in the back room of the stables and sighed wistfully. He'd not be resting his head on his pillow this night.

Thirty-two

"I think I'm with child." Pale and worried, Kathleen studied herself in her friend's bedchamber mirror.

"Oh, Kathleen!" Lizzy turned from the trunk at the end of her bed, where she'd been searching for a particular garment. "That's wonderful!" she breathed.

Kathleen spun to face her. "Is it?" With tears in her eyes, she cradled her abdomen. "I want this baby more than anything. But I've not told Rian about Meara and me. And I'm scared."

Wiping her eyes, she began to pace Lizzy's bedchamber while Lizzy looked on, helpless. "Don't tell him."

"How can I not?" Kathleen shook her head. "I should have told him weeks ago, long before he and I married, but I was a coward. I love him, and I'm so frightened of losing his love."

Lizzy left the area of the trunk to comfort her friend. Slipping her arms about Kathleen, she hugged her. "You've been married for how long? A month and a half? Two months?"

"Two months, three weeks, and five days," Kathleen said. She managed a small smile. "And 'tis been a wonderful life."

Lizzy studied her friend's face and smiled back. "You're in love. I've never seen someone this much in love."

" 'Tis a scary thing. Especially when ya know it could all be taken away."

"When will you tell him?" She pulled Kathleen toward the bed and sat them both on the edge.

Kathleen sighed. "I don't know. That's the thing of it. Do I tell him I could be with child, or do I tell him I'm not Meara Kathleen?"

"When will you be certain," Lizzy asked, her brown eyes filled with concern, "about the babe?"

" 'Tis been five weeks since I've had me courses. I'll know fer certain in three weeks or so." There was a possibility that she was simply late with her woman's time, that she wasn't carrying Rian's child at all. She closed her eyes and hugged herself. That would be worse, she thought. She wanted Rian's baby more than anything or anyone . . . except Rian.

"Are you all right?"

Kathleen opened her eyes. "Sorry." She rose from the bed, feeling restless. "I'm fine." Pacing the room, she paused to look out Lizzy's window, then returned to the bed and back again. Lizzy watched her in silence.

"May I have a cup of tea?"

"Of course." Lizzy rose, went to the end of the bed to close the trunk, then led the way downstairs to the kitchen.

Mrs. Potts, the Foley cook, was there this morning. She greeted the two ladies with a grim-faced nod, then turned back to the stove to stir the contents of a simmering pot.

"Mrs. Potts," Lizzy said. "Mrs. Quaid and I would like a cup of tea."

The woman turned, shot Lizzy a scowl, then swung back to the stove, ignoring her.

Kathleen was appalled at the woman's behavior. She

leaned close to Lizzy to whisper. "Why do you put up with her?"

Lizzy sighed. "My husband likes her. She's been here forever. Says she does the best cooking this side of Green Lawns." She managed a grin. "Henny's is the best in Kent County, though. Everyone knows that, even Mrs. Potts."

It was Kathleen's turn to show concern. "I think ya should get rid of her. She was rude to ya. Is she always so?"

Her friend shrugged. "Sometimes."

"Whenever John isn't around," Kathleen guessed.

"Yes."

Kathleen led the young woman outside to the garden behind the house, where they could talk more privately. "Well," she began, "it seems we are both in a fine kettle of boiled fish."

"She's not too bad, most of the time."

But Kathleen could see that Lizzy's expression said differently. "You should get rid of her. John wouldn't want ya to be treated this way."

"It's John's house. I'm just—"

Kathleen pushed her down onto an iron bench. "His wife, Lizzy. You're his wife."

"Yes, but you know the circumstances."

"Aye, that I do. But he married you, Elizabeth Foley. You're raising the children. His child. He loves you." She held up her hand. "Aye, and don't ye be saying differently. He loves you. I've seen it in his eyes. Might not be the love that you'd wish to have between you and your husband, but 'tis a strong one just the same."

Her old troubles temporarily forgotten, Kathleen went on, "Lizzy, John wouldn't want you to be treated this way. You must tell him. Or you must fire the witch and let John figure it out for himself."

"Could I?" Lizzy appeared to seriously consider the idea. "I'd prefer to do the cooking myself, but I don't think John would hear of that."

"How do you know? Have you asked him? Tried it?" Kathleen was stunned that a woman who was happy with the family that God and fate had given her could be so unsure of her position in the household and of her husband's love.

"I bake," Lizzy said. "He doesn't mind that I do the baking." Her expression filled with hope. "In fact, he loves my cookies and cakes." She met her friend's gaze and grinned. "Perhaps he wouldn't mind it if I wanted to spend more time in the kitchen."

"That's it!" Kathleen grinned back. There was one thing she was sure of, and it was that John Foley cared deeply for his wife. Perhaps not in the passionate or sexual way that he had for his first wife, Millicent, but he did have enormous respect and affection for Lizzy, perhaps more love than either one of them was aware of.

"So what are ya going to do?"

"First?"

Kathleen nodded. Lizzy's eyes sparkled. "I'm going back inside the house and ask nicely for some tea. Then, if she doesn't respond, I'll demand it. If that doesn't work, I'll fire her!"

"Good lass!"

Lizzy tilted her head as she regarded her closest friend. "What are you going to do, Kathleen?"

"Any words of advice?"

"No. I'm sorry, Kathleen. I haven't an answer for you."

"Aye," Kathleen said with a heavy heart. "That's the thing of it, Lizzy. Neither do I. Neither do I. . . ."

The light of dawn filtered through the drapes, giving the room a green glow. Kathleen lay awake, wrapped in her husband's arms, while Rian slept blissfully, with her snuggled against his side. She loved this time of day, when she could watch Rian sleep, those moments when she'd study him and feel her heart fill to near bursting. She'd touch his hair without his knowing, caress him with her gaze, her fingertips, and he'd touch her heart simply by being.

Kathleen smiled as she lifted her head to kiss his shoulder. Soon he would stir and open his eyes and startle her, as he did every morning.

He had such beautiful eyes. And their color changed with his moods. Sometimes they were like the green of the forest. At other times they were a softer shade, like dew-dampened grass, while there were occasions, too, when they would darken until they looked black.

Last night, they blackened to almost midnight, right before he entered her while they were making love. Her skin tingled with the memory.

Now, as she lay there, she allowed contentment to wash over her. Physically, she was feeling fine. In fact, she'd not felt ill when she woke up any day, nor did she expect to any longer. She'd been wrong before. Perhaps she wasn't with child. And although she was unhappy about the notion, she had to remember that, given the circumstances of her relationship with Rian, it was probably for the best.

She had to speak with him. She had to tell him the truth. And it was best if there was no child to become an issue between them. She needed to tell him who she was and have him love her all the same.

A sigh, a shuddering, and a shift in Rian's position signaled that he was awakening. Kathleen propped her head on her elbow. His eyelashes fluttered and then lifted. He blinked to focus, then Kathleen watched a curve come to his sensual lips as he turned to regard her with sleepy eyes.

Her heart thumped hard and then steadied to a softer rhythm. He was so beautiful. He made her breath catch.

"Good morning," ' he whispered.

She smiled. "Aye, 'tis a good morning, isn't it?"

His eyes brightened, becoming more alert. "How long have you been awake?" he asked her.

She shrugged. "A half hour or so."

He pretended to be shocked. "And ya didn't wake me?"

"And what would I be doing that fer?"

"What do you think?" He gave her a wicked grin before he rolled her onto her back and pinned her beneath him on the bed. "Have ya no imagination, woman?"

Her body responded to his instantly. "Aye, I've an imagination, and a good one, as it happens."

He caressed her throat and undulated his abdomen against her lower half. "And what is it telling ya this morning?"

Kathleen gasped as he cupped her breast and teased the nipple. "It tells me that me husband doesn't want breakfast this morning."

"Nay," he said. "I want me breakfast, all right, but me breakfast this morning is you."

A wild thrill lifted her high and sent her soaring as she stroked his back, his buttocks, and his muscled thighs. *"Rian . . . "* She giggled as he tickled her with his whiskers.

"Don't disturb me," he rasped. "I'm just beginnin' me meal."

She chuckled softly as he nipped her nose, her chin, sighing softly as he kissed her eyelids, her ear, her jaw.

"Rian, what if Lucy comes to dress me?" She feigned a gasp, knowing the maid wouldn't come for another hour or so. Besides, she had locked the door earlier when she'd had to get up to relieve herself. She'd been hoping for this, wanting this. And she'd wanted to be prepared.

She hid a grin. But Rian didn't know that. "Rian, please."

He sighed heavily and rolled off her. "Ya won't be happy with making love until ya know the door is locked, is that it?"

She continued to touch him where he lay, and as he sat up, her fingers found him hard and throbbing in the dark curly nest of hair that protected him between his thighs. He groaned and started to climb out of bed. Kathleen grabbed his arm and held tight. "No need to get the door, Mr. Quaid," she said in a silky voice. "I've already locked it."

"Minx."

"I wanted an opportunity to touch you." As she spoke, she found his staff again, surrounded it with her fingers, and fondled its hard, silky length.

He regarded her with an expression that she thought comical. Lust warred with mock outrage, and passion won.

"You want to play this morning," he said. The glint in his eyes made her shiver. A boyish Rian was an irresistible one.

"I'll show you how to play," he rasped.

He flung himself over her, pinning her to the bed. To her immense satisfaction, he began to tease every sensitive inch of her with his hands and tongue until she was gasping and moaning, wild for him.

She couldn't think. Her mind was a blank. She could only feel. And when she tried to touch him, he wouldn't let her. He was the chess master, and she was the solitary game piece.

Only when he'd brought her to climax three times did he allow himself his own release.

As their cries mingled, then ceased, they lay entangled, their hearts beating heavily, their breathing raspy.

And the birds sang outside the window, and the members of the household staff began to stir on the floors below, but Kathleen and her husband didn't move. They couldn't move, nor did they have the desire to. They were sated and content to remain forever in each other's arms.

Thirty-three

She wasn't carrying Rian's child. She was sure now; she'd gotten her courses that afternoon. Given the circumstances, Kathleen knew she should feel relieved, but she wasn't. She was terribly sad and disappointed. She wanted to have Rian's baby.

She was in the kitchen, taking tea with Henny after insisting that the woman stop long enough from her work to keep her company.

The two were chatting easily, unlike employer and employee, more like friends, when Pete erupted into the room, limping and out of breath.

"Pete!" Henny rose from her chair. "What is it?"

"McDermott. Conor McDermott. He's been injured. A scythe fell from its hook on a ceiling beam."

Kathleen set down her tea and stood. "Where is he?"

"He's out in the barn. Master Rian asked me to come for you, as he needs your help."

Pulse racing, Kathleen ran out of the house and hurried toward the barn.

She heard the Irishman cursing before she entered the building and saw McDermott seated on a wooden cask.

"I tell ya that I'm all right. Stop yer fretting! Haven't ya ever seen an injured man?"

Rian spied her as she came in. "Kathleen! McDermott has gotten himself cut. Can ya deal with it?"

Her gaze found the Irishman's, and he scowled at her. "Don't ya think you're goin' to treat me like a lad. I'm not a lad and can take the pain of it."

"Is that right?" she said softly as she picked up the arm, removed the cloth pressed to the wound to stanch the blood, and examined his injury. She turned it this way and that, judging the wound to be deep but even enough to make stitching it a simple task. "Aye, you're a brave one, Conor McDermott. But ya must come inside. I've mending to do, and I'll not do it in a dirty barn, brand-new or not." She pressed the bloody cloth back into place.

" 'Tis nothing," he grumbled.

"Now, that's a surprise, I'd say, to hear ya say that," she replied. "Ya of all people should know that the smallest cut can turn to infection." She ran her finger along his wounded arm. "This one will take it, for certain, if 'tis not properly tended. Will ya not be needing that arm?" She flashed her husband a glance. "Is that so? Is McDermott so talented that he can wrestle a horse or fix a fence post one-handed?"

Rian grinned. "She's got a point there, Conor McDermott."

The man stood, mumbling as he did so.

"Did ya say something, Mr. McDermott?" she asked. She sensed her husband's approval of her handling of the man and sent Rian a glance that promised to thank him later.

McDermott threw up his good arm, gesturing toward the door. "I said if I'm going to stop to get this injury of mine taken care of, then let's be at it! I've got work to do and not all the time to do it in."

Kathleen's lips twitched as she struggled to hide her amusement. It was always nice to tangle with someone from home, for the Irish were often a stubborn lot, and this man had more than his share of stubbornness.

"We'll go into the house through the kitchen," she told the man as he waited for her to precede him toward the house. "I'll not have blood on any of the carpets."

She could feel McDermott's outrage and sense Rian's smile. She paused near the back door. "Do ya have a tolerance fer pain, Mr. McDermott?" she asked sweetly.

"Well, now, Mr. McDermott," Kathleen said as the man walked into the kitchen. "How are you feeling this day?"

"I'm fine," he said. "No thanks to you." He paused to grab a warm cookie from a plate on the worktable. "You enjoyed plying me with that needle, didn't ya?"

Kathleen's gaze twinkled. "Why do ya say that? Did I hurt ya?"

His blue eyes shimmered. "Nay, a little thing like you? Nay."

"I've got to check your wound." She approached him.

" 'Tis fine." He backed away. "I'll check it meself later."

"Afraid?" she taunted.

Glaring at her, he stuck out his arm. "Check it. No one will ever say that Conor McDermott is a coward."

Rian entered the kitchen, met his wife's amused gaze as she unwrapped, then examined, the man's arm, and grinned. "Got ya at her mercy again, eh, McDermott?"

"You've a mean one fer a wife, Quaid. She insists on checking her stitches. Probably wants one to have come loose so she can stick me again. I think she enjoyed sticking me."

Rian went to his wife and slipped his arms about her

waist from behind. He lowered his head and nuzzled her neck.

"Careful, Quaid," McDermott said. "The woman's got me arm."

"And she's got me heart," Rian said happily.

"Are ya done now?" McDermott said when she'd studied the injury, announced that it was healing, and started to wrap up the wound.

"Aye," she said with a smile. "But be careful of that arm."

He nodded. "Aye. I wouldn't want a woman like you to get her hands on me again." He jerked his head toward his employer and friend. "If he can manage ya, then 'tis a fine thing. But I'll keep me distance if you don't mind. Lasses are a passel of trouble," he shot over his shoulder as he left the house the way he'd come.

"Never," Rian said, turning his wife to face him. He kissed her once again. "Never a bit of trouble is me Kathleen."

Kathleen threw him a worried glance as he left. She wondered if he'd feel that way about her if he knew the truth.

She was to wonder the same thing again later that afternoon when she was in the garden and had a visitor.

"Kathleen."

The familiar feminine voice did more than startle her. She turned, saw the stranger, then realized that the dark-haired woman was her cousin.

She grabbed her visitor by the arm and hurried behind a stand of trees and bushes, where they could speak privately.

"Meara! Where did ya come from? Where have ya been?"

"I've been with Robert." Meara's eyes were shadowed. She looked tired and unhappy.

"What happened to ya?"

"Robert took me home to his mother."

"He took ya home," Kathleen said, trying to fathom why Meara had abandoned her in Baltimore. "And?"

Meara hesitated. "The woman is a difficult mother, to be sure."

"What are you doing here?"

"Things weren't going well," she said slowly. "I had to get away for a while, and I didn't know where to go. And so I came here."

"How did ya find your way?"

She shrugged. "Robert brought me. It turns out that one of his friends is familiar with Green Lawns." Meara stepped out from the trees to study the manor house. "Not a bad place to live in," she said.

Kathleen's heart thumped. "Aye, 'tis a fine place."

Her cousin turned from her study of the house to regard Kathleen carefully. "What did Rian say when ya told him I couldn't marry him? I see he gave ya a job. That's a fine thing. I didn't want to leave ya. 'Twas Robert's doing."

"Meara—"

"He said ya'd find a way to get to Abernathy, his plantation. The house isn't as grand as this. In fact . . . Well, actually, Kathleen, I could use me dowry money now. Did ya give it to him already?"

Kathleen nodded. "Ya wanted him to have it. Ya told me so."

"Aye, but I didn't know I'd be needing it."

"Meara. About Rian . . ."

"Where is he? Has he changed much? I wonder. He

wasn't bad-looking, mind you, but he was an irritating lad. Always trying to get me mad, he was."

"Meara, Rian and I—we—ah—married."

"He never gave up. Always calling me names, doing things to anger me. Is it any wonder I refused to marry him?" She froze, as if just realizing what Kathleen had said. *"You and Rian what?"*

"We married."

"Married! I know I told ya to marry him, Kathleen, but I wasn't serious! Whatever possessed ya to marry the man? Why ever would he want to marry me cousin?" Meara narrowed her gaze. "He doesn't know we're cousins, does he?"

"Nay."

Meara stared at her, looking displeased. Her lashes flickered. "In fact, he doesn't know you're not me. Ya married him pretending to be me, didn't ya!" Her face reddened. "How could ya do such a thing?"

"I didn't mean it to happen this way," Kathleen assured her. "He . . . well, he just asked me, and I said I would. I fell in love with him. He's a kind and wonderful man, not at all the man you said he was. He didn't even want your dowry. He took it only after the barn and shed burned and we needed to rebuild."

"You gave him the money as your own?"

"Not exactly." Kathleen looked away, stared off into the shrubbery. "I gave him the money like ya told me to, and he might have thought it was mine. But I didn't actually tell him it was so. But ya wanted him to have it, and I felt he deserved it for the way you left him . . . *left me.*"

Kathleen's temper started to simmer as she recalled how she'd been left alone and penniless in a strange land without family. "Ya didn't care about me, Meara. Ya left me with nothing. Rian thought I was you, and I didn't enlighten him, for I had no place else to go. You left me!"

She shivered and hugged herself, as the memory, the horror, of knowing she'd been left returned to haunt her. "Ya left me with not a thought for your family, me, or Rian Quaid. I went with him, intending to tell him everything, but things got out of hand. I was afraid to be sent away with no one and nowhere to go. Is it any wonder that I stayed here? I'd hoped to confess and find me a job here, but well, it didn't happen that way. I fell in love with Rian, and he with me."

Meara's blue eyes regarded Kathleen coldly. "So ya took me fiancé and made him your own. Then you took me dowry money, and you gave it to him after ya wed him . . . so he would think that 'twas yours to give."

"Something like that."

"What would Rian Quaid say, I wonder, if I were to tell him the truth? That he married the wrong woman, that it was I who should have been the bride?"

"But ya didn't want him!"

She shrugged. "Maybe I got lost. Perhaps ya were the one who left me, stole me money, and then decided to steal me betrothed."

"You wouldn't dare tell him those things."

"Oh, wouldn't I?"

Kathleen studied her cousin's expression and wondered what had happened to Meara's sweet disposition. She sighed.

"What do ya want, Meara?" There must be something she wanted. It was too late for her to get back her fiancé. If Meara loved Robert, why had she come to Green Lawns?

"Want?" Meara echoed.

Kathleen stared at her. "Aye."

"I want me dowry back."

"I don't have it. Rian does."

"Then I want money. Ya need to find a way to get me the funds I—Robert—needs."

"I thought Robert was wealthy."

"He's had some setbacks. Give me the dowry money and me jewelry."

"Jewels?"

"Grandmother's jewels. Find them for me. Surely he hasn't sold them. Give me me things back and I'll leave here with nothing said."

"Are ya blackmailing me?" Kathleen said, her heart thumping. She'd known the day would come when Rian would learn the truth, but she'd wanted it to be told by her, not anyone else, especially not Meara. Now it looked as if it would all come out in the open and she might not be able to stop it, not without betraying Rian further.

She had to stop it, Kathleen thought. She needed more time. To learn such a thing from Meara would be a terrible thing for Rian. Too terrible to imagine.

"What did ya do to your hair?" she said, her chest tightening as she tried to think.

"I darkened it," Meara said. The dark color made her look completely different; Kathleen almost hadn't known her. "I didn't want Rian Quaid to recognize me."

Kathleen scowled. "What did ya think you were going to do when you came? If I hadn't been here?"

She shrugged. "I would have found a way into the house. Perhaps posed as a servant girl looking for work. I would have gotten inside and found the family jewels; then I would have taken them and been gone."

"You would have stolen them?" Kathleen asked with a gasp.

"Well, 'tis not like stealing them when they belong to you, now, is it?"

"But if you'd been caught . . ." Kathleen was shocked by her cousin's naïveté. "You'd asked me to pretend to be you. How would ya have convinced the authorities that ya are who ya are?"

Meara waved a hand in dismissal. "There's me father. He would have vouched for me and told them who I am."

"But you could have swung from a hangman's noose first."

"It didn't happen, so there is nothing to be fretting about. I'm here and you're here . . . and so are me family jewels, I'm certain." She paused, biting her lip. "Rian is too sentimental to part with belongings of a family, even if they are our family's. Unless . . ." Her eyes widened. "Do ya think he would have sold them to repair the . . . barn, was it?"

"I don't know," she said. "I don't know what he did with them."

"Well, you'll have to find out now," Meara said. "And in the meantime, I'll stay on as your cousin."

"No!"

Meara grabbed her arm, squeezing hard. "I'll stay on as your cousin. The companion me father wrote that was accompanying me."

"But ya can't be Kathleen. Rian calls me Kathleen."

Her cousin narrowed her gaze. "How did ya manage that?"

"He called you Meara Kathleen, and I told him I preferred Kathleen, so he said fine, that it suited him, for the name suited me."

"Meara Kathleen," Meara murmured. "I always hated

when he called me that." Her lips firmed. "He did it just to anger me."

"Even before he married me, he was a kind and thoughtful gentleman," Kathleen said, ready to defend him.

Meara's expression hardened. "Was he, now?" Her face suddenly brightened as she glanced beyond Kathleen's head.

"Oh, well, now, cousin. 'Tis happy I am to see ya," she said loudly, for someone a distance away to hear. "I've missed ya and am glad you've asked me to stay."

Kathleen's mouth dropped open before she spun around to see the retreating back of a field hand. *Burns.*

Stunned to have been caught with her cousin, Kathleen never gave a thought to what the man was doing this close to the gardens and the house.

Thirty-four

Kathleen was grateful. Since Meara's arrival, Rian had been too busy to spend more than a few minutes in Meara's company. If he recognized her as anyone other than what Meara had stuck out her hand and introduced herself as—Mary Maureen—he didn't let on. Kathleen decided that he didn't know, for although she and Meara had similar features, the difference in hair coloring disguised the face. She was the only one with red hair now. Meara's hair was dark.

But she had no idea how she would continue to keep Rian from learning the truth. As long as Meara remained a guest at Green Lawns, the threat of Kathleen's true identity being revealed was ever-present.

Which meant that Kathleen had to find a way to get her cousin to leave. Or confess to Rian herself.

As to the first, she didn't know how to do it unless she gave into Meara's demands and found a way to return Meara's dowry money. To her, that would be stealing, and it was bad enough that she'd lied to him. She wouldn't add stealing to her list of crimes.

Her second option was to tell Rian the truth today. Tonight. But she didn't want to do it while Meara was still in the house. And she wasn't eager to stir Rian's ire.

Which put Kathleen in an awful situation.

"Kathleen?" Meara came into the morning room,

where Kathleen had been sitting, attempting to concentrate on her needlework but getting little done because of the worry that plagued her. "May I talk with you?"

Kathleen sighed and put aside Rian's shirt. "Aye. I can't very well stop ya, can I?"

Her cousin took a seat across from Kathleen's. The room was filled with bright summer sunlight. The house was quiet. Henny was at home, at Kathleen's insistence, taking the day to nurse an ill stomach, while Lucy and Lottie were upstairs making beds and dusting the furniture.

It would have been a pleasant morning to Kathleen if it weren't for Meara's untimely return. But Meara had come back and made things difficult. And she didn't know if she could ever forgive her cousin for blackmailing her and wanting her to steal.

"If you've come to urge me again to talk about your dowry money, then you're wasting your time," Kathleen said after a lengthy silence. She grabbed her needlework again and began to ply her needle. "I've been thinking long and hard on this, and if ya want to tell him, then go ahead and tell the man. For I won't hurt or lie anymore to the man I love. Not for you. Not for anyone."

She could feel her cousin's anger as tension filled the air between them.

"Mending your husband's shirt?" Meara drawled mockingly.

Her fingers freezing in mid-action, Kathleen looked up. "Aye. And do ya have a problem with that?"

"With what?" A muscle ticked along Meara's jaw. "That you're mending his shirts or that ya married me fiancé?"

"We've been through this discussion—"

"Well, I'm not finished with it!" her cousin cried.

Throwing the shirt aside, Kathleen stood. "Ya didn't want him! Ya didn't want him, and I do!"

Meara rose to follow her. "I want me money!"

"And I told ya that I don't have it!"

"Then get it!"

"I can't. I won't!' Kathleen cried.

"If ya don't, then I'll tell him. I'll tell him that you're not me and that ya deceived him into marrying you. That ya hit me over me head, stole me money, and left me to die." Her smile was evil. "If it wasn't for a kind and generous gentleman from Baltimore, I'd be hurt and lying somewhere in the gutter. I'll tell him that I couldn't remember who I was because of me head injury. And when I recalled it, I had to dye me hair to keep ya from finding me. Only now that I've found Green Lawns do I feel safe enough to tell him the truth!"

"You wouldn't dare!" Kathleen felt the blood drain from her face.

"Aye, I would."

"You're a wicked lass, Meara Dunne. Your father would be upset with ya if he knew the truth."

Something flickered in her cousin's expression. "Me father isn't here. I told ya that once before."

"But I am, and so ya can take your turn to hurt me?"

The anger left Meara's face as she settled back into her chair. "I don't want to hurt ya, Kathleen. Ya must believe me. 'Tis the money. Only the money. Robert needs it, and so . . ."

"What kind of man would demand money from his wife?" Kathleen tensed when she saw her cousin's face. "You're not his wife yet, are ya?"

Shivering, Meara hugged herself with her arms. "Nay. But he loves me, and he's told me so. Only his mother says he's not to marry me until he has me dowry."

"Oh, Meara." Feeling a wave of sympathy, Kathleen was tempted to go to her cousin. Then she remembered the anger in her cousin's expression, the hatred almost, and she knew that her cousin didn't just want the money. She wanted everything Kathleen had that she'd refused. Meara wanted a man with a plantation such as Green Lawns. And she was jealous of the life that Kathleen now had with her former fiancé.

"What kind of man would tell you one thing, then suddenly change his mind?" Kathleen asked.

" 'Tis not like that," Meara insisted. " 'Tis his mother."

"Then he listens too much to his mother, and he'll never listen to you."

"Nay, he will listen to me. He loves me."

Kathleen sighed. "Perhaps he does."

"Will ya get it, then? Me dowry? If the money's gone, surely the jewels are still about."

"I don't really know what all was in your dowry," Kathleen said. "I gave it to him when the time was right. I might have seen some coin . . . and a ring, I think. But I never looked past what I saw on top."

"Ya must help me."

"The way ya helped me when we first came to America?"

"I told ya I didn't mean—"

"I can't," Kathleen told her. "I can't help you."

"Then I'll have to tell Rian, explain who I am."

"He'll never believe I hit ya over the head and stole your money."

Meara nodded. "Aye, he will. You've deceived him. He won't know what to think, but 'tis sure he'll think ill of ya."

"Why are ya doing this? I told ya I can't help ya!"

"I need something to take back with me. Anything." There was a desperate note in Meara's tone.

Kathleen reached beneath the neckline of her gown's bodice and pulled out her precious locket. "Here. Take this. It must be worth something." It was her mother's locket and worth everything to Kathleen.

Meara fingered the necklace as she studied it thoughtfully. " 'Tis your locket."

"Aye."

" 'Tis not worth as much as the jewels," Meara said. "But 'tis something."

Did that mean that Meara would leave now?

" 'Tis gold," Kathleen said. " 'Tis worth more than something."

"I still think I should tell him who you are. That your name is Kathleen Maguire, not Meara Kathleen Dunne."

"I'll tell him in me own time."

"Humph." Meara rose, swinging the locket by the chain. Kathleen eyed the piece, her stomach burning. She'd given up something of her mother to keep the man she loved. "Will ya go?" she asked.

"Tomorrow. I'll leave tomorrow," Meara said. "But I'll need money."

"Nay!"

"I can still tell him."

"Tell me what?" Rian said as he entered the room.

Kathleen paled. "Rian?"

"What were ya saying, Meara?" He looked at Kathleen's cousin, his eyes hardening as he stared at her. " 'Tis Meara Kathleen, isn't it?"

"Rian—" Kathleen began.

Rian ignored her, his attention solely on Meara. "What do ya want? Why are ya here?"

Meara's face looked white against her dark hair. Her

freckles seemed out of place in a woman of her hair coloring. Rian understood now why something about her had seemed different, yet familiar.

"Well?" he said.

Meara lifted her chin. "I've come for me dowry. Kathleen took it from me. It didn't belong to her. She had no right to give it to ya."

Kathleen could feel the anger emanating from Rian's frame and knew that she was responsible and that he was furious with her. Would he ever forgive her?

"You're saying that ya didn't give the money to Kathleen. That ya had every intention of giving it to me after we wed."

"Aye."

"Liar."

Meara's blue eyes flashed. "The money is mine. I want it."

"Meara!" Kathleen cried, appalled.

"Well 'tis mine," Meara shot back at her. Then she scowled at Rian. "They should never have made the betrothal agreement. It wasn't right."

"Get out." Rian's features were hard, unyielding. "I want ya out of me house now."

Meara stood her ground. "It's rightfully mine," she grumbled.

Rian turned and left the room, leaving Kathleen staring after him with a wildly beating heart and dread burning in her belly.

He was back within seconds with a small velvet pouch, which he thrust in Meara's direction. Kathleen wondered what had happened to the original wooden dowry box. "Get out." he said. "You've got what ya came for. Now go and don't come back. Ever."

Looking relieved, Meara snatched the bag from Rian's

fingers. "I won't need to come back. This is all Robert needs for Abernathy."

Rian tensed. "Did ya say Abernathy?"

"Aye."

"Widham," he snarled.

"Aye, 'tis Robert Widham, Rian," Kathleen began, but he ignored her, as if she were invisible.

The burning in Kathleen's stomach became violet spasms of pain as she fought back the urge to be sick.

Robert Widham! Rian cursed. His stepbrother. His former fiancée had become involved with the offspring of the woman who'd made his father's life a living hell.

He was tempted to grab back the bag and send her on her way penniless, but he knew she would be back . . . and it was worth it to get rid of her.

Kathleen lied to me. The woman he'd loved had lied to him, and he could no longer trust her, as his father had been unable to trust Priscilla when he'd been alive. *Kathleen Maguire,* he thought. *Not Meara Kathleen Dunne.*

He ignored Meara's thanks, watched dispassionately while the woman left. Kathleen stood silently, unmoving, her face white.

He looked at her, saw her tear-bright eyes, and hardened his heart against her. She had lied to him. Deceived him in the worst possible way.

"Rian—"

"Not now," he growled. And he turned from the sight of her. Despite her treachery, her wicked heart, he was still moved by the sight of her tears. He still wanted her, God help him.

"I can explain."

"I don't want to hear it."

"Please—"

He turned on her, his fury taking hold. "What do ya want to say? That ya hadn't meant to play me for a fool? That ya didn't pretend to be Meara Kathleen and work your way into this house—" *My heart,* he thought. "I don't want to hear it. I can't listen to you. Not now. Perhaps not ever."

"But Rian!" She was sobbing now, grabbing his arm, but he shook it off. Her touch, her voice, everything about her, hurt him. He needed to get away from her before he did something he'd regret.

"Nay!" Kathleen cried as the man she loved above all others walked away from her without looking back. She should have told him. Now it was too late. He had obviously overheard her conversation with Meara.

She wanted, needed, to go after him, but it was clear that he didn't want to listen, that he didn't even want to set eyes on her again.

"Nay," she whispered, tears running down her cheeks, her throat constricted, making it difficult to swallow. "I have to explain. I have to make him see!"

But she was afraid. Oh, so afraid that she had lost him. The happiness they had known was gone, and she didn't know if she'd ever find it again.

Thirty-five

Rian didn't come to bed that night. She hadn't spoken to or seen him since Meara left, and Kathleen felt sick and heartbroken.

What was she to do?

She had eaten alone in the kitchen. Kathleen was relieved that she didn't have explanations to make to Henny or any of the men, nor did she have to deal with the servants' speculative glances. But it wouldn't be long before it became obvious to everyone around that something had changed between the master and his new wife, and Kathleen dreaded that time. But not as much as she dreaded the thought of being sent away and never seeing her husband again.

Husband. They were still man and wife, weren't they? Kathleen recalled their wedding vows, when she'd purposely used only her first name, for she had wanted to come as herself and have a real marriage. Aye, they were man and wife, but that didn't mean that Rian couldn't cast her aside.

She caught back a sob. She loved him. How she loved him! And she'd deceived him, hurt him, and now she might have lost his love.

That night, as she climbed into bed, she left a candle burning on the nightstand. Would he come later? Surely he couldn't leave things as they stood? Surely he'd want to confront her?

Or hadn't he loved her enough to care?

Nay, he'd been angry. And beneath the anger she'd felt his pain. Felt and understood it, for she was hurting, too. Didn't he realize that? That she, too, was in pain?

She lay in bed in her prettiest night garment, staring at the ceiling, hoping, praying, that Rian would come, that he'd realize that she loved him and hadn't meant to deceive him, that circumstances had taken things beyond her control.

But Rian never came, and she woke up the next morning with the candle burned down to the candlestick holder. She'd wasted a good candle in the hope that her husband would come to her, but she was alone . . . might always be alone. Her eyes filled with tears. *I might always be alone.*

Her chest tight, her stomach and eyes burning, Kathleen rose from her bed and attempted to gather her composure to begin the day. Only time would tell if she would be sent away. Only time would tell if she would lose her husband, the man of her dreams . . . of her heart.

Thwack! Thwack! Rian lifted the sledgehammer and whacked a fence post into the ground. "How"— *thwack!*—"will I"—*thwack*—"ever trust her again?"

Perspiration ran down his brow as he worked. His fist clenched about the hammer handle with each up-and-down swing. He was angry, hurt, and wanting Kathleen. He was a fool, but he couldn't stop loving her. He'd be a bigger fool if he went on about their lives as if nothing had happened.

"What are ya going to do?" he mumbled to himself. "Send her away?"

The thought of her leaving disturbed him more than he had wished.

He snarled as he lifted the hammer and brought it down hard, splintering wood and ruining the fence post.

"You've got a mighty powerful arm there, Quaid." Conor McDermott approached, his eyes sharp on his employer's face, his brows arched. "Would ya like me to take over before you split all the posts?"

Rian took a calming breath as he eyed the field hand. "I can handle this hammer as well as the next man."

McDermott's lips twitched. "Aye, sure enough. I can see that."

"Very well." Rian handed the man the hammer. "Ya can take over before I hammer me foot as well as the post."

The man nodded as he accepted the hammer and swung to lift it. "I thought you'd like to know that someone has been tampering with the paddock gate."

Rian tensed. "Do you have an idea who?"

"Nay. I went to check on Midnight when I noticed the gate wasn't latched. Someone had wedged the latch in the open position. It would be easy for Midnight or one of the geldings to nose it open. I would have thought it an accident until I examined it closer and saw that someone had skillfully tied it up with a piece of hemp."

"I've had it!" Rian barked, furious with the vandalism and the pranks, made no less annoying by the difficulties between him and Kathleen. "I want to see the men in the new barn today. No, make it this evening! Will ya pass on the word?"

The Irishman nodded. "Aye." He lowered his hammer

arm and regarded his employer with curiosity. "What do ya plan to say to the men?"

"I don't know now, but I'll know for certain when ya gather the men."

Such nonsense had to stop, Rian thought. If he learned that one of his own men was responsible, then he would fire the man and see him jailed for the trouble he'd caused.

His jaw snapped as he made his way back toward the manor house. He needed to speak with Pete; he needed to know if Pete had noticed anything strange lately.

If the incidents hadn't occurred before, he might have suspected McDermott, but the man had worked hard, complained little, and showed responsibility, which Rian liked in a man. No, it wasn't Conor McDermott. He began to sift through his memory for each of his workers' names, sorting, looking for something that might link the trouble to one of his employees.

And then he saw her in the window upstairs. The master bedroom where they had slept together and where she now slept alone. Kathleen . . .

With a muffled oath, he turned and stomped in the opposite direction. He wouldn't go to his office now, he decided. He didn't want to be in the same house with her. Not when she confused him, taunted him, teasing his mind and arousing his desire.

He headed toward the Petersons' cottage, a small structure that his grandfather had built especially for the overseer. If Pete wasn't home, he'd find him later. But he wouldn't sit in his office and wait for the man to arrive, not when there was a chance that she might come and beg him to listen to her.

* * *

The neighbors of the area were gathering for a summer picnic at the Foleys'. The Quaids were invited, and Kathleen had made a salad of fruit picked from the Green Lawns orchards and two berry pies to take along with them.

Kathleen was nervous about the outing. Since Meara's departure and the revelation of her identity, she and Rian had been strangers to one another.

He had managed to avoid her for three days now. Heartsick, Kathleen wanted only to talk with him, explain her side of the situation, but he wasn't ready to listen. And so she stayed away from him lest she anger him further.

The morning of the outing was clear when Kathleen got up, trying not to think of Rian's empty side of their bed, and dressed for the picnic. She was eager to see Lizzy again. Lizzy was the one person she could talk with about Rian, for Lizzy had known the truth for some time and understood how much Kathleen loved her husband.

She took extra pains to be presentable that day, but as she looked into the mirror, she felt that she'd failed miserably.

Dark shadows encircled her eyes, and there was a sad, haunted look in her expression, that of a woman who was suffering.

Kathleen stared into the mirror, fought back tears, and then, gathering her composure, went downstairs to see that her salad and pies were packed and ready for the picnic.

Rian was standing outside, near the wagon they'd be taking when Kathleen left the house. She hesitated before approaching. Heart pounding, she gazed at him hungrily, taken aback by how handsome he was, how much she missed his company and his smile.

He turned to her then, and his expression made her heart bleed. He hated her, she realized. She had hurt him, and he was unwilling and unable to forgive her.

She swallowed against a throat tight with tears. Lifting her chin, she walked silently past him, placed the salad and pies in the back of the wagon, then climbed into the vehicle.

Without a word, he climbed up onto the seat beside her, then, taking the reins, he urged the horses on.

The ride was silent and fraught with tension. Kathleen knew that this might be the only chance of talking with Rian alone, but she couldn't bring herself to speak. Her throat was so tight, she could barely swallow. She was afraid that if she tried to speak with him, her words would be garbled. Or she'd start to sob loudly.

She sat on the seat, her hands in her lap, staring straight ahead, her thoughts and her heart with the man beside her.

And she felt as if she were slowly dying inside.

Thirty-six

They had left early that morning and arrived by mid-morning. Kathleen was so filled with tension that she ached in every part of her body. Here she and Rian were man and wife, and they were worse than strangers. They had become adversaries of a sort, forced to simulate a relationship that no longer existed. And Kathleen couldn't pretend for very much longer.

The silence was oppressive as Rian urged the wagon along the front drive to the Foleys' modest, well-kept home. He had barely stopped the horses when Kathleen was climbing down from the vehicle without waiting for assistance. She could see other guests alighting from their carriages, laughing and talking as they greeted friends, then made their way toward the side yard, where tables had been set up for the event. Kathleen longed for the time when she'd had that ease in her relationship with Rian.

She went to the back of the wagon to get their picnic offerings, and her fingers brushed with Rian's as he reached for the salad bowl at the same time. She jerked back as if stung. Rian said nothing; he used the time of her withdrawal to get the food. With her jaw clenched so hard that she was fighting a headache, Kathleen started to head toward the house.

"Kathleen."

She froze without turning. "We are married. I expect both of us to behave that way. No one needs to see the trouble between us."

She faced him, stared at him with dull eyes, and heard him catch his breath. "If ya wish," she said before turning back. She began to walk toward the house.

"Wait!"

She halted, tensing, and waited for him to reach her side.

"We'll walk in together."

She didn't say anything, but did as she was told, and as they walked toward the gathering, she felt her heart breaking. This man whom she loved desperately no longer cared for her.

What was to become of their marriage? She couldn't live through another week of his anger, let alone a whole lifetime!

"Kathleen! Rian!" Spying their arrival, Lizzy rushed forward to greet them.

Kathleen thought her friend looked wonderful. Lizzy's face was radiant. Her brown eyes sparkled, and her lips curved into a sweet smile.

Kathleen's spirits sunk lower. She didn't want to upset Lizzy on such a wonderful day for her. Whatever people might think of her, they weren't letting her know, for Lizzy looked relaxed and in her element as hostess.

"I'm so glad you could come!" Lizzy said.

" 'Tis happy we are to be here," Kathleen replied, forcing what she hoped was a genuine smile.

"You're looking lovely this day, Mrs. Foley," Rian said gallantly. He bent to kiss her hand, and Lizzy giggled.

"Don't start playing the gentleman with me, Rian Quaid. I'm a woman with a husband. Besides, everyone knows you're smitten with your wife."

Lizzy spun away to greet another guest, a smile on her face, unaware that her comment had created another awkward moment between Kathleen and Rian.

Flashing Rian a glance, Kathleen saw that he was studying her. She gazed back at him blankly, and he frowned, narrowing his eyes.

"Kathleen! Rian!" John Foley came forward to join his wife and their new guests. "So good of you to come."

Rian's cheerful grin made Kathleen's heart shatter. "We wouldn't miss coming for the world. I've been craving Lizzy's treats."

Turning back to them, Lizzy raised an eyebrow. "I heard that. I know for a fact that your wife has been turning her hand to baking."

He nodded. "Aye, she has." He flashed her a look of love that had Kathleen blinking and looking away. "And a good hand it's been."

Kathleen felt a wave of pain. How could he pretend such affection when all he really felt for her was contempt?

In the side yard, they joined the guests, who were having a wonderful time, chatting with friends and engaging in yard games. As children ran about the food tables, their parents admonished them to get away. Some of the women fussed with the placement of dishes, while the men stood off to one side, smoking cigars and watching their familys' antics with indulgence. The weather was perfect, the mood festive. Only Rian and she, Kathleen thought, wished they were elsewhere.

Lizzy and John, spying newcomers, slipped from the Quaids' side, and Rian and Kathleen were alone in the midst of neighbors. Heart thumping, unsure of what to do, Kathleen searched the gathering for familiar faces.

Spying Mrs. Smithfield, she started to approach until a hand on her arm stopped her.

"Kathleen."

She shot Rian a look and met his gaze. He looked at her with less animosity and more curiosity. To her amazement, concern flickered across his expression as he traced the dark circles beneath her eyes with his finger.

"We need to talk," he said gruffly, withdrawing his touch.

Stomach churning with fear, she nodded and looked away.

"You look ill."

Her temper flared as she flashed him an angry glance. "I'm fine, Rian Quaid. Don't ya be pitying me. 'Tis not pity I want from you."

His mouth tightened. "What is it ya want?"

She gazed up at him, her eyes filling with tears. Her throat tightened with pain at the thought that he'd had to ask that question when she'd shown him in so many ways since they were married, and before, how much she loved him.

She turned away, and stared unblinking at the gathering. "Nothing," she mumbled, and walked away.

Let him stop her, she thought. He wanted her to play the perfect married couple with him. Then let him stop her and see how contrary she could be!

She was dying inside. Playing his doting wife would slowly kill her this day, but what choice did she have? She didn't want the neighbors to learn the truth. That all wasn't a happy paradise in the Quaid home.

And she loved him. There was no denying that nothing he'd said or done had affected her deep love for Rian

Quaid. And so she would do as he asked. If nothing else, she felt he had earned it because of the deception.

Spying a woman she'd met and chatted with briefly at the Smithfields' dinner party back in June, Kathleen grabbed a glass of punch and made her way toward her to say hello.

She lost track of Rian for a short time. Then she saw him with a group of men standing under a huge oak tree, smiling and chuckling as they conversed.

As she nodded at Amelia Ways, listening with half an ear to Amelia's description of the new ball gown she'd had specially made in Philadelphia, Kathleen watched her husband.

Longing for him rose to overpower her. Blinking back tears, she managed some appropriate response to Miss Ways's question about Kathleen's wedding dress. Then, when she saw the opportunity, she slipped away to find a seat where she could watch her husband alone. The longing became a painful ache that nearly had her sobbing out loud for all she'd lost.

She rose, left the gathering, and found a private place behind one of the outbuildings, where she surrendered to tears.

Sometime later—she didn't know how long—Kathleen felt composed enough to return to the picnic. She had gone to the well and drawn water to splash on her face, and as she entered the busy clearing, she hoped her eyes weren't puffy and red. She stood there, searching for someone with whom to visit.

"Why, if it isn't Miss Dunne," a dry, feminine voice drawled. "Oh, I'm sorry. I guess it's Mrs. Quaid now, isn't it?"

Kathleen stared at Nancy Sparks, her body tensing. "Aye."

"Well, what are you doing over here when your husband is there—" She paused, looking gleefully sympathetic. "With the ladies?"

Kathleen glanced over to where Rian was conversing with a beautiful blond woman in a bronze-colored watered-silk dress. She looked at Nancy and shrugged. "What can I say," she said. "Me husband is a wonderful man. Every female wants him. Only I'm the one who has him. Lucky me."

Nancy's mouth firmed. "If you don't watch yourself, you won't have him, either."

Fury brought a flush to Kathleen's cheeks. "Is that a threat?"

"What do you think?"

"You think you can win him? Don't ya think he would have chosen ya in the first place if he'd wanted ya?"

The woman sniffed as she focused her gaze on Rian. "From what I hear, he was betrothed to you since you were children."

"And ya think Rian would marry a woman simply because his family wished it? Then ya think little of the man, fer Rian goes after what he wants and gets it. In this case, 'twas me."

Anger flashed in Nancy's eyes and pinched in her cheeks. "You witch," she gasped, her hands fisting at her sides. "You may have won him for the present, but don't think you can keep him. You've not enough to keep him interested in you for very long." She walked off in a snit, leaving Kathleen staring after her with a shudder.

What she'd said was no doubt true, but Kathleen wasn't about to give the woman the satisfaction of knowing it.

Kathleen watched Rian, who was still chatting with

the blond-haired woman. Her vision blurred, and she turned away. He didn't want her; he didn't love her. He wouldn't even listen to her, so his love had been false.

"Kathleen?"

A soft, brief touch on her arm had her turning. "Lizzy!"

"What's wrong?" Her friend frowned as she examined Kathleen's face. "You look ill."

"I'm fine," she said, averting her gaze.

"No, you're not." Lizzy grabbed her arm. "Come on. Into the house. Something is wrong, and I want to know what it is."

Kathleen struggled to get free. "No, Lizzy."

"I said you're coming with me." There was an edge of steel in Lizzy's voice. The sweetness in her expression had turned formidable. But underneath her friend's sternness was caring.

How could she turn away from the only person who understood what she'd been through?

Lizzy dragged Kathleen into the house and didn't stop until they were upstairs in Lizzy's room. She shoved Kathleen onto the bed.

"Now tell me," Lizzy demanded. "Something's dreadfully wrong. I could feel it when you first came, but I didn't want to ask then."

"You could fe—"

"Yes, I could feel it," she interrupted. "I'm you're friend, Kathleen. Remember? I know that you've been worried about your marriage to Rian."

A shaft of pain made Kathleen glance away.

"What?" Lizzy asked anxiously. "What happened?"

"Oh, Lizzy, he knows."

"He knows," she echoed, puzzled. Her brow furrowed. "Rian?"

Kathleen nodded. "Aye. He's learned the truth, and now he hates me. He knows who I am, and now he loathes the sight of me!"

Thirty-seven

"I don't know what to do!" Kathleen cried. "Rian won't listen to me. He doesn't want to hear me side of it. He ignores me like I'm a grubby spot on a barn wall."

"I'm sorry," Lizzy said as she held the sobbing girl. "Perhaps he'll come around. Surely, in time—"

"How much time? 'Tis already been three days! Three days without speaking, Lizzy. . . . In all of the three days, he's barely looked at me! Oh, I'm wrong," she corrected. "He spoke with me this morning. He told me that no one needed to know the difficulties between us and that we were to behave like a husband and wife should."

"You *are* husband and wife," Lizzy said.

"I know that," she said. "But he doesn't see it that way. All he sees is the woman who deceived him . . . not the one who loves him." She grabbed Lizzy's arm. "I didn't mean to deceive, Lizzy. I was afraid to be on me own. Meara had left me. . . ."

"Surely he must see—"

"He overheard Meara!" Kathleen sobbed. She'd already told Lizzy about Meara's visit and her cousin's threat to reveal the truth if Kathleen wouldn't steal back her dowry money, but Kathleen had refused to do so. And as the cousins were arguing, Rian had overheard. How much he'd overheard, Kathleen had no idea.

"It's a cruel thing for a cousin to blackmail another."

"Aye. She threatened to tell him that I'd hit her over the head, then stole her money, so I could come here pretending to be her." Kathleen lifted a hand to wipe away the tears that fell down her cheeks freely. "I didn't want to meet him! She wanted me to pretend to be her to let him down. She'd fallen in love with another man, and she refused to marry Rian. She told me that she needed me to give Rian the dowry so she could leave with Robert without feeling guilty. She claimed that Rian only wanted her dowry."

"Robert?"

Kathleen nodded. "Robert Widham. The man me cousin loves."

"Ro— *Widham?*" Lizzy raised her eyebrows and swore mildly. "Rian's stepbrother."

"He's what?"

"Rian's stepbrother, if it's one and the same man. He's Priscilla's son by her first marriage. Priscilla is Rian's stepmother."

"Oh, no! No wonder he wouldn't listen to me." Kathleen felt a fresh wave of tears. "It doesn't look good, then, does it?"

Lizzy shook her head sadly. "I'm afraid not."

"But you and I both know that I married him only because I love him," Kathleen said. "I didn't marry him fer his money or Green Lawns."

Her friend smiled. "I know you didn't. Never did I see a woman who was torn as much as you over whether or not she should marry the man she loves. No. You married him because you loved him, and for no other reason. And you held on to your secret for that same reason."

"What am I going to do?" Kathleen whispered, exhausted by her tears.

"Give him time."

"How much time?"

Lizzy didn't know. "That is entirely up to you. You'll know whether to stay or leave. You'll learn soon enough if his love for you is as strong as your love for him." She gave Kathleen a hug. "Now we'd best be getting downstairs before your husband misses your presence and comes searching for you."

"Nay. Not a chance of that happening," Kathleen said sorrowfully.

Lizzy frowned as she hugged her friend tighter. "You never know, Kathleen. You never know."

Kathleen went downstairs after she'd repaired the damage to her appearance and searched for her husband in the crowded yard. He was no longer in the spot he'd been in earlier, when she'd seen him with the blond woman.

Heart pounding, she wandered about the yard, searching for him. Afraid of where or with whom she'd find him. As it turned out, she had no cause to worry that he was with that blond woman or another female, for that matter. He and several of the men had found under a shady tree a spot where they'd set up a card table and begun to play.

She saw the group, and unwilling to disturb them, she backed away in search of something to do. But Rian had seen her within several feet. Meeting her gaze, he threw down his cards and rose despite the grumbling of his fellow card players.

"Sorry, friends, but I see my wife, with whom I've had little time for this day," he said smoothly, smiling.

Clifton Reading looked up and over at Rian's wife. "Pretty little thing. I don't blame you for leaving. If I had a wife like that, I'd abandon the whole lot of you as well."

Rian joined in with the men's laughter. Excusing himself, he approached her.

Kathleen stood without moving, staring, unable to look away as her palms grew damp and her head swam. "Rian."

"I wondered where you went." He examined her features. "Are you all right? You look pale."

She sighed. It would be like him to feel responsible for her even while he despised her. "I'm fine."

"Are you certain?"

She met his gaze steadily. "Aye. As certain as I can be for someone whose husband despises the very sight of her."

She heard his jaw snap. "I don't despise you."

"Nay? I find that hard to believe, since you've been doing a good imitation of ignoring me and showing me without words what a common little deceit and liar I am."

"Enough" he growled. He took her arm and forcefully led her far from earshot of the Foleys and their guests. He paused to glare down at her. "I was concerned. Forgive me for being so."

"Concerned about me?" she asked, unconvinced. "Oh, appearances. That's right. We are married, and we're not behaving as a married couple should," she cried. "Well, it wasn't I who wanted things to be difficult with us! It wasn't I who left ya to speak to another man. I've been here, trying to play a proper wife, while me husband was off showing an interest in another woman. A blond woman," she said to clarify things.

Rian's green gaze flashed with anger. "Ya weren't by me side, though, were ya? If ya had stayed with your husband like a good wife should—"

"A good wife!" she exclaimed. "But I'm not a good wife, isn't it so? I'm a bad wife. A terrible wife. I married ya under false pretenses. I gave ya me innocence without thought, without caring, because I had it to give!"

He frowned as she swung about to leave. "Kathleen—"

She froze, faced him. "What?"

"You're me wife. For better or worse." His tone implied that this was the worst. "You're to stay by me side. You owe me nothing else if but that for deceiving me the way ya did."

She gazed at him, long and hard, loving him, hating him, itching to grab him and make him see past the fury that blinded him to the woman who loved him above all things.

"Will ya do that? Pretend to love me even if ya don't?"

She didn't immediately answer. "I will stay with ya for the day. And I'll play your loving wife."

Rian seemed to relax with a sigh. "There, then. We've come to an agreement." He came forward and grabbed her arm. She felt the fire of his heated touch, and she wanted to run from the way he made her feel.

"Have you eaten yet?" he asked casually, as if nothing between them had turned bitter and nasty.

"Nay," she murmured, drawing herself in to feel numb. It would be the only way she could protect herself enough to get through the rest of the picnic.

"Good. Then let's get something to eat. There's quite a fare on the table. Both meats and treats." He smiled at her, and she reeled back under the impact, for his grin had seemed genuine and a bit of the Rian she'd once known before Meara and she had destroyed him.

They rejoined their neighbors, and Kathleen gave the performance of a lifetime. Laughing. Smiling. Gazing up at her husband with adoring eyes. For although she loved Rian and would always love him, the wounds she—and he—felt were too deep for mending.

And she wasn't sure what would happen to their relationship.

It hurt. Rian playing the perfect doting husband, the man he'd been before he'd learned the truth of Kathleen's identity. And Kathleen felt heartsick that it was all just an act. A game.

He continued doting on her for hours, through the day and early evening, when the guests started to depart and the Quaids lingered a bit longer. Rian was so good at pretending, so convincing that Kathleen could almost believe he was genuine. Almost.

But when it came time for them to leave and their wagon was brought around to the front, she knew things would change as soon as they lost sight of the Foley place. When there was no longer a need to pretend.

No longer an audience to witness the travesty that their marriage had become.

Thirty-eight

They arrived home in silence, much as they went. Kathleen entered the house, with Rian following quickly behind her.

"Kathleen."

She froze on the stairs, her hands on the banister.

"I'd like to talk with you."

"What if I don't want to talk?"

His face was grim. "Come into my office, please. We're long overdue for a discussion."

Kathleen studied him, debating whether or not to ignore him and continue on to her room, but in his present mood, she judged, he'd just come up and get her, perhaps drag her down.

With a heavy, audible sigh, she came down the stairs and preceded him to his office. She entered the room and stood off to the side of the door. Rian, following, gave her a look and gestured toward the chair before his desk.

She started to say no but then obeyed. He had something to say to her. He probably wanted her to leave, she thought. Her belly clenched. No! She didn't want to go. Not yet. She wanted him only to love her.

But there was anything but love in his expression as he sat at the other side of the desk.

Kathleen sat in the chair, her hands folded primly in her lap, her eyes on the window behind Rian's head.

"Are ya going to look at me, or will I be talking to the wall over there?" he drawled without humor.

She shot him a fierce look. "Say what ya have to say. I'm tired and would like to seek me bed."

His lips tightened. "I apologize for taking up your time. I thought ya wanted to speak with me, and now I'm giving ya the opportunity," he said, making her blush.

"Four days after the fact!" she cried, rising from her chair.

He stood and rounded the desk. "What did you expect, Kathleen? That I would hear the truth, simply look at you, and say all was forgiven and smile?" His fist slammed on the desktop. "Nay! Ya deceived me and used me, and then ya expected me to be happy about it!"

She had gasped and stepped back as he'd pounded the desk, but now she came forward, her chin raised, unafraid.

"I didn't expect anything from you, Rian Quaid, but fer ya to have a fair ear to listen to me. I'm your wife, and I only wanted to explain."

"My wife," he mocked. "Are you me wife, Kathleen? Or some stranger I've married?"

She blanched at the direct hit. "Ya married me, not a stranger. Ya said it didn't matter about the betrothal agreement. That ya married me fer meself."

"But then I didn't now how you lied, did I?"

"Nay, but—"

"Nor did I have a clue just how deceitful and cunning you are."

"I didn't mean to deceive you! I had nothing! No one and no place to go! When Meara asked me to give ya her dowry and tell about her decision to marry Robert, I didn't want to do it, but I had nothing! If I didn't do what she said, I'd be stranded in a strange land with no money and no family. I had to do it! Don't ya see?"

"And you had to continue the deception for two months?"

She looked away, her eyes misting. "I didn't know how to tell ya. I already cared and—"

"You saw Green Lawns and what I had. You saw Meara's life—what your life could be—and ya decided not to tell me."

"It wasn't like that!"

"It wasn't?" He regarded her as if he clearly didn't believe her.

She spun away and headed toward the door.

"Where are ya going?"

"Anywhere. Away from here! *Away from you!*"

"We're not finished talking!"

She faced him, fighting tears, and the lump that had risen to construct her throat. "I'm finished. We're finished," she whispered.

She fumbled with the doorknob, had turned it to open when his hand clamped down on her fingers, and she gasped as he tugged her around.

"Rian."

"I loved you," he said. He still did, he thought. He stared at the woman before him and saw not the lying, conniving wench who had deceived him but a beautiful, vulnerable woman with a cloud of fiery hair and swimming blue eyes that were the shade of a rain-drenched morning glory. He gripped her shoulders, staring at her as he pulled her close. "I loved you. I loved you and wanted you more than anything on this earth."

"Rian—"

"God help me, I still want you."

He made it sound like a curse rather than a blessing. Heart thundering, she looked away.

He ensnared her chin and tilted it up until he could capture her gaze with his own. "Damn it to hell, I still want you!"

And then he lowered his head, crushed her mouth with his lips, and she was reeling . . . spinning . . . as the memories assailed her, taunted her . . . His scent. His gentle touch. His whispered words of love as they'd clung together, their naked bodies cleaving, straining to become one.

He raised his head, and she could still taste his mouth . . . his tongue . . . still feel the imprint of those lips and teeth. And she swayed closer, wanting him to envelop her in those strong arms and to kiss her again until she was senseless and could forget the difficulty . . . and the pain.

"Kathleen."

She struggled to rise from the sensations catapulting her into the past.

"Kathleen!"

She blinked, then stared. "Aye."

"We've nothing else, but we have that between us, anyway."

Her chest tightened. "Nay, we don't even have that."

He narrowed his gaze. "You're still me wife."

She glared at him, turned, and gave an abrupt jerk of her head.

"Well, we agree on something, then," he said.

She spun back in a fit of temper. "You're a pigheaded mule, Rian Quaid. Ya don't know what we have between us, and ya have too much of that stubborn Irish pride to see it!"

Kathleen left then, hurrying from the room, ignoring his call to come back as she ran up the stairs to her bedchamber. There she locked the door and leaned against it, her breath laboring, her chest constricted.

"Arrogant, foolish pride, Rian Quaid," she murmured as the tears she'd held at bay struggled for freedom. "Ya look at me and can't see that I love ya. That I'm sorry for what I did. And I didn't know what else to do!"

She rushed across the room and flung herself across the bed. She dropped her face to her pillow, then lifted it. "Why did ya have to kiss me? Why did ya have to remind me of all we'll never be?"

Head dropping, she buried her face in her pillow and cried until her eyes were dry and her heart felt empty.

And she wondered whether, if she were cut, there would be anything left within her to bleed.

The man paused at the stable door before entering. When he was sure that no one was within, he went inside to the stall housing the pregnant mare and dropped a few leaves and twigs into the bucket of horse feed.

With a quick glance over his shoulder, he lowered the bucket into the store before the animal. While the horse just stared at him with big, trusting eyes, he edged out of the stall, took another gander about the barn, then watched with satisfaction as the mare began to chop on the mixture of leaves and grain.

He watched with grim pleasure for several seconds before he turned, slipped out the way he'd come, then hurried toward the field where he was supposed to be working. And inside the stable, the mare continued to eat the man's tainted food offering.

Thirty-nine

Kathleen felt ashamed. How could she have responded to him? He'd been punishing her with that kiss. Punishing her and himself.

The house was silent. Rian hadn't followed her to their room, and Kathleen told herself that she was grateful. She got up from the bed, unlocked the door, and peered out into the hallway.

There was no one about. Not even Lucy or Lottie. Henny, she knew, would have gone home to Pete hours ago. And the servant girls would have gone up to the servants' quarters on the third floor.

Which meant that she was on the second level alone. She hadn't heard Rian come upstairs, so she had to assume that he was still down in his study, brooding.

Pain warred with the heat that frissoned throughout her body at the memory of Rian's kiss. She had missed his arms about her. Missed seeing his smile. And savoring his scent. How she'd missed inhaling the odor of him, having it surround her, until she felt safely wrapped in the security of his strength.

She went back inside her chamber, shut the door, and stood a moment, leaning against it. What was she to do? She had had her opportunity to explain, and she'd ruined it. If things didn't improve between her and Rian, then she would have to leave him—and Green Lawns. She didn't know where she'd go, but she'd go somewhere. Anywhere but here.

She moved to the bed and sat down on its edge. Closing her eyes, she said a little prayer that Rian would realize that she loved him and that he'd come to understand that she hadn't deliberately meant to hurt or deceive. She'd been desperate and alone and had taken a chance at happiness with the only man she'd ever loved. She had taken a chance and lost. And the pain of her loss was worse than she'd ever imagined.

Still, she wouldn't have traded those days with Rian for anything. She would remember them always, long after the pain had left. *If the pain ever leaves.*

And she would take those memories and treasure them as she'd cherished the man who had given them to her.

She heard the door open and sat up in bed. Rian approached, carrying an oil lamp, his features hardened by the shadows of dark against light. Clutching the covers to her breasts, she watched him close the distance from the door to the bed.

He was still dressed. He wore trousers and a shirt that was open to reveal his chest and stomach. His hair was tousled, and his feet were bare. He looked too attractive, too irresistible, and she needed him gone.

"Rian," she gasped. "What are you doing here?"

He said nothing as he set the lamp on the night table and then sat at the edge of the bed. His expression frightened her, for he wore a naked look of desire, and there was some other intense emotion there that she couldn't read.

He lifted a hand and touched her face.

"What are you doing?" she asked in a trembly voice. "Why are you here?"

"You're my wife," he said.

She slid toward the opposite side of the bed. "Rian, please."

He looked at her as if in a daze. "You're my wife."

"Aye."

"Come here."

"I think you should leave."

"We are married." He reached across the bed to pull her closer to his side. "I want to kiss my wife."

Her heart stopped, then started to beat faster. "Please go." This strange mood of his scared her. She couldn't tell what he was thinking, but she could see a gleam in his eyes that made her more than uneasy.

Rian gazed down at her, saw her sweet, shining face in the lamplight, and wanted her with a passion that shook him to the core. "I want to kiss you, Kathleen. Just let me kiss you."

She jerked from his grasp, got up off the opposite side of the bed, and moved toward the door. Her eyes were large, round pools of blue in a pale face. "Rian, 'tis not a good idea. Ye're angry—"

He leapt from the bed, startling her. Her hand fought for the doorknob, jiggled it around, and she started to jerk open the door, only to have him stop her. He slammed the door shut and trapped her against it with her back against the wood, his arms on either side of her. Leaning close, he bent to kiss her neck.

"Kathleen," he whispered. His lips played with the sensitive area behind her ear, trailed down her throat to the pulse at its base, which jumped and skittered as her heart began to race.

His warmth and scent filled her senses. His touch infused her with warmth, making her close her eyes and fight against tears. She loved him but was afraid, not of him physically but of having him take her as his wife and of breaking her heart.

"One kiss, Kathleen." It was a husky plea.

Her lashes fluttered open. She blinked up at him, her eyes bright, her lips quivering, her breathing harsh and irregular.

"Please, don't . . ."

"Just one," he breathed before he took her mouth.

She struggled beneath him, fighting the feelings that threatened to overwhelm her. He softened the kiss but deepened it, and with a soft whimper, she gave into him, kissing him back in full measure, loving him, begging for him to love her as he'd vowed to love her on their wedding day.

He lifted his head, stared at her mouth, and with a harsh groan, he captured her lips again. He stroked her with his tongue as his hands found places on her body that made her gasp with pleasure and press into his hand.

He began to nibble on her neck, trailing his mouth downward until he captured a nipple through fabric, wetting and nipping the area until the bud was pebble hard.

"Please," she gasped.

Rising up, Rian gazed down into her flushed face, then bent to swing her into his arms. He gave her a slow kiss as he moved toward the bed.

He dropped her onto the mattress, fell on her, and smothered her surprised gasp with his lips. She clung to him as he devoured her mouth, feasted on her throat, and nuzzled her neck.

"Rian."

"Aye, love. Hold on a minute." He grew impatient to have her. It seemed as if it had been too long. He raised himself up to watch her, settled his fingers on her breast and fondled. His staff grew thick and hard, became a throbbing between his legs, but still he waited. He caressed her with both hands now, stroked her some more.

Her dark lashes fluttered against her cheeks as she arched upward, pressing herself more firmly into his hands. Fire burned in his blood, enveloping him with a raging heat.

She opened her eyes, and the blue orbs glistened, burning, even as she lowered them again to study him from beneath slumberous lids.

And then he felt her soft hands slipping beneath his shirt, sliding down his belly, seeking beneath his trousers in search of his hot, pulsating length, and he rose up with a growl, caught the open collar edges of her nightdress and ripped.

Kathleen started at the sound of tearing fabric, shuddered at the shock of cool air that brushed her naked breasts. Then she watched with a tingling of expectation as Rian rose up and tore off his shirt; then, with his gaze holding hers, he lowered his heated body to warm her.

His weight, hardness against softness, the rasp of his breath against her ear, sent her into a mindless twisting and turning of ascending pleasure.

Caught, enthralled, she clutched his back, stroked his powerful muscles, and her hands went wild with her need to touch and absorb all of him.

The pace of their lovemaking became frantic, desperate. Lips nipped lips; tongues delved, played, and withdrew; and fingers fondled breasts, bellies, then lowered to the hot, throbbing places between their thighs.

"Now," he rasped, as if in warning. But she was already opening for him, pulling him in, gasping as she accepted all of him, shivering and panting as he began to thrust and withdraw hard and fast.

She stared into his eyes, saw the concentration of ecstasy in his features, and was thrown over the edge as he pushed deep.

He groaned as she flew, following her to the gates of heaven, hovering there a moment before slowly drifting down to earth on a white puffy cloud.

She lay there, winded, stunned by the intensity of their lovemaking, still reeling from the reverberating waves of disbelief, now that she'd come back to earth.

Her mind shifted and quickly sought to focus, but she couldn't think. She could only feel the warmth of his damp flesh weighing on her so intimately, the brush of his silky hair against her cheeks, then her throat, as he shifted his head downward.

She fought to take it all in, wondered what this visit, their lovemaking, all meant, and she opened her mouth to ask him and emitted a surprised gasp that shivered along her back and spine as Rian caught her nipple between his teeth.

He rose up to flash her a grin before he started again. This time he loved her more slowly, more thoroughly, until she felt that there wasn't an inch of her he hadn't touched or loved.

And he took her past the pearly gates to a view of heaven she'd never before seen. There he joined her, holding her tight, and the sharing of it changed her. It altered something between them as they joined fully as man and wife.

Forty

She stirred sleepily, then came abruptly awake. Kathleen sat up with a pounding heart when she realized she was naked. Her gaze fell on the dented pillow next to hers, and with a smile, she fell back.

So it hadn't been a dream. Rian had been there. He'd really been there, making wild love to her over and over throughout the night. And life for her had changed.

Happy, eager to see him, she rolled up and out of bed, aware of the pleasant aches and light bruises that had been the result of Rian's desire for her. She grinned. She'd been a bit overeager herself; Rian had the scratches on his back and shoulders to prove it.

They'd come together like starving animals that couldn't get enough to satisfy their hunger. She sighed. And then there had been those tender times when each kiss, each touch, had been a gentle exploration of pleasure points, of souls linking.

The morning air was warm as Kathleen walked across the room to the dresser, where she searched for clean underclothes. She pulled out a fresh chemise and pair of pantalets and fingered them with a smile. She could imagine Rian's hands tugging them from her body, baring her skin inch by inch and following the path with his mouth. She shivered with pleasure. Rian was a perfect lover. Gentle, yet demanding. At other times rough but tender.

And he was her husband.

Holding the undergarments to her breasts, she danced a happy jig about the bedchamber. Then she sat on the bed with a bounce and grinned at the room in general, her spirits soaring, her limbs tingling with anticipation of their next night together.

Kathleen was disappointed that Rian wasn't in the kitchen, nibbling on some breakfast, until the sight of Henny deep in the preparations for lunch, made her realize what time it was.

"You're looking content this morning," Henny commented, pleased.

She beamed. " 'Tis a beautiful morning, Henny. And how are ya this fine day?"

Henny grinned, happy for the change in her countenance. For days now, Kathleen had walked about with sad eyes and a forced smile. It was nice to see that her spirits had improved.

"Will ya be eating?" Henny asked.

"Just a cup of tea, Henny." Kathleen moved to the pantry and pulled out a plate of muffins. "And maybe one of these sweet muffins."

Kathleen hurried through her breakfast and then headed outdoors. She wanted to see Rian, to share a secret smile in memory of last night's lovemaking.

She crossed the yard, passing the mother cat and her kittens near the new barn. She saw a field hand and approached with a smile. "Have ya seen Mr. Quaid?"

The man nodded. "He's beyond the stables in the paddock, mistress."

"Thank ya kindly, Martin," she said, her calling him by name earning her the man's grin. "Top of the mornin' to ya!" she wished him as she continued toward the stables.

She spied him seated on the fence, deep in conversation with McDermott and another man—a stranger. She hesitated a moment near the stables, hoping that Rian would look up and notice her.

But he was too preoccupied for that. Kathleen wondered what Rian's business was about until she heard a horse nicker and snort and saw the rider astride the animal on the far side of the field.

In a ballet of movement, the rider steered his mount in a wide circle, trimming the area down to a smaller one, before expanding it to race about the paddock.

"You have a fine horse there, Quaid," Smithfield said.

Rian smiled. "He's a piece to treasure for certain. Do you have another for me?"

"You can come and take a look," the man replied, eyeing the animal thoughtfully. "And you've others, you say?"

"Will eventually. I have an animal or two, but I'm holding on to them dearly."

"Planning to give me a race for my business?"

"Now, Jacob, you know that your horses are only a side business. You can't handle the demand in all Kent County. There's room for the two of us."

"True enough." An older gentleman, Jacob Smithfield had remained standing when the two young men had climbed onto the fence to watch. "What makes you think you've the knowledge of fine horse breeding," he said.

"I've got me the knowledge for it." Conor McDermott measured the man and found him honest enough.

Smithfield narrowed his gaze and returned the inspection. "What county?" he asked.

"Roscommon."

Rian watched with amusement as Smithfield fired questions at McDermott about Ireland and the Irishman as he answered.

"Rian?"

He stiffened. And saw his wife. "Kathleen, I didn't expect to see ya about this morning." His night with her had shattered him. The depth of his feelings for her was frightening. He didn't want to be his father. He didn't want to make the same mistakes.

But she'd given herself to him so sweetly, an innocent one minute, a temptress the next.

She greeted the other men, then centered her gaze on Rian. "Thought I'd see what ya were doing."

"Fernell is working with Midnight."

Kathleen smiled as her gaze settled briefly on the stablehand and horse. " 'Tis a beautiful animal, isn't he?"

"Aye, mistress," McDermott said.

"Mr. Smithfield, is it?" she said to the other man. "I saw ya at the Foleys' picnic, didn't I?"

"Yes, you did, and it was a pleasure to see you there, as it is now."

"You're a kind sir, Mr. Smithfield. It is me pleasure as well."

Kathleen stood by the fence rail, her gaze on the horse and rider, as Fernell used the reins to control Midnight, stopping the horse, turning him, and with a command, trotting, then galloping him in the other direction. She was conscious of her husband only a foot away, aware that he hadn't smiled at her, as she'd expected him to.

"Ya must be careful of the sun this day, mistress," McDermott said with a smile. "The weather is hot, and the damage to such fair skin would be a heartbreak."

"You've a smooth way with words, Mr. McDermott."

"Just telling the truth, Mrs. Quaid."

Rian pushed off the fence rail. "If you'll excuse me, gentlemen. Kathleen?" He gestured with his hand.

She nodded, then fell into step with him, and they headed back to the house.

"Have you something on your mind, Kathleen?" he asked without warmth.

She paused, feeling hurt. "Are ya not glad to see me this morning?"

"I'm busy. I didn't expect to see you here."

"Rian—" she began, then stopped, struggling to hide the hurt. "I'll go. Ya obviously don't want to see me. After last night, I thought—"

"You thought what?"

Not a gentle word, she thought. Not a tender look. She closed her eyes and fought the urge to cry. "Nothing," she said. "I'll leave ya to your work, then."

She broke away from him, hurrying toward the yard.

"Master Rian! It's Rosebud. Something's wrong with her."

Kathleen heard Jack Peterson's cry and halted to listen.

"There's something wrong with Rosebud! Thomas said to come, and quick!"

Rian caught her gaze before he rushed to the barn to examine the pregnant mare.

Concerned, Kathleen followed. Once inside, she ignored Rian's dark looks and immediately went to the mare to stroke her neck.

She frowned. The animal's head hung low, and her coat, she saw, was slick with sweat. Rosebud was ill. But apparently Rian and the groom, Thomas, couldn't fathom the reason or whether they could save her.

"Isn't there anything you can do?" she asked.

"I don't know, ma'am." It was Thomas who answered.

"Well, someone must know enough to help her!" She had ridden Rosebud during the picnic outing with Rian.

"Jack," Rian said darkly, ignoring his wife's presence. "Go to the paddock and get McDermott. He may know how to help her."

Forty-one

In the end, Conor McDermott identified the culprit and knew what to do about it.

"Wild cherry," he said, frowning as he fingered and sniffed at a leaf that he'd found beside the feed bucket. "We'll have to drench 'er, and we'll have to work fast else we'll lose not only her foal but Rosebud as well." He seemed to be mentally ticking off items on a list. "I'll have to make some of me grandfather's recipe."

No one but McDermott knew what was in the recipe that they hoped would save Rosebud's life. Drenching the mare wasn't an easy task, Kathleen learned. It took all of them to accomplish it. After the Irishman had boiled and cooled his tea of special ingredients, then it wouldn't do but to find an empty wine bottle to put it in. Then, while Thomas and Jack stayed at Rosebud's back, Rian and Kathleen were at the mouth end, where Rian, with her help, had to force open the mare's mouth so that they could dump in the liquid.

Rosebud, once lethargic because of the poison, suddenly came to life when it was time to drench her, and then it was McDermott who replaced Kathleen at the head, forcing open the mouth. Kathleen was the one who nervously, but successfully, poured in the medicine.

Everyone with a hand in the task was tired in the end,

but none, Kathleen suspected, so much as Rosebud herself, who had exhausted herself in her fright.

Kathleen's gown was soiled, for some of the tea had spilled onto her in her first attempt, but it was only a little bit, and there'd been plenty, much to her relief, left over to complete the drenching.

As Thomas stood, mumbling obscenities aimed at the animal after Rosebud in her struggle had kicked him, Rian watched silently as Kathleen wiped her hands on a piece of cloth that McDermott had found for her.

"Nice job, Mrs. Quaid," McDermott praised. "Ya managed the task well."

Kathleen couldn't control her blush. "Thank ya, Mr. McDermott."

"Conor," he invited with a grin.

"Conor, it is, then."

Rian's lips twisted slightly. "What happens next, then?" he asked.

"We wait. And we walk her. 'Tis best to keep her moving so that she doesn't give in to the urge to lie down."

"I'll walk her for a time," Kathleen volunteered. She cared about the animal and wanted to help her.

"Nay," Rian said without feeling. "Thomas will walk her, and when he's done, Jack next."

"But I don't mind—"

Rian flashed her an angry look. "Thomas will walk her," he said in a tone that brooked no argument.

"Fine, then," she said. "I just thought to make meself useful." The urge to cry was great, but she managed to control it.

"You've done a fine job of helping, Mrs. Quaid," McDermott said gently. " 'Twill be a long while before we know whether or not Rosebud has made it. Ya can't wait the whole of the day and into the next night."

Kathleen flashed him a surprised glance. "So long?"

" 'Fraid so, mistress," Thomas said with an approving look at the Irishman. "McDermott's right. I've done a drenching before. Sometimes the animal makes it, while at others—"

"Kathleen," Rian said, drawing her attention. His voice was softer then, but the softness didn't quite reach his eyes. "If you'd like to help, ya can see if Henny can rustle us up some fare to keep us going."

"Us?" she echoed. "Will ya be staying with Rosebud, then?"

He nodded. "Aye, that I will."

And then Kathleen knew why he didn't want her to assist. He'd seen the previous night of lovemaking as a mistake, and he didn't want her around him.

Her chest burned as her heart broke. "I'll see what she has in the kitchen," she said dully before she headed back to the house.

She was good enough for a tumble but nothing else. Kathleen sat alone in her bedchamber, near the window, and stared out into the night. That was the conclusion that she'd reached about Rian's thoughts. He wanted her physically. In fact, he probably couldn't help his desire, but that didn't mean he had to like it.

And he doesn't, she thought with sadness. He wanted her in his bed, where he could satisfy his body's urges, but later, when the sun came up, in the bright light of day, he didn't want her about. She could only think that he hadn't forgiven her and wasn't about to do so soon, if ever. So, he must want her out of his sight and out of his mind until his lust for her raised its ugly head and had him coming to her again to satisfy himself.

Well, I cannot live that way. She pushed back her chair and stood, then paced the room. *He'll never forgive me. His pride is wounded, and he is half Irish, after all, and being what he is, there is the curse of that pride . . . that unforgiving, stubborn pride.*

What was she to do? She loved him and couldn't imagine herself without him, but she couldn't tolerate the way things stood now. She had her pride, too, didn't she? And her pride, although it might be stubborn, was a fine thing to protect her, for it wouldn't allow her to take less than what she deserved as a loving wife.

So, she'd deceived him! She hadn't meant to. She'd been forced to play the role of Meara because of circumstances beyond her control. She knew it, and now he knew it. If that fact bothered him still, then it was too bad. She couldn't change the way it was, and she couldn't live with the way things stood. Which meant only one thing. That it was time for her to go. To leave Green Lawns and find a life for herself elsewhere.

She didn't have money or anything of value. She'd given Meara the only jewelry she'd owned. Meara, who could have had everything and was foolish enough to let it all slip through her fingers.

"I hope she is happy with her Robert," Kathleen said, "for she has made her bed and now must lie in it, just as I must lie in mine alone from this time on."

Kathleen sat down on her bed and stared at the far wall. She thought of her husband, the smiling, loving, doting man who'd given her gifts, who'd come to her for kisses and hugs, and who'd longed to see her big and round with his child.

She sniffed, then started to weep, for all that would never happen, for all she had lost.

She would have to go soon, she thought after she'd cried until she had no more tears. They would all be busy with Rosebud for a time yet. She had to think and plan and find transportation to a place where she could find employment. A city, perhaps. She would need some kind of job that would finance her food, some personal items, and lodgings.

Baltimore? Or was there a place closer? Closer but not too close? Near enough where she could find work but not have to worry that Rian or anyone here would see and recognize her?

It wouldn't concern Rian what the neighbors would think. He'd be glad she was gone. Hadn't he told her he didn't care what people thought as long as things were right in his own mind?

And in his mind he'd decided that she was not worthy of him. She had sinned by deceiving him, and he wasn't able to forget or forgive her.

"Mr. Burns?" Kathleen hailed the man as he circled the house and cut through the rose garden. "May I speak with ya for a minute?"

The man halted, then approached. "What is it I can do for you today, Mrs. Quaid?"

"I've a need to go to Chestertown." She'd heard of the city, and it was far away, but she wasn't sure how far. "My husband is busy, as you must know, with tending our mare Rosebud. Do ya think you can be the one to take me?"

She'd thought through the night and into the next morning. The solution she'd managed was clear and simple. She would get to Chestertown or some other place, and then from there she would find a way to go to Baltimore or another big city where there would be employment for a healthy woman such as herself.

She knew that she'd never be able to convince Captain Bitmen to take her across the Chesapeake, straight into Baltimore on the *Windslip*. She would have to go the roundabout way. And if she found employment in the next county, then she would take it as long as it was respectable work and she could make do.

"You want me to take you to Chestertown?"

"Aye, Mr. Burns. Is that a problem for ya, then?" He seemed only mildly surprised, she thought. Chestertown must be a reasonable request, then.

"No," he said quickly. "No problem at all. I've got a day off coming to me. I can use it to go there myself and buy some supplies."

Kathleen smiled, and the man's blush relieved her misgivings about going off with a worker who might be forward or a danger to her. That Mr. Burns had been so easily embarrassed had convinced her that he was a kind and gentle man. She could trust him to take her to Chestertown, and then it would be easy enough to say that she'd found a friend to visit with there for a day or two. Then he could return to Green Lawns without her.

Forty-two

Rosebud was coming around. It was still touch and go, and they wouldn't know if the foal inside her would make it, but the mare herself was improving. After hours of walking with her, tending to her, and giving her another drenching, the animal seemed more alert, less lethargic. And she'd raised her head so that Rian could look into her eyes and see the way she was before the poisoning.

The danger to the mare had passed. Now it was left to watch and wait to see if Rosebud would carry the foal inside her to full term. And to find out how the crushed leaves and twigs of a wild cherry tree had happened their way into Rosebud's stall and into her belly.

Rian stood outside the stables in the dark of night, taking a breath of fresh air, trying to relax after twenty-four hours of being on his feet with Rosebud. He was exhausted but had no thoughts of finding his bed. He wanted to stay close to Rosebud for a while yet. If the mare made it but the foal didn't, they would know soon enough. He needed to be close for the stillbirthing should the foal inside his mother die from the cherry poison.

"Quaid."

He tensed until he realized it was the Irishman. "McDermott. Why haven't ya gone to your bed?"

"For the same reasons as you, I imagine," he said.

McDermott joined him in the night air. " 'Tis a soft night with nary a breeze to disturb it."

Rian smiled. "Adding poetry to your skills now, are ya, Conor?"

The man grinned. "A man uses what he has to use, but I didn't mean to charm your stubborn Irish heart. I was feeling my mood shift in the night air. 'Tis a welcome change after the day and night we've had."

"Aye." Rian had to agree. The situation had been worrisome. It was a blessing to stand back and know that you'd done your best, even if your best isn't the answer. If the animal died, knowing you had done your best was all that a man could ask of a body, especially oneself.

And it was at times like this that he knew when he'd been less than a man, done less than his best to fix a difficulty or right a problem. As with Kathleen. He loved her—by God he did—but did he show it? Nay. For she had wounded his heart and his pride when he'd learned that hers wasn't the name he thought it was. Still, she was the same woman, wasn't she? And it was the woman herself that he'd fallen in love with, not the name. The woman herself who pleased him, took him to the heights of pleasure and back, time and time again, giving all of herself.

The more he thought of it, the more he knew that he'd been wrong. He'd loved her with his body, but he'd held back his heart and mind, fearing that he'd fall victim to the same trap that had ensnared his father. But Kathleen wasn't Priscilla. There was nothing similar about the woman who was his wife and the evilness that was Priscilla's heart. And so he had judged her without using his brain, without considering his heart. For if he had looked deep into his mind and his heart, he would have seen it all long—that Kathleen Maguire was the meaning behind his living. She was his other half, his life mate, the soul he'd searched for, without his knowing, his entire life.

"You're quiet," McDermott said, reminding Rian that he wasn't alone.

" 'Tis that kind of night."

"She hasn't come back since ya sent her away."

Rian stiffened, stared at him, but there was nothing of disrespect or prying in the man's demeanor. The only thing he saw in the man's bright blue gaze was friendship and concern. He allowed the tension to leave him. "Aye. She hasn't. I'm afraid I was a bit harsh with her in me concern for the animal."

McDermott stared at Rian and judged him to be a smart man. "Ya were worried about the mare. Nothing wrong with that."

"Aye, but then so was she. And she helped us in a way that most men would have shied from."

"Aye." McDermott grinned. "That she did. She's a good sort, your wife is. A brave lass with a tough temper but a bigger heart."

Rian regarded the man with raised eyebrows. "Who made ya such a smart one that ya can see the way of it with her?"

"We Irishmen are an intelligent lot" was the softly spoken answer.

"Are you lumping me in with that lot, then, McDermott?" Rian said. "Ya know I'm a bit of a Brit myself."

"Says who?" McDermott replied. "You're more Irish than any lad I've seen on the far side of County Roscommon. Even your voice gets thick with the sound of home, Rian Quaid. Nay, you're not a Sassenach, no matter who your mother was or where she came from. You're your father's son. A true Irishman." He paused to grin. "So ya see, there is something good about you, although me employer you might be. And you're good together, you and the tough, fiery-haired lass. I don't know what it is that keeps ya from showing how ya feel to her, but you'd best recognize and discard it. She's a keeper, your Kathleen. And if she weren't married to ya, then I'd give me a time or two to try me hand at attracting her heart. But it's your heart she wants. I can see it in her eyes, and she yearns for it as no woman I've seen yearning for a man."

Rian tensed and turned, about to get angry with the man.

"Now it wasn't me intention to be mean or disrespectful in me observations, Master Quaid. There is no reason to get yourself all hot and mad at me. I've simply given ya me thoughts, and the rest is up to you. So take them in kindness and care for them as ya may."

Rian thought long and hard on McDermott's words hours after the man had left him for his bed, long after he'd found his own place in the stable to lay down his head for a snooze.

As he lay on his back, staring at the ceiling rafters, a bed of straw beneath him and the scent of horse and hay thick in the night air, he knew what he wanted, and what he wanted was Kathleen. He had done a terrible thing by taking her body but rejecting her love. He had accepted her love once, when it was freely given and he'd believe her to be Meara Kathleen, the woman he'd been engaged to, the woman who'd been the spoiled girl he'd so much enjoyed teasing. But it wasn't Meara Kathleen he loved. It was Kathleen Maguire, her cousin, generous with her spirit and with her love. He hadn't rejected her because she had misled him, for if truth be told, he had known that she wasn't the same person. The Meara Kathleen he'd known when he was a boy had been willful and selfish, and from what little he'd had the misfortune to see of her, Meara hadn't changed at all.

Rosebud nickered, and Rian climbed to his feet and went to the next stall to place his hand on her belly. Nothing seemed out of place. Rosebud was resting comfortably, and her belly wasn't contracted or distorted, although he knew that didn't necessarily mean that the foal was safe. Still, satisfied that all was as it should be, at least for now, he returned to stretch out on his bed of straw.

Kathleen. She had wanted him, and if she still did, she was his to keep forever and always.

Rian smiled. He found he liked the idea of forever and always with Kathleen. And he wanted to have children with her, to raise them and to grow old together.

The urge to see her had become strong. With a new surge of energy, he jumped to his feet and started toward the house. But then he stopped when he was outside and saw the moon, the stars, and the dark house that was his. It was late, and he couldn't go to her and slip into her bed again without talking first. It wouldn't be fair to her. He had done that before, and she had welcomed him, but he wouldn't be so welcome now. He had taken her with his body and worshiped her with his mouth, but he had kept back his heart once the sun came up.

Tomorrow, he thought as he reentered the stables. Tomorrow he would find the time to be alone with her, an occasion where he could tell her he loved her and have the rest his body needed to show her how much.

His heart lightened. His mind felt free. When he lay his body down again, it was to find the sleep that had been eluding him and enjoy pleasant dreams of loving his Kathleen and basking in the return of her love.

Forty-three

She hadn't realized that Chestertown was so far away, and she was glad that she'd written a note that said she was visiting Lizzy and would be staying the night.

Burns—Geoff Burns—seemed a capable driver of the wagon they'd borrowed from Green Lawns. He'd been quiet for most of the journey, almost pensive, but Kathleen had decided that the responsibility of transporting his employer's wife was daunting to him.

"Mr. Burns, how much longer until we get to Chestertown?" she asked. The day was lengthening. The sun was low in the western sky, and Kathleen thought it odd that there was no sign of life on the roads they'd taken. But she didn't want to point it out, for the man seemed flustered enough as it was, and, grateful, she didn't want to add to his discomfort.

Burns turned in his seat to stare at her. She shivered and had her first inkling of uneasiness. "Not much farther from what I can tell." He gestured toward a winding bend in the road ahead. "Just around that curve and on a piece and we should be there soon enough."

"I see," she said, relaxing. They were almost there. "Thank ya, Mr. Burns."

He simply grunted, then focused his attention on the horses again.

The forest had a lush beauty to it that was pleasant to

the eye and senses but vastly different from that found in County Roscommon. The green of one tree she studied was the exact color of Rian's eyes. Her heart fluttered as a wave of pain struck deep. She took a deep breath, bucked up, and righted herself. She couldn't think of him now. To do so would only make her weep, and there would be days, weeks, for weeping, when she was finished after a long day's work and longing for her husband's arms.

The wagon rounded the bend, rumbling over rough road, sending rocks and sand in all directions. One particular bump took Kathleen unawares, and she had to grab hold of the side of the wagon to keep from toppling off. To her dismay, Burns neither acknowledged the rough road or apologized for her inconvenience, strange behavior indeed for a man who seemed embarrassed and nervous about dealing with his employer's wife.

Kathleen's uneasiness returned as she shot him an unobtrusive glance. She couldn't wait to make their destination, where she could settle in somewhere and be free of the man. As the sun set, deepening the shadows cast by the thick of the forest, Burns's face had taken on a sinister cast, and she was beginning to regret that it was he she'd asked to take her.

Kathleen saw a weathered sign up ahead, and nearly cried out with relief. Burns pulled the conveyance onto a road that turned abruptly off the main thoroughfare. This road bumped and jolted the wagon until Kathleen felt sure she would fall. And then she saw it—a house of sorts. Not a fine manor house but one that had been neglected and needed painting. A structure so dark and ugly that Kathleen wondered if it might be haunted.

"Where are we?" she asked, her heart thumping. "Why have we stopped here? This isn't Chestertown."

She knew it wasn't, for Henny had told her that Chester-town was a busy place with lots of people. The only inhabitants of this residence looked to be the wild animals and the trees and anyone else who might lurk behind those dark wooden doors.

"It's an inn, Mrs. Quaid," Burns told her. "I've miscalculated the trip, and we've a way to go yet. It's not a good thing to be traveling in the dark, so I thought we could stay the night at this fine place. It doesn't look to be much on the outside, but inside it's got plenty of warm beds and a generous enough fare."

"An inn?" she said. He nodded. "In the middle of the forest?"

"And where else would a traveler making these roads stay?" he replied.

"True enough," she said, and forced a grateful smile that she was far from feeling.

He pulled up to an open area where he could tie up the horses. He didn't say a word as he took care of the animals and then helped her alight from the carriage.

"Have they no stables, then?" she asked.

"I couldn't say, mistress. The last thing I heard about Abernathy was that there'd been a fire that damaged the barn, but it may have been rebuilt." His grin looked wicked. "I thought I'd ask the innkeepers. If there's a place for the horses, I'll see that they get straw and feed."

She nodded. It all sounded reasonable enough. Still, she couldn't control a shiver as she walked up the path to the front door and waited as Burns knocked.

The sound of brass against wood seemed to reverberate inside the house. Kathleen slipped her arms about her middle, examining her surroundings and finding them wanting.

The door behind her suddenly opened. Kathleen

gasped and spun toward the house as Burns addressed the tired-eyed servant who gazed at them without emotion.

"Yes?" the woman said. Her garments were faded, and on closer inspection, Kathleen realized, with a start, that they were threadbare. What kind of good establishment kept their servants in such poor fashion? she wondered.

The next thing she knew, they were being reluctantly invited inside. Kathleen's attention went to the furnishings in the foyer: the dark, heavy wood that seemed too large and cumbersome for such a small area; the scent of lamp oil that clung to the air as does wood smoke on a damp night.

"I'll get the master," the servant said.

"Have ya a room for us?" Kathleen called as the woman started to leave.

The servant halted and turned. "I'll get the master" was all she said, for the second time.

She stood next to Burns, this time feeling as if the man were harmless, a safe haven in a strange inn in which the servants were overworked and in poor health and dress and the house was darker than the lengthening dusk outside. Suddenly she saw a shadow of a man leave an archway of a room down the hall. The figure approached on silent feet, his bearing straight, erect. Almost familiar, Kathleen thought with a strange tingling along her spine.

He came forward, into the light of a sconce burning on the wall near the stairs. As he stepped into the glow of the oil lamp, Kathleen could only stare at him.

"Robert!" she gasped.

He smiled and wore an expression that said he'd been expecting her. "Welcome to Abernathy, my home."

Forty-four

"Henny, has Kathleen come down yet?" Rian was eager to see her. It was early, just barely past dawn. It was wash day and a Saturday, and Henny had come to get a head start on the tasks at hand.

"No, she hasn't, Master Rian." She gave him tea and watched with pleasure as he accepted the cup with a nod of thanks and bent his head to sip from it. "The girls will be busy downstairs this morning. Perhaps you'd like to check on the missus?"

The cup froze inches from Rian's chin. "Check on her?" He saw the twinkle in her eyes and was mortified to feel himself blush. He set the cup on the worktable. "Aye, I think I should check on her. 'Tis been a long two nights in the stables." He started down the hall for the stairs. "Downstairs, ya say, Henny?"

"Yes, Master Rian. And all day, perhaps. There's a lot to be done in the main part of the house. I believe it will be quiet upstairs all day."

Encouraged, buoyed by the fact that he would soon be holding Kathleen, telling her that he loved her, Rian bounded up the steps and hurried down the hall to the master bedroom. He thought about bursting in and then remembered how he'd frightened her the other night.

Well, he wasn't going to do this wrong. He would knock, and if she didn't open the door, he would enter silently, carefully, and glide toward the bed to wake her with a soft kiss.

He rapped his knuckles lightly on the wooden door. Then he paused a minute to listen before knocking again. When she didn't come to the door in answer, he turned the knob carefully, pushed the door open slowly, and entered the room.

The window drapes were drawn against the morning light, and he moved through the dimly lit room, knowing by habit rather than by sight how to get to the bed.

His fingers itched to touch her. His lips ached to kiss her, and his heart began to pound as he thought of the upcoming discussion they would have.

"Kathleen?"

No answer.

"Kathleen, love. 'Tis me—Rian." He paused, aware of his racing pulse. "Your husband."

He sat down on the edge of the bed, reached an arm across to the lump beneath the covers, touched it, and found a mound of softness too pliant to be Kathleen.

Straightening, he sprang from the bed, threw open the curtains, and hissed at what he saw. Or didn't see.

Kathleen wasn't there. But there on a pillow lay a piece of parchment. His chest tightening, his stomach burning, he picked up the note and began to read.

And felt his gut wrench and his eyes film as he realized that she was gone. Despite what the note had said—that she had gone to visit Lizzy—Rian knew differently. She was gone; she had left him.

"She would have gone to Chestertown, I'm thinking," McDermott said.

Rian bobbed his head. He could barely think straight;

he could only feel. And the feeling was a numb terror that blackened his daylight and made him want to howl with frustration. Kathleen was gone, and so, too, was Geoff Burns. She must have convinced the field hand to drive her to the nearest town. And he agreed with McDermott; the likely place would be Chestertown, for Kathleen would need employment, and it was the best place to begin her search.

"Rian," McDermott said, "I don't want to unnecessarily alarm ya, but I've got concerns about Burns." He explained about the trouble he'd had with the man's behavior. About the feelings he'd had that something about the man wasn't right, but he was loath to say a word, since the man was ordinarily a good worker who knew his tobacco.

"How do we know she left with Burns?"

The Irishman's features hardened. "Burns's belongings are missing, and so is the wagon and two of the horses we left in the paddock. Jack saw Burns about the vehicle yesterday. When Jack happened to walk by, Burns told him that he was checking the wheels, that he'd seen a crack in one of the wheel spokes and he'd thought to repair it before it split and caused an accident. It had sounded logical to Jack at the time, so the boy didn't think to say anything to his father. It was only when we discovered that Burns had gone that Jack worried about the incident and came forward."

"So you think Burns took Kathleen," Rian said with mounting alarm.

"Given her note, I think that Kathleen might have asked Burns to drive her. We can't be sure that he kidnapped her." McDermott studied his employer. He was the only man who knew about the trouble between Rian and Kathleen. And he knew little of the circumstances other than what Rian had told him—that Kathleen had written that she'd gone for the night out to the Foleys' place. But Rian had known that the Foleys were out of the area, having gone to Philadelphia to see John's sister.

Kathleen must not have known or had forgotten that Lizzy was gone, and since she didn't come home, Rian knew that Kathleen hadn't gone to the Foleys'. She'd run away from him.

Because of the way he'd treated her.

"We'll find her. And Burns," McDermott said.

Rian nodded.

"Would ya like to spare a few men to search, or would ya prefer to keep this between you and me?"

He thought, and quickly. Kathleen might be in danger, and he wanted his wife home, safe and sound, where she belonged. "We'll use whoever ya think. I love her. I want her home."

McDermott nodded, then went to round up a group of workers to help in the search for Kathleen Quaid and Geoff Burns.

"Meara, what are ya doing here?" Kathleen asked, startled.

"What do ya mean what am I doing here?" her cousin said. "What are you doing here? This is *Abernathy*, Robert's and my home. I belong here. Ya knew I lived here. What are ya doing here? Have ya come to make trouble?"

Kathleen shook her head, her mind reeling from the shock of the new situation she'd been thrust in. "I don't understand." She transferred her gaze to Robert. "Ya knew we were coming," she accused. "How?"

"Because Burns—he works for me."

Kathleen heard Meara's gasp and ignored it. "He works for you?" She felt a clawing panic. "Why? Why would an employee of yours be working at Green Lawns?"

She stiffened as realization dawned. "You," she said. "You were the one behind the accidents on the plantation. The fire. The fields. The poison . . ."

"The poison?" Robert raised his eyebrows. "I know nothing about a poison."

"Aye, ya do indeed. Ya had someone give wild cherry to Rosebud and nearly killed her and her foal in the process."

"Don't be addlepated, Kathleen. Robert wouldn't do such a thing. He's a sweet man. Kind and true."

"The fire, perhaps," Robert said, ignoring Meara's gasp. "And I may have had a thing or two to do with the mischief in the tobacco field. But poison? Why would I want to poison the livestock that I might need?"

"Robert—" Meara began.

"Be quiet, Meara," he said easily and with such affection that Meara instantly shut up and snuggled against his side.

"Was it you?" Kathleen shot the question to Burns. "Did ya poison Rosebud? Give her wild cherry to kill her and the foal she's carrying?"

"I might have," Burns said with a smug smile.

"Stupid!" Robert burst out angrily. "Why would you do such a thing as that? I never told you to do it."

"No, but I did." Priscilla Quaid entered the room, walking easily on both feet. Her son stared at her, taken aback at the sight of his mother's mobility. For months he'd thought her crippled, had lavished the attention necessary to care for an ill mother. But she had lied to him. Playacted. Because it suited her to have him at her beck and call.

"Mother!" he snapped.

"Quiet, Robert!"

"I will not—"

"Now!' she shouted. He jerked with surprise when she pulled a lady's pistol from within her skirts. "So, you're Rian's wife." Priscilla smiled. "How nice! Now we've both the fiancée and the wife. How wonderful for us." She waved her gaping-mouthed son into a chair. "Quaid will come now, don't you see, Robert? He'll come because we have something he wants, something he loves. And he'll want her back at all costs. And lucky me, I'm the one who will decide who goes where and what we'll get in return for her if I decide to be generous."

"Mother, what is this? You're talking strangely." Robert started to rise. "You're ill. Perhaps you should lie down."

Priscilla laughed. "Sit down, Robert!" She waved the gun at him, forcing him to sit. Frightened, Meara crouched on the floor beside him, terrified of the situation and Priscilla.

Kathleen studied the woman carefully and thought that here was a lady who respected courage. Bolstering herself with thoughts of Rian and the quick decision to go back if she ever got free, she drew herself up to her full height and looked Priscilla straight in the eye.

"You had the barn burned, the fields tampered with, and the mare poisoned, didn't ya?" she said.

"I had a list of things I wanted done, yes." Priscilla smiled. "You are a smart woman. Smart and pretty. Rian made a wise choice in you for a wife. Too bad you'll not have a chance to make babies together."

With the barrel of the pistol still aimed at Kathleen and ready to shift toward the others should they move, Priscilla ordered Burns to come closer. "Well done, Mr.

Burns," she said. "Where's Pete?" she asked. "Did he come with you?"

Kathleen perked up. "Pete?"

"You didn't know that your foreman was working for me, too?" She made a scolding sound with her tongue. "Pete has a loyalty to me since my days at Green Lawns. He's more than an adequate lover. And eager to be rid of his bold-faced wife."

"Nay." Kathleen couldn't believe it. She didn't want to believe it, for Henny's sake. Dear Henny. If it was true, then Henny would be hurt, and Rian and Green Lawns could be in danger.

"I don't believe you," she said, narrowing her gaze.

Priscilla shrugged. "Believe me or not, I care little." She gave her a look. "Why should I lie? What would it get me?"

Dread formed a knot in her stomach. "Pete?"

The woman laughed. "He's a man, after all, and men are so easy to manipulate when it comes to making love."

"Love?" Kathleen said. "I hardly think you know what the word means—"

"Silence!" Priscilla was angry now. Her gray eyes gleamed with fury. Her mouth twisted into an ugly sneer.

"This is ridiculous, Mother," Robert said. "A few harmless pranks to annoy Rian are one thing. Even burning a bit of his fields I understood, but poisoning the horse? Threatening Kathleen?"

"Robert," his mother said slowly as if speaking to a dim-witted child. "You must listen to your mother when I tell you that I know what's best. I aim to get us Green Lawns so that we can sell this place." She snarled the last word and looked about the room as if everything about the house disgusted her.

"What are you going to do with me?" Kathleen asked.

"Why, nothing. For now. We'll simply enjoy each other's company until Rian Quaid decides to put in an appearance."

"He'll not come," Kathleen said, sounding confident.

"Oh? And why not?"

"We've quarreled. He found out that I'm not Meara, and he's furious. He'll not forgive me." She silently prayed it wasn't true, and she also prayed that Rian wouldn't come. She didn't want him in danger. She'd rather figure out a way to escape first or die trying.

"You'd best hope that you're mistaken, young woman," Priscilla said. "For if Rian Quaid doesn't come to us, then we'll have to go to him. And I made a vow when I left that if I ever returned to Green Lawns when the place wasn't already mine, I would destroy it. It and everyone who lived within the walls of its manor house."

Forty-five

Rian was surprised to see his foreman. "Pete! What do ya think you're doing?"

"I'm going to help find the missus," Pete said.

"Nay, Pete. You've mending to do yet. We'll handle the search. You stay here and take care of business—"

But Pete was firm. "I care for the missus. She's been good to my Henny and me. I'll go, and I'm asking you not to stop me. I can ride. I'll not let my leg hinder me or any of you; that I can promise."

Rian studied the man, saw his determination, and his respect for the man had him unwilling to disappoint him. James Peterson had been a loyal worker for the Quaid family for over thirty years. He wasn't about to tell the man he had to stay behind, especially not after what he'd said about Kathleen. He knew all to well what it was to love her. If it had been Pete telling him to stay behind, he would not only have objected, he would have shot any man who'd tried to keep him from searching for the woman he loved.

"All right, Pete. Saddle up, then. We'll be leaving as soon as you're ready."

The man nodded gravely, then limped off.

Rian turned to catch McDermott watching him silently. "Well?" he asked. "Have you an objection to the man coming along?"

McDermott shook his head. "It isn't for me to say one way or the other. 'Tis your wife." He bent to pat his mount's neck. "Pete's able enough, as long as he can manage the distance."

Rian stiffened. "You think they got that far?"

"Can't say. I don't know how long they've been gone. Whether or not they left this morning or yesterday."

"What do you think?" Rian didn't want to think that they might have had over a full day's head start on them. If Burns had taken Kathleen against her will, he would have had plenty of time to make his escape.

Pete came riding up on a chestnut gelding. His face was grim, and his gaze looked determined. "Henny's worried about Kathleen, but I assured her we'd return within a few days."

Rian nodded. And he was sure that Kathleen wasn't the only one that Henny would worry about. "We'll bring her back," he said, having to believe it. Kathleen was his life. He has lost her once; he would find her and keep her.

Meara was appalled. Her new mother-in-law was more devious and evil than she'd first given her credit for, and the woman was threatening her cousin, Meara's flesh and blood. And she had threatened Robert, her own son.

Something had to be done, and quickly. They were all seated in the parlor as if they were sharing a tea. Priscilla sat in the Queen Anne chair near the fireplace, while Kathleen, Burns, Meara, and Robert were scattered about the room but on the opposite side of Priscilla. The woman continued to hold and wave the gun, and from her position she had the ability to use the pistol on any one of them that upset her.

Now that she and Robert had married, she had less reason to fear his mother. But Kathleen had every reason to fear her. Kathleen was the one who'd married Rian. If Rian didn't come, Kathleen would be the one who bore the brunt of Priscilla's anger.

Since she'd returned from Green Lawns with the family jewelry that had been a part of her dowry to Rian Quaid, Priscilla had been more than nice to her. When Robert had insisted that the two of them marry and soon, Priscilla had posed no objection. In fact, it had been she who had sent for the minister to come and perform the ceremony.

And so now she was Robert's wife. She glanced over at him with affection. He was really quite handsome. And without his mother about, he was a fine man and a kind husband. If his mother weren't about, their lives together would be perfect.

Mrs. Robert Widham, she thought, rolling the name about in her mind. She was Mrs. Robert Widham. And her cousin was now Mrs. Rian Quaid.

Meara knew she could not live with herself if she allowed Priscilla to harm Kathleen. She had already done her cousin wrong—twice. Once, by leaving her at the dock—her and not Robert's idea. She had lied to Kathleen about that. And the second time had been when she'd threatened to blackmail her if she didn't return the jewels.

But she'd been desperate then. She'd loved Robert and wanted to wed him. The only way to get permission to marry him was to give his mother what she needed.

But now Priscilla was getting out of hand. Having her dowry hadn't been enough for her. Nor was it enough just to improve Abernathy. Priscilla wanted Green Lawns for the Widhams, or no one, especially Rian Quaid, could have it.

She had to get Robert alone. Robert looked shell-shocked. Poor man, his mother had stunned him, first with her deviousness and then with her ability to walk.

Poor Robert, she thought. Aye, she had to find a way to get him alone. He didn't like what was happening. She could see it. If only she could speak with him privately, she had ways to charm him, to prove her love for him—a love that was truer than the crumbs of affection that his mother tossed to him whenever it suited her to have him near.

Priscilla would have to go, or she would have to find a way to manage her. Meara stared at the woman with thoughtful consideration.

They would have to forget the idea of getting Green Lawns. That property belonged to Rian and Kathleen. Besides, they didn't need it. With the jewels they had, there would be cash enough to fix up Abernathy and make it a grand place for crops and outbuildings, orchards and babies. Babies, she thought with an inner smile. Aye, she wanted Robert's child.

But she would have to take care of the grandmother first. The house wouldn't be safe for a child as long as Priscilla was about, with her strange beliefs and her gun.

Rian and his men rode toward Chestertown and realized that it would be well past dark and into the next day before they even got within miles of the place. From up on his mount, Rian studied the surrounding woods and wondered if they should make camp for the night.

He was reluctant to stop. If it had been only him—and McDermott, perhaps—he would have continued. He

wouldn't have given a thought toward rest if not for the
men who accompanied them, especially Pete, with his
throbbing leg and his quiet acceptance of the pain. So he
mentioned the idea to McDermott to see what he thought
about it. He kept Pete in the dark, because he didn't want
the man to feel inadequate or that he'd let Rian down.

"I've given some thought to setting up camp," he said.

McDermott eyed the area thoughtfully. "It would be
best to find a clearing off this road," he said. "There
may be bandits about, and we wouldn't want to be taken
unaware."

Rian nodded. He hadn't given that possibility much
thought, but he realized that McDermott was right. It
would be best to find a clearing well out of sight of the
road. No need to draw attention to themselves. There
were five of them, it was true, but there could easily be
nine or ten men working to take one's money.

They set up camp, and there they rested until dawn
was but a hint in the cloudless sky. Then they headed
back toward the main road to Chestertown, where they
could proceed as planned.

What would he do if he couldn't find her in Chestertown? Rian wondered.

He fisted his left hand. He didn't want to think of
that. He had to believe he'd find her there. And find her
soon.

They came to Chestertown by midmorning, about ten
o'clock according to the clock in the lobby of the hotel
they entered.

"Is Mrs. Quaid registered here?" McDermott asked.

"Who wants to know?" the man said. He had squinty
eyes behind wire-rimmed spectacles. His mouth drooped,
and his features looked stubborn. If the man didn't want

to tell you something, he wouldn't, Rian thought. He had to convince the man that the knowledge belonged to him.

"Mr. Quaid," he said, stepping up to the desk.

The man jumped. "Mr. Quaid, is it?" he asked in a scratchy voice.

"That's right," Rian said sternly.

The fellow looked at him with curiosity. "She's traveling alone, you say?"

Rian narrowed his gaze. "Nay, she's traveling with her brother," he fabricated. "His name is Burns. Geoff Burns."

The innkeeper nodded his head as he bent over the register book. His eyes skimmed the page, searching. "I was out yesterday, and so I don't remember the names myself . . ." He looked and looked again somewhere else, and he took his time about it until Rian lost his patience.

"Mr.—"

"Sewell," the man said. "Chester Sewell."

"I've got business to attend to, Mr. Sewell. Do you think you could help us? We haven't got all day."

A hazy film came over the man's small eyes. "I'm doing my best to find you your information," he said, sounding insulted.

Rian realized that the last thing he wanted to do was offend the one man who might help him locate his runaway—or kidnapped—wife.

He reached into his coat pocket and withdrew a coin, which he set down carefully before the man's book. "For your trouble," he said with a smile.

The man's gaze gleamed as he snatched up the coin with grubby fingers. He read the book quickly, then turned it in Rian's direction. "No, there's no woman by the name of Quaid here," he said. "Nor is there a Geoff Burns."

Rian sighed. "Have ya an idea of another place they might be staying in?"

The hotel manager shook his head. "You can try the Blue Jug down the road, outside of town. But I doubt you'll find your wife or her brother there. The Blue Jug's been half-burned. The only rooms left are for family and for a number of regulars. If your wife and brother came to the area, they'd stay here and no other place." He wrinkled his nose. "Unless . . ."

"Unless?" Rian asked impatiently.

"Have you tried the White Swan?"

"Aye." They had, in fact, tried the White Swan Tavern before coming to this place.

"Then your missus must not be here."

Rian sighed heavily. It was just as he'd feared. Kathleen and Burns had gone elsewhere. Where might they have gone?

He thought about it for a time as he and McDermott joined the others, who waited on horseback outside the building.

"Not there?" Pete asked.

" 'Fraid not."

Pete scowled. "What next?"

"I don't know. I'm giving it some thought."

Where would he go if he were Kathleen and he had no family and no place to go? he wondered. Downs Cross Roads? Millington? Was it possible that she'd chosen a place that was close to Green Lawns? If she'd wanted to leave him, it didn't seem likely that she'd have to stay in an area nearby. Which was why Chestertown had been a likely place.

Rian tensed. Kathleen had family in America. Meara

might not be the ideal one to turn to, but she was family all the same.

Meara Dunne. And Meara Dunne was here in Maryland, in Cecil County.

At Abernathy.

He didn't want to go there, vowed never to step foot on his stepmother's land, but he would go for Kathleen. *Only for Kathleen*.

"Any idea where ya want to go next?" McDermott asked.

"Aye," he said. "We're going to Cecil County and a place called Abernathy. She has a cousin there. And 'tis likely that if she's gone by her own choice, she's gone to Abernathy and her cousin Meara Kathleen."

Forty-six

Kathleen was tired, hungry, and she had to relieve herself. But she hadn't dared to speak up until now.

"Mrs. Widham," she began. "Is there someplace where I can—" She blushed. "An outhouse, perhaps?" It was embarrassing to have to ask in the company of others, but what else was she to do?

The woman glared at her. "It's *Mrs. Quaid.*"

"I apologize, Mrs. Quaid. I didn't know." She had known but had forgotten. Besides, how could she have known that the woman still went by the name of a man she seemed to hate? She must have hated Michael Quaid, for she certainly hated his son.

"Robert," Priscilla said. "Take Mrs. Quaid to the necessary."

Kathleen's cheeks turned a darker shade of red.

"I'll take her, Mother Quaid," Meara volunteered.

Priscilla's lips formed a straight line. "I don't believe that would be wise of me, dear. You're her cousin. You may try to help her—"

Meara flashed Kathleen a look before meeting her mother-in-law's gaze. "I got me dowry money back."

The older woman smiled. "I know, dear, and you're a good girl for doing it, but all the same, I think I'll have Robert take Mrs. Quaid."

Robert patted his wife's hand in reassurance as he rose from his seat. "I'll be happy to take her."

"And don't be long. I'd hate to see anything bad happen to Ms. Quaid's cousin." The implied threat was to the both of them.

Kathleen felt a chill and saw the same feeling reflected in Robert's eyes. Robert had realized that his mother was unstable, and he was afraid of her.

They went out the back door to the outhouse in the rear yard. Robert apologized for his only living parent as he gestured for her to go inside and promised to wait a distance away to give her privacy. "She's really not a terrible person," Robert said. "She wants only the best for her children."

"She wants Green Lawns," Kathleen said.

He sighed. "Yes."

"And you?"

"I don't want anything that belonged to Rian Quaid," he said sharply. His expression softened. "Except Meara. But she's mine now."

"You really love her, don't ya?"

He nodded, his gaze dreamy. "Yes, yes, I do."

It was embarrassing for Kathleen to enter the outhouse, relieve herself, and then come out to where the man was waiting for her. True to his promise, Robert stood at a discreet distant away, and she realized that he was as uncomfortable with the situation as he was.

Knowing that the man loved her cousin the way he did, she decided to trust him. "Robert, your mother can't keep us prisoners."

"I know."

"We're tired and hungry. Do ya think ya can manage to convince her to feed us?"

Robert himself looked exhausted as he inclined his

head. "I'll see what I can do, but I doubt she'll listen to me." He lifted a hand to rub his neck. "Mother has always been . . . difficult."

Kathleen felt sorry for him. "You've got to help us get out of here."

He looked torn. "She's got the gun. How am I to do that?"

"I don't know," she admitted. "But we've got to think of something."

He shook his head. "We'd better get back. I'm uncertain what Mother will do if we linger."

Kathleen nodded, and they started back to the house. She paused and laid a hand briefly on his arm to halt him. "Robert. You've got to find a way."

His expression hardened, then became shuttered, as if he were unwilling to discuss it. "Get moving." He gave her a little shove.

With a hitch in her breath, Kathleen obeyed him.

They'd found her! Rian and McDermott stood in the woods near Abernathy and watched as Robert Widham conversed with Kathleen out in the rear yard. Rian's first thought was to rush forward and make his presence known. But then he saw Robert push Kathleen, and it took all of his control to remain where he was. He was angry now. There was murder in his heart and fury clouding his eyes, for there was something amiss here.

If Kathleen had come on her own, why was Robert mistreating her?

As the pair reached the house, the door opened, and Geoff Burns stepped to talk with them. Rian saw red, and he started to bolt forward, but a large hand stopped him.

"Nay, Rian," McDermott said. " 'Tis better to take them when surprise is for us."

Rian shot an angry look toward the Irishman, and his fury eased some. McDermott's face was grim, almost frightening in its intensity. If he felt like murder, McDermott must have a fouler means of accomplishing it.

So they crouched where they were and waited while the rest of their men stayed away, about a hundred yards or more behind Rian and McDermott.

Priscilla had moved them to the kitchen. Hungry herself, she'd consented easily enough when her son had suggested they needed food, and she'd ordered them all to head to the kitchen without trouble.

Seated at a table normally used for food preparation, they were crowded together, with Robert, Meara, and Burns on one side and Priscilla, with her gun, on the other.

"I don't think you need that pistol, Mother," Robert said as the tired woman, who'd let Kathleen and Burns in when they came, placed platters of hard biscuits and three-day-old muffins before them. Kathleen grabbed a biscuit and slathered it with the strawberry jam that tasted surprisingly good despite the fact that she'd had to remove a layer of mold from the top before she could use some.

As she bit into the biscuit, she was grateful for the food. She chewed and swallowed the hard dough and felt herself already gathering strength as well as hope that something would happen and they would all get away.

Kathleen watched Priscilla carefully as she ate. The woman looked old. Perhaps she'd tire and fall asleep.

But Priscilla didn't appear in the least fatigued. In fact,

she seemed alert and restless, which made for a more dangerous adversary, Kathleen realized.

Rian wasn't going to come. There was no reason for him to do so, for he had no idea where she was; and if he had, he would have been glad to see the last of her. She had disappointed and hurt him, and he was unwilling to forgive her.

A longing for him rose up and tightened her throat, and she set aside the last bite of her biscuit.

"Food not good enough for *Mrs. Quaid?*" Priscilla asked with a sneer.

" 'Tis fine," she managed to choke out. She cleared her throat and tried again. "Especially the strawberry preserves. I haven't tasted anything that good at Green Lawns."

Kathleen realized immediately that it had been the right thing to say.

"Of course not," Robert's mother sniffed. "We grow the best strawberries on the eastern shore."

Kathleen could feel her cousin's gaze on her. She turned, stared at her, and was surprised to see regret in Meara's eyes, as if she were sorry for the trouble she had caused her.

Kathleen attempted to smile, but it was a weak effort. She wanted to get free. She wanted to go home to Green Lawns. If all she'd get, as Rian's wife, was a tumble in his bed, then she would take it. She loved him. And she'd never get over her love for him. If she could return, she'd try again to make him see that. And if he still remained a blind and stubborn fool, then she'd accept what he could give her, even if it meant she'd be seeing only the harsh side of his wounded heart.

Restless, with energy she needed to burn, Priscilla rose from the table and wandered about the room. The hairs at the back of Kathleen's neck bristled as she watched her. Priscilla's eyes had grown wild-looking, her movements jerky. If the woman didn't find a way to calm down soon, Kathleen feared that Priscilla's sanity would shatter and they would all suffer and die for it.

"Mrs. Quaid," she said, "is there something I can get you? More tea, perhaps?"

"No." The woman halted near the back window, shoved aside the window curtain, and peered out into the light outside. The kitchen inside was as dark and gloomy as the rest of the residence that Kathleen had seen.

How could anyone live in this darkness and not go mad?

Her gaze caught her cousin's expression, and Kathleen realized that Meara's thought mirrored her own. *No wonder she wanted her dowry,* Kathleen thought. This place needed more than repairs; it needed furnishings and painting as well.

She studied her cousin Meara thoughtfully and was amazed. Meara had surprised her. Her cousin truly seemed deeply in love with her husband, and it was her love for him that had driven her to attempt blackmail.

Like me love for Rian made me keep me identity a secret.

Meara, who had been spoiled and selfish for most of her life, was willing to live in this sorry monstrosity of a house because she loved her husband and thought she could truly make it a home. Kathleen could understand that. Hadn't she done things she knew she shouldn't have? All because she loved a man to distraction and didn't want to lose him?

Priscilla made a disgusted sound and moved from the window. She wasn't gone from that spot for five seconds when she was back, sliding aside the curtain fabric to press her nose against the glass. She stiffened.

"What!" she cried suddenly, drawing everyone's attention. She turned to face them, a grimace on her face, her eyes shining. "Quaid," she said. "He's here." She hefted the gun and aimed it at Kathleen's heart. "How touching." She scowled. "And you said he wouldn't come."

Priscilla's slow smile was chilling. "I knew he would come." She approached Kathleen and shoved the barrel of the pistol against Kathleen's right breast. "Get up and be quiet about it."

Terror such as Kathleen had never known gripped her hard, strangling her ability to scream.

"Now move," the woman said, poking her once before stepping back slightly so that Kathleen could obey.

Kathleen pushed back from the table carefully, then eased herself from the chair. "Mrs. Quaid—"

"Silence!"

Obeying her, Kathleen clamped her lips shut. The whole scene seemed like a scene from one of her worst nightmares, only in this dream everything was all too real. She could smell the musty mold that clung to the kitchen walls and the tea that steeped in a cracked pot on the worktable. Even the little sounds penetrated to increase her horror: the clatter of a teacup onto its saucer as someone finished a drink of tea; the sound of dripping water as the servant woman had overfilled a dented washbasin past its leaky spot. And then there was the harsh rhythm of her own breathing and the wild hammering of her frightened heart.

Rian. Oh, Rian, go away! She's got a gun. She wants ta kill ya!

Priscilla instructed Kathleen to go to the back door. Flinging the door wide open, she shoved Kathleen into the threshold, a gun at her back. "Rian Quaid!" she shouted. "I've got your pretty wife here! Come out. I know you're there. I saw you!"

Frozen with fear, unable to move, Kathleen searched wildly for a sign of her husband. She wanted to warn him. She wanted to save him, and she'd do anything—anything—to keep him safe.

"Quaid! Do you hear me?"

Rian stepped out from the bushes up close. "I hear you very well, Priscilla. You don't have to shout."

Priscilla eyed him warily. "Stay back!"

He looked cool, calm, amicable even, but Kathleen recognized the anger in him, the fury, in the set of his jaw and the shade of green in his eyes.

"Are you all right?" he asked her softly.

"Aye—"

"Silence!" Priscilla barked. "Both of you!"

"Now, Priscilla, is that any way for you to treat a guest?"

"Guest?" Her harsh laughter was loud and grated along Kathleen's spine. All the while Priscilla and Rian talked, Kathleen was conscious of the gun at her back and the unstable mind of the woman who wielded it.

"What's on your mind, Priscilla?" Rian asked quietly. He stood within a few feet. Priscilla was so busy studying Rian's face that she didn't see the way Rian reached out to lace his fingers with Kathleen's.

"What do I want?" the woman echoed. "We want our due! My due! I want Green Lawns."

"It doesn't belong to you, Priscilla," he said easily. "You know why it doesn't, yet you can't seem to accept it."

She snarled, then prodded Kathleen's back with the pistol. Kathleen cried out at the force of the blow. Rian used Kathleen's cry and the opportunity of their linked hands to jerk Kathleen out of harm's way. He slammed Priscilla's wrist with his fist, knocking the pistol away.

Her scream of outrage echoed in Kathleen's ear. Heart thumping, Kathleen spun, ready to go for the gun, but Meara was already there, lifting the pistol from the ground, while Robert had grabbed hold of his furious, cursing mother, subduing her wild struggles.

Rian eyed the trio—Meara, Robert, and Priscilla—prepared to fight, but Meara came to him and handed him the pistol. "I'm sorry," she said with tears in her eyes. "For everything."

Surprised, Rian could only stare at her, then nod.

McDermott rushed onto the scene then, having heard Priscilla's angry bellow. "Is all well, then?"

"Aye," Rian said. "But will ya see to Burns and my stepmother—the woman who is responsible for all this?"

Kathleen waited patiently for Rian to give his men orders.

"Rian."

He turned to examine his wife. "Are ya all right, then?" he asked, his voice thickening with the sound of Ireland.

"Aye," she said breathlessly. Her blue eyes glistened. A smile trembled on her lips. "Ya came."

He flashed her a grin. "Aye. Did ya think I wouldn't?"

Her expression sobering, she nodded. "I'd hurt ya and thought ya'd be glad to see the last of me." Her voice was soft, her words choked with the onslaught of tears.

"Nay, lass," he said warmly. "I'll never be glad to see the last of ya. You're a fire in me blood and a tenderness in me heart. Why would I want to lose the one thing—the one person—in the world who gives me life meaning?"

He heard her little intake of breath. "In truth?" she asked.

As he pulled her into his arms. "Aye, in truth," he said as he buried his face into her red hair. "As God is me witness, I'm telling ya that I love ya with all of me heart, and I won't ever let ya go." He stiffened and set her back a space. "Unless you've made it your final wish to leave me?" His green gaze had turned black with emotion as he waited for her reply.

She gave him her warmest smile. "Nay, me home is with you, the man I love. And ya must believe me, Rian Quaid," she said, "that I've always loved ya, from that first day, which is why I married ya and was afraid to tell the truth."

"If 'tis time for more truths, then I have another one to give ya," he said as he studied her mouth. He focused on her lower lip. "I knew you weren't Meara Kathleen. You were nothing like your cousin. Oh, aye, ya looked a bit like her and all, but inside ya were as far from the girl that I knew back then that I knew you couldn't have been her."

Kathleen frowned. "Then why—"

"I was afraid, me sweet, wonderful wife. Me father had made a disastrous mistake for a marriage. He married her." He pointed to Priscilla, who now sat, sniffling, in a chair while her angry son guarded her without sympathy or forgiveness.

"I was afraid to give my heart, for I didn't want to be vulnerable. I thought that if I could just wed and bed ya, I'd have some control over me feelings . . . me heart. But I was wrong. I had lost me heart to ya from that first time we'd kissed . . . and even before. And now you've got it forever, and I'm no longer afraid."

He drew her close, kissed her tenderly, then again more fiercely. "I love you, Kathleen Mary Quaid."

Kathleen smiled. "Now that's what I've been waiting me whole life to hear." She touched his cheek and placed a tender kiss on his chin. "And I love you, Rian Quaid, me husband."

Epilogue

Priscilla was not only bitter and angry; she was delusional as well. She'd never had an affair with James Peterson. Kathleen was to learn the truth of it later when Priscilla saw Pete and didn't recognize the man as the one she'd called employee and lover.

It was McDermott she saw first as the man she'd bedded all those years ago. Although McDermott would have been a boy in Ireland at the time Priscilla had claimed a relationship with him, she wouldn't sway her story or change her mind.

It was actually quite comical for Kathleen to see. First, there was McDermott, standing there wide-eyed and looking nonplussed for the first time that Kathleen had ever seen. And then there'd been Pete, who had come along behind with the others. Poor Pete, who had looked terrified by the woman's story, fearful that they would all believe her and tell Henny so, even though Priscilla didn't know his face or anything about who he was.

The fire in the barn had been set. Priscilla had had a hand orchestrating that incident by contacting Burns directly without telling her son. Robert had thought that only a small field fire had been set, one easily seen and managed.

Robert was ashamed of his part in Rian Quaid's difficulties. He had loved his mother and had been forever trying to win her approval, but no matter what he did, he'd never been successful. He'd had no idea of the depth of his mother's madness. He'd understood that his mother had been bitter about Rian's inheritance, but he himself would have been quite content with his Abernathy estate.

Now he understood why his mother hadn't trusted him with the funds of his inheritance. Until he'd learned the truth in recent months, his mother had told him that the money would come in time, that when it did, they would have everything they needed to make their lives grand.

And Robert had believed her. He'd had no idea that Priscilla had spent his inheritance on a plan to capture the heart and the home of Rian's father, Michael Quaid. When she'd finally won her man, she'd learned that Michael wasn't as generous with his money as her first husband, Rodney Widham, had been. Michael spent the bulk of his profits reinvesting in Green Lawns, to make it a better, grander, and in the end, more profitable place. Then, when Michael had died, leaving Priscilla with nothing more than a bit of funds to see her through and her children with nothing but what was left by their natural father, Priscilla was furious. Her fury and bitterness had eaten away at her until she'd been driven to madness and enlisted her own affection-starved son into her evil plan of revenge and destruction.

Kathleen thought of the whole sorry incident as she lay in bed with her husband. It was early. The sun had barely made its appearance, and it was that special time that Kathleen so loved, when she could study Rian without his knowing and rejoice in the love he gave freely and in joy over the tiny life that she now knew grew inside her.

She rose up to prop her head on her elbow. With gentle fingertips, she caressed the skin of his belly, sliding upward to graze a male nipple within its golden swirl of hair.

I love you, Rian.

An eye popped open. She gasped as he tugged her flat against him, caught her bottom lip between his teeth, and nibbled. She pushed away from him, laughing.

"Did ya think I don't know when me wife is staring at me body?"

Kathleen blushed. "I was touching ya, that's how ya knew."

He smiled knowingly. "Ya were looking at me long before ya touched me, sweet lass."

"I was n—" She bit her lip. "All right, so I enjoy viewing me husband. Is there a crime in that now?"

He grinned as he tumbled her to the bed to gain better access to her soft skin and feminine curves, which he took his best advantage of seeing with his fingers and lips as well as his gaze.

"Rian."

He raised his head. "Aye, love?"

"You're crushing our babe."

"I'm crush—" He stopped as he saw the teasing twinkle in eyes of bright blue. "Our babe is but a tiny thing. There's nothing I can do to his mother that he would nay like." Rian grinned. "But I've neglected to greet the babe, haven't I?"

She nodded, her lips curved with pleasure. "Aye, that ya have."

"Then I'd best remedy that one." He raised Kathleen's nightdress, placed his hand over her flat belly, and gently rubbed.

Kathleen caught her breath at the touch of his hand on her. There was such a warm and comforting feel to him. He had a loving hand. He'd be a good father to the babe inside her.

He lowered his head onto her belly. "Good mornin', little one," he said, and then he kissed her there, right below the navel.

As he rubbed her belly lower, kissing his way this way and that, Kathleen groaned and arched upward. "Rian."

He lifted his head. "Aye, love?" There was a look of false innocence in his green eyes.

"Well, now that you've started something, are ya going to finish the job or no?"

Rian gave her a heart-pulsing, knee-weakening smile. "Aye, I'll finish the task," he said cheerily. "With pleasure."

And he did just that . . . much to each other's satisfaction.

ABOUT THE AUTHOR

Candace McCarthy lives in Delaware with her husband of twenty-six years and has a grown son, who is soon to be married also. She has written fifteen books for Kensington Publishing. Her works include *Fireheart, Irish Linen,* and *Heaven's Fire* and the tales of two sisters—*Sweet Possession* and *Wild Innocence.*

Candace has won numerous awards for her work. She was extremely pleased to have received the National Readers' Choice Award for her book *White Bear's Woman.* She loves to read and garden, and she enjoys music and doing crafts. It was her enjoyment of romance novels that prompted her to first put pen to paper. *Irish Lace* is her seventeenth book.

You may write to her at P.O. Box 58, Magnolia, Delaware 19962. Candace enjoys hearing from her readers. Check out her Web site at:

http://www.candacemccarthy.com

And if you liked *Irish Lace,* you'll want to read Candace's upcoming tale entitled *Irish Rogue,* about—you guessed it—Conor McDermott, Rian Quaid's new hire.

Discover the Romances of
Hannah Howell

Embrace the Romances of
Shannon Drake

Put a Little Romance in Your Life With
Constance O'Day-Flannery